Women's Studies

Interdisciplinary Themes and Perspectives

Women's Studies

Interdisciplinary Themes and Perspectives

Vidyut Bhagwat

Diamond Publications

Women's Studies
Interdisciplinary Themes and Perspectives

Vidyut Bhagwat

First Edition : 2012

ISBN 978-81-8483-448-2

© Vidyut Bhagwat

Printed at
Repro India Ltd.
Mumbai - 400 025

Cover Design
Sham Bhalekar

Printed & Published by
Diamond Publications
1255, Sadashiv Peth, Lele Sankul
Nimbalkar Talim Chowk, Pune 411 030.
Ph. (020) 24452387, 24466642
diamondpublications@vsnl.net
www.diamondbookspune.com

Sole Distributor
Diamond Book Depot
661, Narayan Peth
Appa Balwant Chowk,
Pune 411 030. Ph. (020) 24480677

Rucha, Vanraj, Kaushiki, Deepa, Anil, Mayuri,
Dhammasangini, Sanjyakumar, Sneha · for all these new
generation students, I dedicate this writing with a hope of
carrying the torch of new thought ahead.

Foreword

Despite the efforts of social reformists and intellectuals over several generations and different legislative measures adopted, the problems of gender discrimination have continued to persist in post-independent India, although with diluted severity. The traditions are resilient particularly when certain vested interests are involved in them. In the light of this social reality, it was indeed a very perceptive and thoughtful move of the UGC to have launched the Women's Studies programme in the VII Plan period by establishing Women's Studies Centres in quite a few universities. The objectives enshrined in the policy framework of Women's Studies Centres included, promotion of research about the problems related to women in a more systematic and scientific way, activities generating consciousness about the rights of women as human beings and also as equally important members of society in their own rights.

The Department of Sociology of University of Pune has always been in the forefront in undertaking innovative academic enterprises. It gave very positive response to the UGC's initiative and established Women's Studies Centre. During the last 25 years or so, the Centre has undergone different phases of its development and has given a very assuring performance in meeting its original mandates and also those which were added later on. The Centre was originally a part of Department of Sociology. Subsequently, it carved out for itself a separate identity.

The Center soon earned recognition at the national level as a dynamic centre of academic and extension activities in the arena of women's studies. Its vibrancy was evidenced in various programmes it launched. One of them, that I particularly applaud, is the launching of Certificate and Diploma courses in Women's Studies. This endeavor gave an added prestige to the Women's Study as an independent academic discipline. The added dividend it rendered has been that the students of these courses got trained to do disciplinary thinking about the women's issue.

The Women's Studies Centre in the University of Pune got a new direction and added dynamism when Dr. Vidyut Bhagwat was appointed as its Director. Dr. Bhagwat has a background of Marathi literature. She has well cultivated sharp literary sensitivities. Her doctoral work in Sociology imbided in her the scientific vigour much needed for serious studies. There is thus a good blend of literary sensitivities and scientific discipline in her. A person can be an authentic feminist scholar if he/she has empathy as a strong personality attribute and a passionate approach. Dr. Bhagwat has both.

Dr. Bhagwat's scholarly contributions have helped the Centre to create space for itself on the national map.

One gets glimpses of the sweep of academic interests which Dr. Bhagwat has as a feminist scholar, if one merely scans through the articles of this book. One may not agree with all that she has written, but the insight and concern with which she has developed these varied themes indeed deserve appreciation. I am sure this book will be an important addition to the collection of scholarly books of any ardent student of feminism and of all that it stands for.

The newly emerging discipline of Women's Studies is in the real sense of the term enriching our understanding of complex issues behind women's and men's everyday life conditions. Particularly, this Globalization, Liberalization stage of Capitalism is asking us to closely look at our families, kinship, caste and community networks as well as rural/urban divide as it is perceived today. In this very fast growing and changing world a lot is happening to our structures and ideologies and new challenges are coming up. I am sure; writings of Vidyut Bhagwat will help to create nuanced understanding to deal with the new challenges.

I indeed take it as a privilege to write a foreword for such scholarly work.

Uttam Bhoite
Professor of Sociology (Former)
University of Pune

Acknowledgements

While expressing in English, I was always haunted by a feeling that because I think in Marathi, my English expression is always under the shadow of Marathi. This is why I kept postponing bringing out a collection of my English writing. But my friends who were comfortable with English expressions in the academic circle like Sujata Patel (Sociologist), Kamala Ganesh (Anthropologist and Sociologist), Laxmi Lingam (Feminist Scholar in the area of Women and Health), Sharmila Rege (Feminist Researcher exploring dalit feminist standpoint) and Maitreyee Chaudhari (Sociologist) had always encouraged me by saying that my 'Marathi' - 'English' confluence had its own strength. A support like this is really a motivating force behind bringing out this collection.

Honestly, this kind of collection was brought out determinately and urgently because, my friend for last thirty years Rajendra Vora (Raja) who was always looking forward towards retirement for doing some kind of interdisciplinary work, passed away suddenly. His going away snatched the assumption of a definitive tomorrow from me. Political Economy of Liberalization, growing facelessness of violence and insecure feeling in the everyday life practice is around all of us, but now after friends going away, I became sure of the thought that, whatever is to be done has to be done today.

Prof. Uttam Bhoite, was teaching Sociology in the University of Pune when I entered as an interdisciplinary researcher and teacher. His love for rural Maharashtra and Marathi language, his ways of dealing with various kinds of people with compassion, in fact helped Women Studies Center to survive in its infant stage. I am truly grateful for his foreword.

Suhas Palshikar (Political Science), Sanjay Sonawane (Education), Vijay Khare (Ambedkar Thought Center) and many teachers form Maharashtra and outside Maharashtra attending orientation and refresher courses in the Academic Staff College; have always given positive support for my frameworks of presentation. If this had not happened, I would never have published this collection.

Student's Organizations particularly 'Yuva Bharat', Vilas Sonawane and many students with whom I always had dialogues in the context of language and particularly about domination of perfect English have also helped to make this collection possible.

Sugeeta Roy Chaudhari who was very closely associated with the Women Studies Center as a student and a teacher helped to carefully proof read the texts. Sugeeta otherwise is an expert copy editor in her own right. I thank her profusely for all the help that she willingly gave.

Vidyut Bhagwat

Introduction

In the last two decades, as a feminist - located in the field of women studies, as the subject of feminism came to be challenged and radicalized, I tried to read the present and to re-read, and rewrite the social history of Maharashtra through gender perspective. This involved reading Marathi literature both Medieval and Modern, discovering texts, recovering submerged voices to understand the different parameters of systemic subordination of women. I would like to start by outlining my social location, the institutional and personal journeys undertaken that have both opened up and limited my academic endeavor.

I was born in a lower middle class family which migrated to the fringes of Mumbai in 1940s. At times it was municipal schools, at times committed leftist teachers who trained me into thinking innovatively. As a daughter born in a family with middle class aspirations, the boys were sent to Sciences and Technology and I was 'put into' Literature that took a combination 'Marathi' - 'Sanskrit'. This was all seen as natural and given. 'Finish your B.A.' and 'get married to a foreign settled engineer or doctor and then while raising your children in UK and USA, your literature background will help you to protect our culture' - so said my parents and elders. Looking back at this life plan, trap set for me by people around me, I can now see both - how in my caste and class location this was seen as the most suitable path and how women alter, evade or overthrow such life plans set for them.

I evaded this trap of studying literature to protect 'our culture' by reading literature in a creative and innovative manner and using the new space of conjugality that love and inter-caste marriages were opening up in the Nehruvian era. Of course marrying into a Brahmin progressive family living in the heart of Mumbai metropolis with writers of children's literature and producers of new mass mediated woman's programmes; the family had good cultural capital.

Marriage provided the space for pursuing my studies in Literature, to read, write and thus complete my post-graduation in Marathi literature. In the 1967 we studied literature in a compartmentalized descriptive manner, treating all that was pre-colonial as medieval and *Bhakti*, Colonial as Marathi prose reborn with English incarnation and thus modernity in Marathi literature seen as a gift of European Enlightenment. Studying and reading different literary texts several times remained at a verbal level and a sense of creative discovery was lost in this process. The history of Marathi literature then became a matter of memorizing, without contextualizing historical stages in the political economies that were shaping them. I felt vacuous and uneasy when I completed my studies and immediately joined as a part time lecturer in the Anjuman Khairul Islam's Poona College, because I truly wanted to become a teacher and wanted to be connected with the students' community.

Increasingly through this new job I could see myself as a teacher, my students were all from poverty stricken families particularly Muslim families who had to learn different 'Marathi's and the cultures that go with it. The student's were mostly migrants from drought prone rural areas and were from the newly migrated working class families in Pune city. Marathi literary texts which were to be taught to these students invariably needed decoding at various levels. Awareness towards standardization of Marathi language and its relationship to the dialects like 'dakhani' which my students spoke at homes, took me towards doing more research in language and linguistics. Marathi literary texts that I was handling as a teacher seemed far away from the everyday life of these students. These students energized me to transform received understanding and to read further - to interrogate cannons. I wanted my students to think creatively and critically. This was the period of the magical 1970s where the new movements and collectives were emerging and as a part of many of these initiatives, I began to more seriously and historically pursue questions of domesticity, housewifery, motherhood and companionate marriage. As frameworks of my life these were simultaneously suffocating - but also creating a space for my journey into the archives. Bhalchandra Nemade, A. V. Joshi, P. S. Rege, Mardhekar, Namdev Dhasal, and D. K. Bedekar allowed me to imagine myself as a hero of my time carrying multiple tasks. Dalit Literature provided moral stamina to encounter literary studies with many questions and interrogations.

At times I was a part time teacher, a full time mother and at times I 'succeeded' in getting a full time safe job as a language teacher in the Central Governments 'Unity in diversity' scheme. Those were the times of students' movements, dalit movement, and overall hope and one moved among these spaces almost easily learning and unlearning. We all were somehow sure, of bringing transformations in our society and in the process changing the givens of man-woman relationship.

Initially after having read Simone-de-Beauvoir, Betty Friedan, feminist classic texts of the times, I was able to relate myself to those texts easily and also could make rational meaning of Indian women's writings. This were the times in the academy when the sharp divisions between and within social sciences and humanities were being questioned in small group meetings and study circles. Ram Bapat, Jayant Lele, Sitaram Raikar, Vijay Tendulkar, Shyamala Vanarse and many others involved in these discussions contributed in showing the gray areas in rhetoric's of 'opening the disciplines'. That period was of great optimism and border lines of different disciplines were slowly opening up. This became a space in which for me as a researcher a dialogue between social sciences and literature began to unfold.

After 1975 actively participating in the women's movement in Maharashtra helped me to write feminism in a disciplined way. I remember in 1980s Prof. Maitreyee Krishnaraj had begun an academic project of studying basic concepts in the Feminist Discourse at RCWS, S.N.D.T,

Mumbai. Our efforts to write about these concepts in the Indian context made us think in multiple ways. I wrote on the concept of 'Sexual Division of Labor'. This writing in English and reading systematically on the debate about labor and political economy boosted my confidence and gave me a feeling of learning something new-both at the level of content and method. While reading both the languages and material within it I increasingly felt that Marathi literature and overall writing was not in tune with the changes occurring around it. In fact many chauvinistic voices in Marathi seemed as if to easily reaching the mass of people but in no way gave emancipatory message; women particularly were seen as numbers and patriarchal frameworks were being remoulded. Slowly in this process my alienation with English language reduced. I wanted to know and understand 'Woman question' in an internationalist framework and was convinced that unless I had my feet rooted in the regional ethos and my understanding gained through various feminist writings which were available to me in English I would not be able to grasp issues sufficiently.

Early feminist writings and feminist thinkers had invariably dealt with popular literature of its time to develop new ideas. I also felt like treading the same path. I had an opportunity to work on a project undertaken by The Indian School of Political Economy where there was an effort to train rural women into leadership. We documented common women's narratives of everyday life about their perception of being a woman. A collection of essays by ordinary, minimally educated women was published as 'Because I am a Woman' and we conducted training workshops for these women. In short, while writing 'Feminist social thought' as it developed in the western world, a continuous dialogue with various women's groups with the help of friends like Dr. Neelam Gorhe, Samar Nakhate and many others helped to keep my feet firmly grounded.

In the late 1980s I participated in the project of documenting women's writings in India from different regional languages under the guidance and editorship of Susie Tharu, K. Lalita. The two volumes were published by the New York Feminist Press, but what was more enriching was the search for women's writing, efforts to delineate not a unilinear but meaningful tradition of the same became a preparatory ground for much of research in the 1990s. I see the eleven essays that are included in this book as products of this protracted journey - both personal and political.

In 1987, the Department of Sociology in the Pune University started a 'Women's Study Center' with the help of UGC. When I joined the center 1990s the site of this work was unsteady and temporary but, colleagues like Sharmila Rege, Vaishali, Swati, Anagha and many others as students helped in developing interdisciplinary teaching programmes in Women Studies. We started teaching a Certificate Course at a post-graduate level and it was supported by students from different disciplines as well as housewives, who wanted to understand the 'woman question' and at the same time their own lives.

Indian Feminist thinkers like Kumkum Sangari, Sudesh Vaid, Prem Chaudhari, Uma Chakravarti, Nivedita Menon, V. Geetha were of great help in developing the content of our teaching. Gail Omvedt and Gabriele Dietrich and writings of Maria Mies were also helpful. Along with this, right from *Mahanubhav* and *Varkari* Women's writing in Marathi were taught in our classrooms in English. The essays included in this book have emerged from this context of teaching social history of Maharashtra from a gender perspective in a state University in the early 1990s.

In short, these essays are rooted in engagement with democratic women's movement and what later emerged as a field of women's studies in higher education. These essays traverse through different stages of women's studies. I hope the articles will allow the readers to review limitations and explore new possibilities opened up by the progressive challenges to the given category woman as a subject of feminist research. My essays outline the centrality of history and literature to practice women's studies as a discipline.

Section I
Gendering Social History : Medieval and Modern

These essays map the field of social history of 'medieval/modern Maharashtra', looking for hidden, submerged voices of '*sant*' poetesses (retrieving women *bhakta, sants* in medieval Maharashtra as well as seeking to establish caste and gender as structuring) and thus crucial for creating a comprehensive understanding of the history and contemporary practices of the *Varkari* movement in Maharashtra. (Essays 1, 2, 3, 4)

The essay on Tarabai Shinde's '*Stree-Purush Tulana'* and works of Pandita Ramabai read the texts as feminist classics and interrogate the dominant taken for granted interpretations of their lives and works in the Marathi public sphere. These essays will provide to the reader a historical review of the woman question in modern Maharashtra and outline the limitations of middle class, Brahmanical reform. (Essays 5)

Essay 6 which deals with the 'Patriarchal Discourse' in 19th century Maharashtra takes again a historical review of how structures of patriarchy in Colonial India were complexly reformulate - with some layers persisting, others changing.

Essay 7 which is a book review is specially included in this collection because it is a response towards an English translation of Tarabai Shinde raising many nuanced questions about the relationship between English and Indian rather than regional language. The interpretation of Tarabai Shinde's negotiations as non-modern is thus questioned in this text.

Section II
Literature as Social History

Section II carries two essays that seek to point out how literature can be read as social history. As a student of Marathi Literature we were trained to read literary text 'in the framework of images of women'.

But slowly with the help of the interdisciplinary field of Women's Studies, I have come to a conclusion that there was a relative absence of Marathi literary criticism which would create new we do not have good literary criticism which would create new critical assumptions, reading through historical circumstances and ideologies. This has resulted in a serious lack of critical appreciation of important writings of Marathi authors. My essay on Wada Chirebandi is an effort towards building up feminist literary criticism and without assuming the usual divide of West and East. I have tried to read Elkunchwar's text as an articulation of complex relations between mode of production and reproduction as they make a social formation.

The second essay in this section is about Mumbai as a metropolis appearing in dalit literature. There was always and still is constant debate about Mumbai being multicultural, multilingual. But the working class community which built the base of Mumbai is always a core of Bombay/ Mumbai. My essay searches for the voices of different dalit expressions relating their selves and politics to the city.

Section III
Histories of Women's Studies - Institutional and Intellectual

A significant part of my academic career is spent in establishing Women's Studies in a State university – taking Women's studies from what in the university registers was a UGC sponsored temporary programme to a respectable teaching Department. This section outlines the macro and micro politics - tensions and traumas, dilemmas of strategizing and negotiating - in the everyday life of our public institutions. (Essay 10)

Essay 11 is a part of these processes of building up Women's Studies in the Contemporary context. In 1975, women's movements in various regions began spelling out feminist politics and dreamt about bringing all women of India together to combat patriarchal structures and ideologies sharing pain of each other. But in 1990s major challenges were posed to categories of Women's Studies as a political and intellectual field.

My essay, which has outlined dalit feminism as a way out is to be read in the context of narrowing democratic space of all social movements and a need for a very strong and firm and broad-based women's movement which will subvert the populist essentialsing meaning *'Baichi jat'* (of woman caste) and create unity amongst all women in India, giving new meaning to the reality of *baichi jat!* (a meaning that emerges from understanding Jatitil Bai - Women within caste structures).

This collection of essays is published with an intention of introducing Maharashtra social history through gender perspective for those students who come from different regions and different nations to do Women's Studies in India. Some glimpses of debates and discussions might be useful while studying and researching in the field of Women's Studies. With these essays, I am seeking to put away the burden of the last twenty years work and start a fresh. The site of Women's Studies with its interdisciplinary ethos is so challenging that a new creative turn for my work will be helped by critical responses to this collection.

Vidyut Bhagwat

Contents

Section : II

Section : III

Section : I

Gendering Social History : Medieval and Modern

Chapter - 1

Heritage of *Bhakti* : *Sant* Women's Writings in Marathi*

After a prolonged neglect by Indian as well as western intellectuals, the *bhakti* tradition is at last getting the necessary critical attention. Both as a part of this newly found interest in general and due to the impact of the post-1975 women's movement and women studies programmes, a good body of work on *bhakta* women, particularly *sant* women,[1] is now being published. As is natural, the assessment of their collective and individual work is carried out in terms of competing theoretical and ideological paradigms. The search by contemporary feminism in India for indigenous roots and the mobilisation of *bhakta* women's poetry to fill this need is one such effort. It is fraught with several dilemmas. Nonetheless, one could see it as part of a pattern in a range of fields in post-independence India, which have turned the searchlight on past traditions in their quest for an identity. It is in this context that the present article focuses on *bhakta* women who were a part of the *bhakti* tradition prevailing in the Marathi-speaking areas in the later medieval period in Indian history.

The initial part of this article consists of a brief review of the *bhakti* tradition specific to the Maharashtra region in the period between 13th and 17th centuries'. It then goes on to trace key interpretations of the *Varkari Sampraday* (as the *bhakti* tradition is known in Marathi) and the *Varkari sants* by scholars. Contextualising the neglect of *sant* women's lives and writings, the article moves on to note the key elements

* I would like to thank Kamala Ganesh for her patience, and Ram Bapat and Sharmila Rege for their valuable help. Swati, Anagha and Vaishali were a constant source of encouragement in my struggle to complete the paper.

in the post-1980s feminist scholarship on the contributions of women *sants*. In conclusion, the article suggests that *sant* women's resistance to patriarchies and resistance to caste hierarchies were inseparable. It underlines this early feminism in India as having a predominantly *dalit-bahujan* character, that is, representing non-Brahmin peasant and artisan groups.

The *Varkari Sampraday* of Maharashtra

Spanning a period of over five centuries, the *bhakti* tradition in Maharashtra began with the generation of *sants* like *Dnyanadev* and *Namdev*, *Muktabai* and *Janabai*, and reached its zenith with *Tukaram* and *Bahenabai*. Its spread and impact covered the entire space of political economy, culture and language occupied by the Marathi-speaking world, and included even parts of Karnataka and Andhra. The *sants* entered almost every home through *Vithoba*—a domestic deity par excellence.

The Marathi *sants* were neither sectarian conservatives nor Shaktas practising *tantra-mantra*. They were open to all castes, including untouchables and women, and insisted on sharing the language of the masses. *Sants* were very much a part of the peasant communities of their time. Jayant Lele (1981: 107) notes that they were 'a community of active producers . . . *Jnaneshwar* explicitly rejects the renunciation of productive life and ridicules the claims of liberation through rejection of activity.' The *sants*, while celebrating human productive activity, were a part of the community of the oppressed. They consciously preferred to write in a language that highlighted the everyday practices of common people. Their idiom of writing was direct and dialogical, thus reaching out to women as well. The women of the period, especially those who were in search of creativity and freedom, realised that the doors of the *Varkari Sampraday* were open to them.

Romila Thapar notes the historical role of *bhakti* as a departure from the earlier indigenous religion. *Bhakti* soon became a new vehicle of religious expression. The main features of the *bhakti* tradition lie in its drawing from the Puranic tradition of *Saiva* and *Vaisnava bhakti* and from the Sramanic religions, a deep sense of God-centeredness, and the worship of a specific icon or idol. Some sects rejected brahmanical *sruti* and *smruti*, and insisted on the equality of all worshippers in the eyes of the deity (Thapar 2000: 970). A.K. Ramanujan (1989: 9-10) clarifies that:

> There are many kinds of *bhakti* though we speak of it in singular . . . One way of looking at *bhakti* movements is to see them as a counter system, opposed to classical, orthodox systems, say in their views about caste, gender or the idea of god. For example, the *Vedic* Gods are not localised, but in *bhakti* they are worshipped in local forms in temples. The Gods... are as human as they are divine.

If modernity is seen as the first social philosophy that allows ordinary people to dream of freedom and self-determination, then it is not surprising that *bhakti* paved the way for India's early modernity. Lele has pointed out that given the nature of India's peasant economy, the direct producers were battling for sustaining their economy as a moral economy. He examines the role of *bhakti* in this light as an expression of that modernity (Lele 1995: 53). The radical *sants* challenged brahmanism, caste hierarchy, untouchability and Islamic orthodoxy. They built a broad unity of the masses, cutting across class, caste and gender lines. It is well known that the dialogue between Islam and earlier indigenous religions is reflected in various *bhakti* and *sufi* traditions. Though some of the leading *bhaktas* were *Brahmans*, its broad following consisted of *Shudras*, in particular the middle castes. *Bhakti* was thus neither elitist nor cultist. *Bhakti* in Maharashtra always remained a mainstream movement of peasants and artisans offering a most potent source of critique of brahmanism.

If we look at the variations in the expression of *bhakti*, north India produced *nirguna* (abstract) *bhakti*, whereas south India adopted *saguna* (concrete) *bhakti*. Maharashtra represented the confluence of the northern and the southern traditions.

What then are the salient features of the *Varkari bhakti* tradition? What features constitute the specificity or peculiarity of Marathi *bhakti*? One of the striking features in this context is the range of castes and occupations that came together within the *Varkari Sampraday*. Their articulations were in the idiom of their caste-based occupation, their everyday life practices. *Sena Nhavi* (a barber) would carry his critique of caste discrimination by upholding his occupational skill: 'We are the barbers, we do "*hajamat*" minutely.' *Gora Kumbhar* was from the potter community, *Savta* was a gardener, *Chokha Mela* was a *Mahar*,[2] *Narhari* was a goldsmith, *Bahira* came from *Jatved*, *Jagannath* from the *Vadwal* sub-caste. *Jnaneshwar* and his sister *Muktabai* belonged to an excommunicated Brahmin family. *Namdev* was from the *Shimpi* (tailor) caste. His disciple *Janabai*, from a *Shudra* caste, was a part of *Namdev's* household as a bonded domestic servant. The community of *sants* in Maharashtra, therefore, were from the artisan and service *jatis*, and the *bhakta* community included women from both high and low castes. The crucial feature of this formation, therefore, was the fact that every caste contributed to the knowledge building process on equal terms. Thus, *Chokha Mahar* analyses the discriminatory system, saying:

> While for one there is only food for subsistence
> For another sweetmeats.
> Some do not get even grains despite asking
> For one there is wealth and titles of kingship
> While another begs for alms from village to village,
> This is the law of the 'home' you created
> Says Chokha, O Hari this is my karma!
> (My translation)

Chokha often asserts his '*Mahar*' identity and states, 'They curse me as a *Mahar* and blame me for polluting the deity.' But then in open defiance argues :

> Who is pure and who is untouchable?
> My Vitthal is different from both of these
> Who gets polluted by what?

Everything of birth is pure.
If five senses pollute the one body
In which they are housed
Who in the world is pure then?
Says Chokha my Vitthala is different
Formless and different standing on the brick.
(My translation)

Sant Eknath (1533-99), a *Brahman* from *Paithan*, notes:

God baked pots with Gora
drove cattle with Chokha
cut grass with Savta Mali
wove garments with Kabir
colored hide with Ravidas
sold meat with butcher Sajana
melted gold with Narhari
carried cow clung with Janabai
and even became the Mahar messenger of Damaji.
(Zelliot 1987)

Varkari sants composed in various folk meters like *ovi, abhanga, bharud, virani and palna*, collectively developed by women and men. Generally, the *ovi* meter is treated as *Dnyaneshwar's* contribution and the *abhanga* as *Tukaram's*. The *ovi* originates in the rhythm of the songs sung by women at the grinding stone. *Janabai, Soyrabai* and *Bahenabai* had used *abhanga* meter for their free and hard-hitting compositions. *Tukaram* had imbibed this tradition. *Virani* were songs of pain of separation, and *palnas* or lullabies were also a favourite form of articulation for both men and women sants. Eleanor Zelliot (1987: 91) has noted:

A great many of *Eknath's* three hundred bharuds are in the persona of untouchables, passing Muslim fakirs, acrobats and travelling entertainers, religious personages from unorthodox sects, prostitutes and unhappy women—a wide sweep of the non-sanskritic world around *Eknath*.

Bhakti was centred on *Vithoba*, the God who was more or less like anyone from the toiling class, man or woman. *Vithoba* was seen as a common Marathi peasant, free from excesses of miracles. He did not expect any kind of sacrifice, in animal or other forms, and was a friend, a motherly figure. *Irawati Karve* even sees him as her 'boyfriend'. Right from *Dnyaneshwar*, all the sants talk to him in a conversational mode. For Janabai, he becomes a helpmate in carrying domestic chores. Vithoba was no doubt a homely god. *Varkari Sampraday* built up a strong egalitarian, democratising, anti-hierarchical ethos of *Vithoba bhakti*. Celebrating earthly joys, their *bhakti* had a robust peasant-like directness of expression.

Modern Interpretations of the *Varkari Sampraday*

The arrival of colonialism marked the rise of print culture and, in consequence, a new intelligentsia. The new rulers—Elphinstone, for example—as well as a band of Christian missionaries needed to know Marathi for the implementation of their desired projects. The evangelical missionaries began to distribute translated scriptures on a massive scale. The new intelligentsia's response appeared in the form of printed texts of key *sants* like *Dnyaneshwar* and *Tukoba*. The process began in full vitality from 1844. *Sadanand More* (1996: 225) points out that *Tukaram's* writings appealed to the religious as well as literary taste of the missionaries and colonial officials as his writings were direct and simple, lucid and trenchant in their critique of brahmanism. A leading liberal British official like Alexander Grant confessed in the Royal Asiatic Journal that *Tukaram's* poetry revealed a high sense of morality and authentic spirituality based on *bhakti*.

Missionaries treated *bhakti* as a bridge to Christ for commoners in Maharashtra. Eminent social thinkers like Justice *M.G. Ranade* turned to *bhakti* as an alternative to utilitarianism. He also argued that *bhakti* provided the energies that resulted in the rise of *Maratha* power under Shivaji. His own *Prarthana Samaj* initiative drew its sustenance from the *bhakti* tradition and above all from *Tukaram*.

Mahatma Jotirao Phule had a complex relationship with the *Varkari Sampraday*. He founded the *Satyashodhak Samaj* as an alternative to the *Prarthana Samaj*. But he knew the potential of the *Varkari Sampraday* in resisting casteism and untouchability. More has demonstrated that while Phule kept himself aloof from the *Varkari* tradition for reasons of his own, his *akhandas* are in fact organically linked with *Tukaram's abhangas*. *Lokmanya Tilak's* interpretation of the *Bhagavad Gita* is a confluence of *bhakti* and *karma*. *Tilak* stood against the rituals of the *Varkari Sampraday* and followed *Sant Tukaram* in his forthright critique of hypocrisy.

Anthropologist *Iravati Karve* countered *Rajwade's* and *Ketkar's* denigration of the *Varkari* endeavour as unscientific and backward. She in fact participated in the *vari* or pilgrimage to Pandharpur and then defined Maharashtra as 'that region where people visit *Pandhari*' (Karve 1962). *G.B. Sardar* refuted the charge of the *Varkari Sampraday* being non-intellectual and praised *Tukaram* for his honesty and transparent self-expression (Sardar 1969). *D.K. Bedekar*, an eminent and creative Marxist scholar, read *Tukaram* and the *Varkari Sampraday* in a democratic, secular framework.

Jayant Lele argues that in order understand the revolutionary potential of the *Varkari Sampraday*, one must enter the world-view of the peasant with gentle humility and alertness. He sees *Varkari Sampraday* as an example of an immanent critique of brahmanism. 'It rejects both counter culturalism and ritualism. As a discourse of the underprivileged, it penetrates the falsehood of an ideology through the eyes of suspicion but it does so in order to extract and expose the encrusted truth of that ideology through the sensitive ears of a believer' (Lele 1995: 80). For him the *sant* poets of medieval Maharashtra offer a most important methodological lesson of unmasking the hypocrisy and falsehood of orthodox beliefs, but they also teach us to develop the art of listening. *Sadanand More* considers the *Varkari* tradition as the core of Maharashtrian culture and sees *Tukaram* as a social critic and a poet of a high order with matchless clarity of expression and an utter fidelity to his own integrity as a free and radical human being and *bhakta*.

Sant Women and Their Poetry

Almost till recent times, women's *bhakti* writings were more often than not studied only in terms of literary expression. The rigorous critique developed by them to challenge all kinds of caste and gender ideational hegemonies were either altogether neglected or pushed into the background. In reality, the *Varkari* women had dared to enter the *Varkari* movement as equal partners. They drew fearlessly from their domestic life-world and wasted no opportunity to challenge the unequal order that subordinated them. We have a long line of woman *sants* full of radical intent, critique and expression - *Mahadaisa, Baisa, Ausa*, and then *Muktabai, Janabai, Soyara-Nirmala, Sakhu, Premabai* and *Bahenabai*. From the 13th to 17th centuries, there is an uninterrupted tradition of radical women *sants* and *sant* poets.

Some writings of *sant* women were translated and printed in the early 20th century. For example, Justine Abbott's preface mentions that the first printed edition of the 17th century sant poetess *Bahenabai's* work was edited by *Dhondo V. Umarkhane* which appeared in 1914 and was soon out of print (Abbott 1985: 9). Eventually in 1929, Justine Abbott published a translation of chosen portions of her autobiography. 'To introduce to the west a name there absolutely unknown but worthy of being known', he had chosen such portions 'as seemed best adapted to give to the English reader the thoughts of this Indian woman that found expression in her verses nearly three hundred years ago.' (ibid.: ix)

It would be apt to say that this writing of women *sants* was seen for a long time, in fact up to 1975, only as a part of the spiritual realm, and women *sants* like *Muktabai* and *Janabai* were treated as women who had already transcended the physiological division of humans into 'man' and 'woman'. But in this process it was ignored that women *sants* were very much a symbiotic part of the *Varkari* masses. They were also a part of the social historic reality of the Marathi-speaking region. After the rise of women's movement in India, gender-sensitive academic and political discourses made conscious efforts to write women into history. Initially, women *sants* were treated as add-ons to the list of male *sants*.

Muktabai, Dnyaneshwar's sister, was designated at one level as *'mahayogini'*, highlighting her spiritual status, but her very complex writing is yet to be analysed seriously. Thus, these historical accounts did not recognise the agency of women *sants*. Moreover, mainstream history was preoccupied with 'women in early India' as enjoying a high status, a position of honour and dignity. This homogenisation had created a category of 'women in India' with *Gargi* and *Maitreyi* being seen as exceptional women seers and knowledge makers. The predominance of this homogenised category further blurred the agency of *sant* women of the medieval period. Their expressions were relegated to the sphere of *'bhakti'* as only devotion, contrasted to the sphere of 'knowledge'. Women *sants'* lives as well as writings were either not contextualised or rendered a tokenist treatment.

There have been serious controversies as to whether there was one *Dnyaneshwar* or two. *Namdev* is acknowledged for his organisational brilliance and skills. But the women *sants:* were always clubbed together with the male *sants* as their dependants. As I have observed elsewhere, 'we always talk of *Mahadaisa* of *Chakradhar*, *Jani* of *Namya*, 'little' *Muktai* of *Dnyaneshwar*, *Bahenabai* of *Tukaram* . . . This is a classic instance of how the hegemonic order manages to reappropriate emancipatory drives for its own legitimization' (Bhagwat 1995: ws-25). As a result, as late as 1957, Neera Desai acknowledged the *bhakti* movement as an important movement, but concluded that the *bhaktas'* 'total conception of woman's status was not quite free from the admixture of the then prevailing attitude towards womanhood'. Hence, in her opinion, the overall effect of the movement on women was rather limited (Desai 1957: 34-47).

During the 1980s, in the overall context of 'gender politics' and the second wave women's movement in India, there seems to be a proliferation of scholarly writings on *sant* women. A.K. Ramanujan in 1973 translated love poems and published the *Classical Tamil Anthology* (Ramanujan 1973). In 1989 he talked extensively about *sant* women in an interview for *Manushi*. He began studying the detailed history of *Mahadeviakka*, a *Virasaiva* woman, and an extraordinary picture emerged before his eyes. He saw 'marriage' as an issue in the lives of Indian women *sants* in a way that it was not for male *sants*, both upper and lower castes. He saw the women going through five phases: (a) early dedication to God in the form of a particular deity; (b) denial of marriage; (c) defying social norms; (d) initiation by the guru; and (e) marrying the Lord. He notes, 'The upper caste male's battle is with the system as a whole, often internalized as the enemy within, whereas a woman *sant's* struggle is with family and family values.' The woman sant remains feminine because 'she has nothing to shed: neither physical prowess, nor social power, nor prudity, nor even spiritual pride. She is already where she needs to be in these sants' legends' (Ramanujan 1989: 324).

Since *bhakti* movements, radical in their beginnings, eventually got routinised, Ramanujan suggested that the *sant* writings have to be constantly reinterpreted and rescued from the domestication that they undergo. In his opinion, *bhakti* writings do offer alternatives, humane and creative ways of being and acting. Hence, he gave immense importance to the lives and poems of women *sants* for studying Indian women's voices, for finding alternative conceptions in Indian civilisation (Ramanujan 1989: 14).

Jayant Lele in his edited work on *bhakti* movements (1981) makes pertinent observations about women *sants* in the context of the tradition-modernity debate. He argues that when *dharma* speaks only as an oppressive moment, as a duty from which the joy of performance has been stolen, it becomes coercive. He sees *sant* women's rebellious posture vis-à-vis the social order in the context of their reality as communally exchanged young brides in an alien patriarchal/patrilocal family, in an often hostile household. He points out:

> A sensitive woman under conditions of oppression, looks upon god as an alternative to her husband, she does not, I think, look upon the former as a mere alternative, but a determinate negation of that very being which a husband is not, but should be. The worldly husband symbolizes the lure, the bondage, the oppressive reality of family life, while the god as husband and lover signifies liberation

... Their involvement with the lord was an all-consuming affair . .. They rejected repressive marriage and not marriage, oppressive sex and not love making (ibid.: 12).

According to him, women *sants'* love transcended the prison gates of legitimised duty, false modesty, enforced honour and oppressive kinship.

Feminist Engagement with *Sant* Women's Poetry

In the 1980s feminist scholars of the second wave of women's movement were grappling with an extremely troubled situation in India. The statistics of deteriorating women's status; the experience of Indian women's overall victimisation and sexual exploitation complicated by their locations in different communities, castes, classes; an absence or invisibility of women's collective resistances in historical narratives; an urgent need of writing cultural historiography in order to combat naturalising or essentialising 'the woman question': all these presented immense complexities. A nuanced understanding of recasting of Indian women during the colonial period (Sangari and Vaid 1989) was attempted. This also led to researching 'women in early India' and challenging the myth of the 'Golden Age' (Chakravarti 1989). The search for women's voices in Indian history sought to make them audible as specifically women's voices. This was the context within which women *sants'* lives and writings were foreground and studied by feminist scholars of different ideological dispositions.

In the late 1980s, feminism emerged as a critique of biologism and the sexual division of labour. It rested on the assertion of the right to chosen political affiliation and social identities above birth-bound ones. Women's membership of any community and even of the state was seen as problematic due to their patriarchal modes. The roots of misogyny were rightly traced to traditional as well as modern male-dominated cultures. The stereotypical abuse of the weaker sex along with deep-seated phobic anxiety about the woman's body and its reproductive ability was critically analysed by feminist scholars and activists. Sexism was defined as a process providing a rationale for the disempowerment of women in all spheres of life, secular and spiritual.

In this milieu, it is not surprising that the special issue of *Manushi* celebrating its 11th year sought to resurrect women *sants* as exercising individual choice and creating alternative tradition. Women *sants* were seen as 'extraordinarily courageous and creative women who asserted right to their own life as they defined it'. Their writing was seen as a celebration of their individual choice and their religious path as an escape from the narrow confines of domesticity (Kishwar 1989: 7).

Uma Chakravarti situates gender relations within the context of caste, class and delineates the issue of the control of female sexuality as the central issue. *Chakravarti* acknowledges *bhakti* as a rich tradition

> Particularly significant for women both for variations and commonalities in its social and religious implications. Here the dominant brahmanical ritual world is attempted to be turned upside down, boundaries operating in the social world collapse, and the shackles imposed by rigidly hierarchical social order are stretched to provide breathing space for some men and women (Chakravarti 1989: 18).

She warns against homogenising *bhakti* into a neat unified tradition and simplifying its social content, and suggests that the extent to which *bhakti* dissolved gender lines needs to be investigated further.

Kumkum Sangari provides an analysis of *bhakti* thus:

> In an economy where the labour of women and the surplus production of the peasant and artisan are customarily and 'naturally' appropriated by the ruling groups, high Hindu traditions sought to encompass and retain the management of spiritual 'surplus' and to circumscribe its availability along lines of caste and gender. In this spiritual economy, the liberalising and dissenting forms of *bhakti* emerge as a powerful force which selectively uses the metaphysics

of high Hinduism in an attempt to create value grounded in the dailiness of a material life within the reach of all (Sangari 1990: 194).

Susie Tharu and K. Lalita compiling an anthology of *Women Writing in India* (1995: 35) argue that, 'We might indeed learn to read them not for the moments in which they collude with or reinforce dominant ideologies of gender, class, nation, or empire, but for the gestures of defiance or subversion implicit in them.'

Tharu (1991: 57) observes:

> The path of devotion set up no barriers of caste or sex. The women poets of the *bhakti* movements did not have to seek the institutionalized spaces religion provided to express themselves and women's poetry moved from the court and the temple to the open spaces of the field, the workplace and the common women's hearth.

Tharu and Lalita do acknowledge *sant* women's writing as expressing a new sense of self-worth, new dignity to domestic chores, new self-confidence and even their access to a wider world, but note that their options were limited. They, too, doubt whether patriarchal controls were radically questioned and lives of ordinary women changed.

Vijaya Ramaswamy's work *Walking Naked: Women, Society, Spirituality in South India* appeared in 1997, mapping the spiritual history of women in the context of societal structures though historical time and space. Her study looks at the issues of gender inequalities in the context of dominance and power, and the debates over female sexuality and education.

In Marathi, Indumati Shevde's *Sant Kavayitri* (Women *Sants*) was published in 1989 under the guidance of Suma Chitnis, the editor of the series of books *Stri Muktichya Maharashtratil Paulkhana* (Footsteps of Women's Liberation in Maharashtra). It was, in Shevde's own words, an effort to search for the seeds of contemporary women's movement in the past in order to create an understanding of the struggles of contemporary women in search of 'self'.

During those years I, too, was engaged in researching the complex weave of *sant* women's compositions in Maharashtra. 'Man-Woman Relations in the Writings of the Sant Poetesses', written in 1991, is an effort to show how women sants were talking differently as women and hence even as *sants*. 'Marathi Literature as Source for Contemporary Feminism' (Bhagwat 1995: ws-24) argues that:

> The feminist movement in the [Maharashtra] state ignored its own tradition of a succession of women sants and other women writers who had inverted, and occasionally even subverted, the classical ideals of womanhood embodied in the hegemonic texts. The movement paid a price for this failure; it appeared to be based on dry, upstart ideas lacking roots in the soil.

Postscript: Personal Reflections on *Sant* Women's Lives and Poetry

The last decade has posed several challenges to feminist scholarship in India, and new directions and issues have been opened up. As Rajeshwari Sunder Rajan (2000) has argued, feminist scholarship's move from victimisation of woman to resistance and agency of woman has emerged in the context of majoritarian religious politics and its mobilisation of women, and the failure of the state and its laws to ensure women's safety or rights. The other important context of the 1990s, at least in western India, has been the challenge posed by *dalit-bahujan* feminist perspectives and organisation to feminist and non-Brahman historiography and epistemology. These challenges have led us to reflect on questions like: What constitutes resistance? Can the resistance to patriarchies and brahmanism/caste hierarchies be neatly separated even if only for analytical purposes? We are impelled to reflect on what we hide when we privilege the voices of women sants as voices of female resistance, as if they are unmarked by their caste location. For instance, *Soyarabai*, a Mahar *sant*, questioned untouchability: 'O God, every human being carries impurity along with purity, then why should some human beings be treated as untouchables?' (Pawar 2003) Or *Janabai*, as a bonded slave, as a *dasi*, that too of a *Shudra* caste, consciously stated, 'I am low-born and kept outside the temple.' Her declaration that *Chokhamela*, the *Mahar sant*, was the only true *Vaisnava* is important in understanding her as a member of the *Varkari* community. When we read their voices as voices of specifically female resistance, we edit out the fact that early feminism in India had *dalit-bahujan* beginnings and that these women were resisting the principles of brahmanical patriarchy. In fact, their consciousness, expressed through their poetry, spanned different locations of gender and caste, and thus offered a universalist and humanist critique of oppression.

No doubt there has been important feminist historical research and emancipatory interpretations of the lives and works of women *sants*. However, the caution that most feminists express about reading 'too much' into these voices may at least partly be explained by the fact that there has been very little work on the 'living tradition'. The meanings that these women *sants* have in the lives of contemporary *bahujan* women as well as the co-option of the egalitarian tradition by the latter, needs documentation. The imprint of the egalitarian practices from the Varkari movement in the literature of the early decades of the 20th century are apparent, for instance, in the autobiographical accounts of *dalit* women. *Shantabai Kamble*, for example, in her 1990 work *Mazya Jalmachi Chitterkatha* (A Kaleidoscopic Story of My Life) recalls early childhood memories of practices of untouchability in the movement. Her dismay at being asked about her caste and then served water from a distance by a fellow *Varkari* and her disappointment after being told by her mother that the untouchables could pay respects only at the steps of *Chokhoba* and *Namdev* at Pandharpur is a case in point.

I would suggest, therefore, that the essentialisation of *sant* women's writing as 'women's writing' has often rendered invisible their resistance to brahmanical patriarchy and that this needs to be brought to the foreground. I do not suggest thereby that there is some readymade indigenous *dalit-bahujan* feminist solution in *sant* women's writing that can deal with multiple patriarchies of the contemporary situation. An analysis of *Bahenabai's* contributions can help explicate the argument in this context: *Bahenabai* (1628-1700) was the last great woman sant in this tradition. Born in a poor Brahman family, married at the early age of 3 or 4 to a 30-year-old *Vedic pandit* of a *Shakta* cult, beaten up by her husband, *Bahena* chose a *Shudra* guru and actively participated in *bhakti* by becoming a Varkari. Her writing consists of historical accounts of the *Varkari Sampraday*, a commentary on *Vajrasuchi*, a Buddhist text attacking dogmatic brahmanism by Ashwaghosha, an autobiography that is an important source for the social history of Maharashtra and almost 729 *abhangas*. As Dilip Chitre (1998: 5) notes, 'The crisis that arose in *Bahenabai's* life was noted simply as *bhakti* of "the god vs. duties of the *pativrata*" kind.' Her struggle was a complex weave of questions on varna hegemony, self-perception of brahmanism, true meaning of the *Veda* and the discipline of ritualism. This Marathi Brahman woman changed the conservative frame of mind of her husband, redefined the concept of *pativrata-dharma* (wifely duty) from 'loyalty' to 'pursuing a higher goal' for both men and women, chose a *Shudra guru* and actively participated in the *Varkari Sampraday*. In university courses in Marathi literature, we were taught to read her texts and underline her skills in drawing a balance between the fulfilment of her wifely duties and achievement of spiritual excellence. The context of her times was thus completely lost. There is a need to highlight the system of her times, which treated women as subordinate beings having no right over material or spiritual property and no right to the knowledge-making discourse. Her whole life then is a quest of building an open community. She thus redefines the concept of a Brahman not as born, but as one who understands truly *'Brahma'*, that is, truth that is universal for the whole of humanity.

Bahena challenges brahmanical patriarchy through a subversion of meanings of the pillars of its coercive structure. Her *'brahm'* is *'karma'* that is, active intervention. 'Wifely duty' for her is recognising her own self. She takes a *Shudra guru* and challenges the very presence of god in brahmanism.

She writes (and I have translated the following songs from Javdekar's *Sant Bahinabaicha Gatha*) (1979: 126):

> One who recognises her own self
> She is the true pativrata
> One who treats worldliness and other worldliness on par
> She is the one who holds the sky.

She tells us about the beatings that she suffered.

> Whenever it pleases him, he beats me a lot, binds me like a bundle of sticks. (*abhanga* 161)

She tells us that:

> The husband says we are Brahmans
> We will always recite Veda
> Who is this Shudra Tuka?
> My wife is spoiled by him.
> (*abhanga* 32)

Bhakti was her chosen path towards bringing freedom and equality for both women and shudras. She raised questions like:

> My husband earned a living through practising Veda
> Where is God in this?
> (*abhanga* 575)

She tells her God that her body was tortured at the hands of her husband:

> But my mind has taken a vow
> I will not leave singing for devotion
> Even if I die.
> (*abhanga* 588)

She had a large following of people. Her husband detested this popularity. She says

Every moment his hatred grows
Will she be possessed by the God?
Will she be fed by the God?
Baheni says this is how he worried
The God understood all this.
(*abhanga* 31)

She challenges brahmanical patriarchy's vicious propaganda about the sinful birth of women and *Shudras*, and refuses to be deceived by the mirage of rebirth. She says:

A pativrata when she serves her husband
Blesses both the families
Baheni says my soul is rested eternally
By my husband putting a stop to
The cycle of birth and death.
(*abhanga* 38)

Bahenabai lived on for many years after her husband's death and worked till the end for the suffering community of *Varkaris*. She actually managed to convert her husband to the *Varkari* sect and persuaded him to accept *Tukaram* as his *guru*.

I suggest that woman sants were very much a part of the early modernity of India. Hence, their struggles and negotiations within their cultural context will have to be understood and reinterpreted as emancipatory cultural histories. Drawing them out solely as women's voices often excludes their agency in challenging the political priesthood of their times and blurs their historical relevance as early voices against brahmanical patriarchy. Their voices more than being 'specific voices of women', are expressions of freedom and equality emerging from their lived experiences as women in specific communities. Their message thus has universality. These voices against patriarchal political priesthood are a demand for a new world, to be realised not in the next life through *karma*, but in the empirical world. This heritage of *bhakta* women's voices as renderings of nascent modernity has several clues for today.

Our present is marked by a world order that collapses capitalism into democracy, equating freedom with choice and equality with access. Third world women's issues are thus being equated to issues of poverty and their agency is being collapsed into efficient management of poverty and a mirage of 'choices'. In India majoritarian fundamentalism opposes the ideas of secularism and equality, labelling them as 'Western'. This challenge has underlined further the limitations of several academic trends, which pose undifferentiated 'collective tradition' against the 'modernity' of the West. Feminist scholarship that seeks to redefine democratic politics must, in retrieving emancipatory collective traditions, separate the brahmanical and the non-brahmanical, and inegalitarian from egalitarian aspects. The voices of freedom and equality of the bhakta women, which were at once directed against the intrinsically inter-linked caste system and patriarchy, contained an urge to transform the world. It is this tradition of equality and rights in the 'early modern' period that provide a rich heritage and can become a resource for redefining feminist democratic politics.

Notes

1. *'Bhakta'*, literally means 'devotee', refers to the community of believers and worshippers in the *bhakti* tradition. *'Sant'* or sant refers to the leaders of the movement whose devotional poetry became emblematic for the *bhakti* movement. Marathi words like *bhakta, bhakti* and *sant* are popularly used and understood by English speakers in India.
2. Mahar is an ex-untouchable caste in Maharashtra which until the 14th century was compelled to drag dead animals. But under Malik Amber's regime, after the decline of the Yadav period, the Mahar caste became known as the Vatandars and later as a part of Shivaji's military.

Original Source

Culture and the Making of Identity in Contemporary India
Ganesh, Kamala and Thakkar, Usha (Eds.)
Sage Publication, New Delhi,
2005
(pp: - 164-183)

References

Abbott, Justine E. 1985 [1929]. *Bahinabai: A Translation of her Autobiography and Verses*, New Delhi: Motilal Banarasidass.

Bedekar O.K. 1978. *Adhunik Marathi Kavya: Udgam, Vikas ani Bhavitavya* (Modern Marathi Literature: Origin, Development and Future), Mumbai: Lokvangmay gruha Pvt. Ltd.

Bhagwat, Vidyut. 1990. 'Man-Woman Relations in the Writings of Sant Poetesses', *New Quest, 82* (July-August): 223-32.

_____.1995. 'Marathi Literature as a Source of Contemporary Feminism',

Economic and Political Weekly, 30(17): Review of Women's Studies, ws-24-29.

Chakravarti, Uma. 1989. 'Whatever Happened to the Vedic Dasi?: Orientalism, Nationalism and a Script for the Past', in Kumkum Sangari and Sudesh Vaid (eds.), *Recasting Women: Essays in Colonial History*, New Delhi: Kali for Women, pp. 27-87.

Chitre, Dilip Purushottam. 1998. *Baheni Mhane Hat Ghatala Mastaki* ('Baheni Says I Have [Earned] Blessings'), Shri Kshetra Dehu: Bhagwat Prabodhan Sanstha.

Desai, Neera. 1957. 'Impact of Bhakti Movement on the Status of Indian Women', in *Women in Modern India*, Mumbai: Vora and Company, pp. 34-47.

Javdekar, Shalini (ed.). 1979. *Sant Bahenabaicha Gatha* ('Story of Bahenabai'), Pune: Continental Prakashan.

Kamble, Shantabai. 1990. *Mazya Jalmachi Chitterkatha* ('Kaleidoscopic Story of My Life'), Pune: Sugava Prakashan.

Karve, Iravati. 1962. *Marathi Lokanchi Sanskriti* ('Culture of the Marathi People'), Pune: Deshmukh.

Kishwar, Madhu. 1989. *Manushi*, Sp. 10th Anniversary issue, January-June, New Delhi.

Lele, Jayant. 1981. 'Community, Discourse and Critique in Jnanesvar', in Jayant Lele (ed.), Tradition and Modernity in Bhakti Movements, Leiden: EJ, Brill, pp. 104-12.

————— . 1995. *Hindutva: The, Emergence of the. Right*, Madras: Earthworm Books.

More, Sadanand. 1996. *Tukaram Darshan*, Pune: Gaj Prakashan.

Pawar, Urmila. 2003. 'Hidden Behind the Curtain: Women in Maharashtra Who Made History Too, article translated by Kunda Pramila Neelkanth, and excerpted in *IAWS Newsletter*, pp. 26-30.

Sunder Rajan, Rajeshwari. 2000. 'Introduction: Feminism and Politics of Resistance', *Indian Journal of Gender Studies*, 7(2): 153-65.

Ramanujan, A.K.1973. *Speaking of Siva*, Harmondsworth: Penguin Books.

————— . 1989. 'Talking to God in the Mother Tongue', *Manushi*, 50-52: 9-14.

Ramaswamy, Vijaya. 1997. *Walking Naked: Women, Society, Spirituality in South India*, Shimla: Indian Institute of Advanced Study.

Sangari, Kumkum. 1990. 'Mirabai and the Spiritual Economy of Bhakti' *Economic and*

Political Weekly, 25(27): 1464-75.

Sangari, Kumkum and Sudesh Vaid (eds.). 1989. *Recasting Women: Essays in Colonial History*, New Delhi: Kali for Women.

Sardar, G.B. 1969. *The Sant Poets of Maharashtra: Their Impact on Society*, New Delhi: Orient Longman.

Shevde, Indumati. 1989. *Sant Kavayatri: Stree Muktichya Maharashtratil Paulkhuna*. Mumbai: Popular Prakashan.

Thapar, Romila. 2000. 'Imagined Religious Communities? Ancient History and the Modern Search for a Hindu Identity', in Romila Thapar (ed.), *Cultural Pasts: Essays in Early Indian History*, New Delhi: Oxford University Press, p. 970.

Tharu, Susie and K. Lalitha (eds.). 1991. *Women Writing in India: 600 B.C. to the Present*, Vols. 1 and 2, New York: The Feminist Press,

Zelliot, Eleanor. 1987. 'Eknath's Bharuds: The Sant as Link Between Cultures', in Karine Schomer and W.H. Mcleod (eds.), *The Saints: Studies in a Devotional Tradition of India*. Religious Studies Series, Delhi: Motilal Banarasidass.

Chapter - 2

Marathi Literature as a Source for Contemporary Feminism

Till very recently Indian women were treated as a silent lot in Indian history. No one had expected them to possess a voice of their own. The notion of recording their alternative conceptions of culture and power simply did not exist. Nor was there any idea of studying Indian women's successive critiques of ideology for the purposes of the present. Almost overnight we are experiencing a sea-change. Anyone who wishes to study Indian women is talking not only about their evergreen creativity but also about the vigour and quality of their expression. We have gone even further. Instead of talking about one monolithic tradition of Indian women's protest and creativity, we acknowledge the immense variety of their projects and voices. We are demanding new research on these differences with the hope that comparisons with other regions and languages may in due course of time yield a coherent and meaningful body of knowledge.

I too was part of this process of growth. I also took an inordinately long time to realise that I was a part of a tradition that I could bank upon; a rich tradition which opened for me, when in need, new cultural vistas and made available fresh conceptual frameworks in dealing with the problems of the present. Now I think I know something about this tradition in Maharashtra, as available through Marathi literature. I, therefore, need to tell you how I made this kind of a theoretical journey. My observations will obviously be rooted in my background and be limited by it. But hopefully they may make some progress in a new direction in women's studies.

I was born and brought up in an urban middle class family in Mumbai. My parental family shared more or less the same values which pervaded families of similar social status. It was neither an orthodox nor a progressive household. The needs and priorities of the male members, namely, of my father and two brothers, always took precedence over the interests and aspirations of my mother and myself. But this was taken almost as a natural state of affairs by us all. It was not that I did not realise the secondary importance which was given to me in comparison with my brothers. I did entertain some resentment about it. But no senior woman relative of mine, including my mother, nor anyone in the large circle of my schoolmate girls ever thought it fit or worthwhile to discuss similar experiences of their own. In the final years of my school life, when I was 12-16 years old, I came under the influence of two remarkable teachers—a man and a woman—who introduced me for the first time in my life to the larger universe of social and political thought and practice. I began to take animated and uninhibited interest in all social and political events which impinged upon my existence. Still no one, even in this new circle, paid any attention to women's problems, predicaments and perspectives. The ill treatment experienced by women was no doubt noted and talked about. But it was believed that the emancipation of the society as a whole could eventually put an end to all women's problems. When I left my schooldays behind and entered the realm of collegiate education, I still did not experience much of a change in terms of my experiences as a woman. As a teenager and then as a young woman, I had to take some extra precautions in my deportment and expression to avoid eve-teasing and occasional male harassment. The need for these additional disciplinary controls was routinely absorbed by me. Again no one in my domestic or public circles made me see these additional burdens as a problem. At the university level, I specialised in Marathi language and literature. My teachers and fellow-students owing loyalties to competing ideologies and political programmes often used to utilise the entire body of Marathi literature to seek support for their positions. The radicals used to unearth and analyse protests against the traditional social order and/or the orthodox literary canons. Interestingly, the differentiations and the specificities related to the caste or class of these texts and authors were thoroughly discussed. In this whole game, it was a quite common practice to draw upon relevant material from women writers—ancient and modern. Yet no one took note of the voices of women as women. In sharp contrast to the attention paid to the caste or class dimensions, the gender dimension of the whole literary and social history was not mentioned. In a nutshell, my formal education left me sex-blind in tackling problems of culture and power.

After the first three to five years of my married life. I once again began to participate in contemporary radical movements around me. Both within India and outside radicalism was in ascendency. The students, the youth, the blacks, the women and oppressed minorities of all kinds had taken the path of revolt. In India various kinds of grassroots organisations and movements were coming up in a big way. A major and a very welcome and creative change was taking place. The young radicals from all quarters were throwing off the shackles of dogmatic versions of Marxism, democratic socialism, and for that matter even liberalism. They were adopting new conceptual frameworks and experimenting with new strategies of action. Problems of the various oppressed sections of the Indian society—the tribals, cultural and religious minorities, slum dwellers, landless labourers, the non-organised sections of the toiling masses, etc— were highlighted and discussed in depth. In most cases a conscious attempt was made at the theoretical and practical levels to reappropriate in a dynamic manner the emancipatory content of traditional texts and of the tradition itself within which they are embedded. A creative release of the essential core of tradition into a new context was sought. The Marxists as well as the liberals endeavoured to utilise the revolutionary potential in tradition to justify their new strategies and concerns.

The contemporary feminist movement in Maharashtra also arose in the wake of this development. A number of dedicated women's groups with different ideological perspectives emerged - first in Mumbai, then in Pune and soon in other urban centres and finally even in the countryside. Women's studies programmes were also inaugurated. Yet the feminist movement in Maharashtra differed from other radical movements in one crucial area. The non-feminist radical movements were increasingly refusing to treat tradition as a deadweight opposed to modernity and emancipation. They were trying to develop a critique of tradition which would lay bare its essential emancipatory core. For a long time feminists ignored their own tradition of a succession of women *sants* and other women writers who had inverted and occasionally even subverted the classic ideals of womanhood embodied in the hegemonic texts. The movement paid a price for this failure. It appeared to be based on dry, upstart ideas lacking roots in the soil. It is only recently, when the movement lost some of its momentum, that I began to worry about this lacuna. In my restlessness and also as a part of my other commitments and interests, I turned to literature for comfort and, honestly, even some kind of an escape from the harsh realities of social life. Suddenly I discovered the tremendous potential of the Marathi tradition which asserted women's right to lead a life of their own. This realisation not only provided me with new sources of energy and ideas but opened my eyes to whole areas where women's studies can achieve remarkable progress and fruition. Accordingly I present here the way I came to see the continuity of women's protests in Marathi literature right from its inception to the present day.

I. Pre-colonial period

The first phase of women's literature in Marathi covers a period from 13th century AD to the beginning of colonial rule at the end of the 18th century. During these six centuries we come across a long line of women saints. They followed one after the other with amazing regularity. Some of them are known and cherished in all Maharashtrian households. I soon realised that they were known in a certain curious manner. These women were without exception referred to in relation to their male gurus or mentors. For example, we always talk of *Mahadaisa* of *Chakradhar*, *Jani* of *Namya*, 'Little' *Muktai* of *Dnyaneshwar*, *Bahinabai* of *Tukaram*, *Venabai* of *Ramdas* and so on. This is a classic instance of how the hegemonic order manages to reappropriate emancipatory drives for its own legitimation. I began to ask myself a question. Why had feminists not perceived a theoretical challenge when they came across these male-oriented identifications of these bold women writers?

Mahanubhav women

I first realised this when I began to consult the writings of the heretic *Mahanubhav* sect which emerged in the second half of the 13th century. A succession of *Mahanubhav* women writers including *Mahadamba, Kamalaisa, Hiraisa, Nagaisa* have left for posterity us a rich store of authentic protest literature. As Raeside has observed, the *Mahanubhav* doctrine is '. . . designed only for the *sanyasi*. There is no provision for lay hangers on, no ritual, no real sense of community, no tangible objects of worship — except of course for *Chakradhar* (the founder of the sect) himself as the latest incarnation at God' (in Tulpule 1979: 592). *Chakradhars* radical measures included a ban on the ritual isolation of menstruating women, a common feature of Brahmanism. *Chakradhar* himself had rebelled against various indignities meted out to women. One episode in *Leelacharitra* recording the story of his life goes this way. A brahmin had five daughters. All of them were widows. The neighbours habitually used to refer to them as *'Pandas'* (literally prostitutes). But *Chakradhar* himself always used to identify them as the *'panchaganga'* (five Gangas or rivers) (Kolte 1982: 405). *Chakradhar* has received high praise from modern social reformers and even literary critics. Ausa, his equally courageous woman follower, did not receive equal attention. *Pinda-dan*, the ritual offering of food to the soul of the dead, is laid down in the shastras as the duty of the son or, in his absence, of some other male member of the family. Women were denied the right to offer *pind-adan*. Yet Ausa declared that

> I am the daughter and
> I am the son too
> (*Kolte* 1982: 399)

This expression of exemplary defiance of the oppressive patriarchal order was not emphasised even in the *Mahanubhav* tradition. Another *Mahanubhav* woman, Baisa, also rebelled against the gender-based rules which permitted natural bodily movements and expressions for men but imposed severe restrictions on women in the name of privacy, grace and modesty. *Baisa* used to take her exercise of 250 *'sashtanga namaskars'* (prostrate salutations) unmindful of the men who might be gazing at the 'private' parts of her body (Kolte 1982: 415-17). Tradition praises *Chakradhar* for saying that a woman has no need to be ashamed when she has to bare her breast to feed her infant nor to feel embarrassed while bathing her child upon her exposed thighs, the common Indian practice (Kolte 1982: 227). Once again the silence maintained about *Baisa's* practice and the praise offered to *Chakradhar* stand in marked contrast.

Varkari women sants

We must turn to the *Varkari* tradition to understand the full depth and grandeur of women's protest in Maharashtra. Among the mass of people in all parts of Maharashtra and particularly in rural areas, the *Varkari* sect and its tradition remain today a source of inspiration and comfort. As Deleury a French ex-Jesuit scholar, has pointed out, it is not a church but a movement: '. . . –there is not centralised organisation, no hierarchy, not general councils, no credo, no sacraments (in Tulpule 1979: 2). Maharashtra's cultural ethos is to a considerable degree shaped by this religious upsurge of the 13th century, it was a part of the larger *bhakti* (devotion) movement which arose first in the Tamil region around the sixth century, and later spread from there to encompass Kannada, Marathi, Hindi and other language areas. It played a role similar to that of the Protestant movement in Europe. As Lele puts it, 'The *Varkari* poets spoke for a community of the oppressed ("sanvasarasranta") their critique of ideology through a philosophy of devotion in life (*"bhakti"*)' (Lele 1981:33). A.K. Ramanujan has made it clear that '*bhakti* movements are also social movements. We should not forget that here all sorts of crucial human experiences are cast in religious idiom. In *bhakti* "man is a man for all that" and women are very much a part of the scene. Feelings are more important than learning, status and privilege. In fact status, panditry even maleness and the pride that goes with such things are seen as obstacles to a true experience of God. Once such a position is taken, anyone at all is qualified to experience God. To be human is to be qualified' (Ramanujan 1973: 10). It is no wonder that radical intellectuals and movements in Maharashtra have tried to appropriate this rich heritage to further their causes as champions of the working class, the peasantry, the scheduled castes, the tribals. So too, later on, did radical nationalism use this tradition against alien domination (Sarda 1969; Patil 1982).

The *Varkari* movement produced a long line of women sants. Women of all castes and regions in Maharashtra—*Janabai, Muktabai, Gonai, Rajai, Ladai, Kanhopatra* and *Bahinabai*—have left a rich body of literature. This is no accident. All men sants in the *Varkari* movement always supported the cause of women. *Eknath* is considered to be one of the four pillars of this tradition. Zelliot has translated one of his songs *'Amba satvar pav ge mala'* (Zelliot 1987: 98-99).

> Save me now Mother—
> I'll offer you bread, Bhawani
> Father-in-law is out of town—
> Let him die there
> I'll offer you bread, Mother Bhawani
> Mother-in-law torments me—
> Kill her off,
> I'll offer you bread, Mother Bhawani
> Sister-in-law nags and nags
> Make her a widow
> I'll offer you bread, Bhawani
> Her brat cries and cries
> Give him the itch
> I'll offer you bread, Bhawani
> I'll give my husband as a sacrifice
> Free me mother!
> I'll offer you bread, Bhawani
> Eka Janardan says
> Let them all die
> Let me live, alone!

The song offers a classic example of the Varkari understanding of women's problems. Zelliot writes, 'A woman's plea to the Goddess for deliverance from husband and in-laws is one of *Eknath's* most popular bharuds today—in spite of the fact that it counters the image of the devoted wife!' The *bharud* (a moralising burlesque) can be interpreted in metaphysical terms as an allegory for casting off various sins and worldly attachments. It can also be interpreted as a comment on the necessity for women *bhakti* sants to give up husbands and homes to achieve the freedom to devote themselves to the worship of their Lord, as *A.K. Ramanujan* has pointed out. The *Eknath* touch is that it also reads as a married woman's bitter, ironic and quite funny cry for release. Both *Amba* and *Bhawani* are common Maharashtrian names for the Goddess.

When I started reading sant literature, I came to realise that it is a large reservoir of an imminent critique of patriarchal oppression. Recently the feminist movement and the women's studies centres in Maharashtra have made some efforts to interpret and analyse this tradition (Desai 1985; Sherade 1989; Bhagwat 1990). A lot more can be done in this direction.

Since research carried on by leading feminist scholars like *Kumkum Sangari, Sudesh Vaid, Uma Chakravarti* and *Kumkum Roy* usually appears in English, it rarely reaches activists in the women's or Dalit movements. The latter tend to shy away from studying *Bhakti* literature for fear of being branded 'brahman' or 'Hindu'. If however, we listen to the women sants, we would certainly secure valuable insights into the history of Maharashtra as well as into contemporary problems.

Take *Janabai*, for example. She was born into a *shudra* (low caste) family and functioned as a dasi, that is, as a bonded domestic servant. While the tradition insists that the household in which she worked brought her up benevolently as one of its own, the fact remains that *Janabai* always identified herself as *'Dasi Jani'*. Her poetry is full of references to the hard chores which she had to perform, which deprived her of the space necessary for a dialogue with her own emancipatory God. In one of her oft-quoted *'abhangas'* (devotional songs), *Janabai* says:

> As a kite roams in the sky
> And still thinks of its young ones

> Or as a mother is trapped in the household work
> And yet longs for a child
> Or as a female monkey climbs from tree to tree
> And yet clasps its young ones
> So is mother Vithoba to us, says Jani.
> (*Shri Namdev Gatha* 1970: 940)

Through total surrender to *Vithoba*, the heretic, ritual-free God of Pandharpur, *Janabai* recovered her status as a free and autonomous human being. Her poems offer us a combination of a deeply felt sorrow, a product of the fact that she was born as woman, and a confident assertion that she could in real life undermine the cultural confines which denied identity to her kind. In another famous *'abhanga'*, she declares:

> I will let my saree slip
> From my head to the shoulders
> Hold my head high and walk
> Into the market-place
> Taking cymbals in hand and veena on shoulder I will go
> Let me see who forbids me
> I have opened a shop in Pandharpur
> Put oil on my wrist now
> Jani declares herself a prostitute
> Leaving you O God, this 'home'
> (*Shri Namdev Gatha* 1970: 171)

Ramanujan comments on this song: '... Such a throwing away of clothes is a throwing away of concessions to social conventions, defences and investments. Nakedness signifies being open to the experience of God' (Ramanujan 1989: 13).

> I am completely relaxed
> I am exulted, happy in all respects
> I am indifferent to distinctions
> Of sex or body
> (*Shri Namdev Gatha* 1970: 963)

She states categorically:

I am known to the world
As merely Nama's maid servant
I am not learned
I have not listened to discourses
Nor have I contemplated
I do not understand proprieties or
improprieties of this world
(*Shri Namdev Gatha* 1970: 971)

And yet the stamp *Namayachi dasi* (Namdeo's maid) has sealed her true message to this day. It is for us as students of women's studies to release it.

Then take *Muktabai* When I read her, I was struck by her profound statement that:

Do you desire self realisation?
Then do not blindly follow others.
Search for the truth in your own self
There lies wisdom.
(*Tatiche Abhanga* 1978: 12)

The strength of her character and conviction is attested by the following myth which is popular in *Varkari* circles. It is recorded in the *Hari vijay*, a popular text of the *Varkaris*. Once when *Muktabai* was bathing in the nude, *Changdev*, a reputed male *yogi*, happened to come that way. When he saw her, he turned his back in shame. *Muktabai* found fault with his behaviour, as he was known as an accomplished yogi. She told him quite bluntly that:

One is not ashamed to stare at
The niches in the wall
Do the cows grazing in the
Fields have any clothes!
I too am like the cows.

Why are you embarrassed at my sight?
As Ramanujan has remarked, '. . . By exposing the difference between
male and female, by becoming indifferent to that difference, she is liberated
from it—and liberates anyone who will attend to it (Ramanujan 1973:
13)'.

Bahinabai was the last great women sant in this tradition. Even though
a brahmin by birth, she accepted Tukaram, a great *Varkari* sant of *shudra*
origins, as her *guru*. This created a crisis in his personal life. As Feldhouse
relates '. . . with wounded pride, unable to understand devotional religion,
and full of the prejudice of his high caste and superior sex, *Bahina's*
husband prepared to leave her...' (Feldhouse 1982: 569). In a perceptive
account of *Bahinabai's* life and work Hardy has noted: 'it is certainly
true that some general complex, say *"bhakti"*, was operative in *Bahina's*
environment independently from whatever personal application an
individual might use it for. Nevertheless *Bahina* shows quite clearly that
such complexes become alive only in specific, individual contexts that
might in fact modify them considerably . . . And this resource itself was
by no means pre-given to her, it came about through unconscious struggle
and personal choice. The result too throws light on her Hinduism'. She
emerges as a woman who had come to terms with the problem of life,
ready to take on a positive, active note, and who at the same time knows
that . . . life has come to an end for her' (in Fridhelm 1982: 177). Bahinabai
was strong enough to defy the traditional ideal of a 'pativrata' (a loyal
wife) defended by the orthodox patriarchal order. She chose to interpret
her 'pativrata dharma' (wifely duty) in a startlingly novel manner. She
says:

> You cannot approach God
> If you do not love your husband

But then she adds that

> A true wife is she who is aware of her own self
> Being married she has to fulfil her family duties;
> But she must have the craving for spiritual salvation too.

> It is possible that the husband
> Children and others may not approve
> But she must not give up her true path

She asserts:

> She whose mind constantly contemplates God
> Is recognised in the three worlds as the dutiful wife
> (*Sant Bahinabaincha Gatha* 1979: 205)

She, therefore, concludes that women as also men who live their worldly lives with a sense of *'nijananda gnana'* (supreme self realisation) are true wives. The path of a true wife is as necessary for a man as it is for a woman. A measure of *Bahinabai's* achievement can be gained from the fact that in the end she actually managed to convert her husband to the *Varkari* sect. She persuaded him even to accept *Tukaram* as his *guru*!

Bahinabai also interpreted her duty towards her child in a revolutionary manner. She bore only one child and regretted this bitterly. Using a strategy totally different from the stereotype handed down by the patriarchal order through the centuries, she transformed her child in her mind and treated him as a companion in a former life. *Bahinabai* must have gained this audacity and independence of mind through her close contact with the living tradition of emancipatory resistance waged by the outstanding women saints from the 13th century to her own 18th century.

In my opinion women's studies have much to gain from following seriously Ramanujan's advice: 'anyone who wishes to study Indian women, listen to their voices, and find alternative conceptions in Indian civilisation, often startlingly different from what one is used to in our classics, should turn to materials like the lives and poems of the women saints, women's tales, songs, riddles, games and proverbs in oral traditions all over the country and the myths and cults of goddesses' (Ramanujan 1989: 14).

II. Colonial period

The years 1818-1984 span the period of colonial domination. Colonialism gave rise to a new English educated class of intellectuals. In the words of Lele, 'The new intellectuals had the task of justifying not only their own subaltern existence but also an alien regime, looked upon with suspicion both by the indigenous ruling class and the common people' (Lele 1989: 35). This new intelligentsia absorbed some of the utilitarian, individualistic, radical bourgeois ideas from its western counterpart. Its enthusiasm for spreading female education at all levels had striking results. There appeared a new body of creative and critical literature in Marathi, both by women and about women. According to Dandavate, during the years from 1873 to 1920 some 300 women produced books, pamphlets, occasional papers, poems, short stories, novels and essays devoted to a variety of topics (Dandavate 1921: 2-3). A good idea of the depth and quality of women's protest and the level of consciousness can be gained from the writings by three outstanding 19th century women—*Tarabai Shinde* (c.1850-1910), *Pandita Ramabai* (c. 1858-1922), and *Anandibai Joshi* (c. 1865-1889).

Tarabai Shinde's now famous essay *'Stree Punish Tulana'* (A Comparison of Men and Women) with a subtitle 'An Article Penned by *Tarabai Shinde* with the Purpose of Making a Comparison between Men and Women and Intending to Explain as to Who—the Men or Women—Are the More Brave' remained virtually unknown until 1975 when it was accidentally found by the well-known scholar of Marathi literature, S.G. Malshe. Till then only a reference to it in one of the essays of Jotirao Phule had kept its memory alive. *Tarabai* is beyond doubt a very original, courageous and brilliant critic. Her bold exposure of patriarchal oppression was so far ahead of her times that the public lapse of memory in this case cannot be an accident!

Tarabai Shinde inherited the tradition of the counter-cultural revolt by the oppressed non-brahmin castes of Maharashtra under the revolutionary leadership of *Jotirao Phule* (1827-1890) who challenged all aspects of the brahmanical hegemony and gave a bitter and comprehensive exposure of brahmanic ideology. He took the radical step of starting the first school for girls as well as the first school for *shudra* and *atishudra* (non-brahmin *sawarna* castes and untouchable castes) children—both boys and girls. At the theoretical and programmatic level, Phule worked for a broad alliance of all non-brahmin castes and women against the orthodox Hindu social order. *Tarabai Shinde's* booklet was published in 1882 in response to an article that had appeared in *Pune Vaibhav* with regard to a hotly discussed incident. A young widow named *Vijayalaxmi* had been sentenced to death by the court for committing infanticide. *Pune Vaibhav* printed an article making a vicious attack on *Vijayalaxmi* and women in general for their 'modernistic', 'loose' morality. Tarabai's essay picks up every single accusation made against women and demonstrates how men invariably are themselves the perpetrators of the very vices they so often locate in women. *Tarabai* must have been familiar with the various themes in the contemporary social reform debate in Pune and western Maharashtra. O'Hanlon has pointed out that 'what these different male perspectives shared in common, however, was the focus itself upon women's immorality other than that of the men willing to consort with them, and upon women's conduct in general as the central and sensitive barometer of the health of the tradition'. More importantly O'Hanlon remarks with great insight, 'In slightly different ways, both perspectives (orthodox and liberal reformist) created a position for women in public discourse at once of acute responsibility and of powerlessness, confined within an essentialized nature and deprived of any recognised presence of power of agency on their own account'. *Tarabai Shinde* offered the first fully worked out analysis of the ideological fabric of Hindu patriarchal society. She also has the distinction of being the first Indian feminist literary critic. *Tarabai's* exposure of male stereotypes of women appeared almost a century before Simone de Beauvoir's *The Second Sex*. Some idea of her thinking may be gained from the following arguments:

God brought this amazing universe into being, and He it was also who created men and women both. So is it true that only women's bodies are home to all kinds of wicked vices? Or have men got just the same faults as we find in women? I wanted this to be shown absolutely clearly, and that's the reason I've written this small book, to defend the honour of all my sister countrywomen. I am not looking at particular castes or families here. It's a comparison just between women and men (O'Hanlon 1994: 75).

And again:

But every day now we have to look at some new and more horrible example of men who are really wicked and their shameless lying tricks. And not a single person says anything about it. Instead people go about pinning the blame on women all the time as if everything bad was their fault. When I saw this, my whole mind just began churning and shaking out of feeling for the honour of womankind. So I lost all my fear, I just couldn't stop myself writing about it in this very biting language (O'Hanlon 1994: 7).

She goes on in the same tone:

Because you men all are the same, all full of lies and dirty tricks. But I come from the weaker side of nature, so you will see all sorts of faults in this book still, all I've done here is write down what I see with my eyes (O'Hanlon 1994: 77).

The utter independence of thought and person that *Tarabai* had achieved can be judged by the lines which immediately follow the above passage. She continues:

I am not going to ask all the usual things here—don't just ignore this book, read it carefully, give it some support and so on. All I ask if you're really someone with an open mind, think about it carefully and see if what I say is true or not. But if you just kick your horses forward to protect those fancy reputations of yours I've got no remedy for that. Still, I will myself always struggle and strive for the good of my own kind, and keep on sowing the seed of good conduct in their minds (O'Hanlon 1994: 77).

With the solitary exception of *Jotirao Phule* no one even in *Satyashodhak Samaj* (the radical non-brahmin movement) established by him cared to take Tarabai's work seriously. In fact, *Krishnarao Bhulekar*, a close associate of Phule and the number two man in the *Satyashodhak* movement, made a violent attack on the book, not devoid of personal abuse. It is no wonder the essay was allowed to be forgotten. *Tarabai's* narrative device is simple. She takes one by one every single representation by men of female nature in authoritative *Sanskrit* and vernacular literature, cultural and religious canons, and refutes them pour:int by point. A similar strategy was adopted a century later by Simone de Beauvoir in *'The Second Sex'*.

Why is it that the contemporary feminist movement in Maharashtra (and elsewhere in India) and the existing women's studies programmes have failed to conceive of a programme of analysis of the entire structure of Indian masculinist culture? It seems to me that there must be something in our approach that has made us blind to the possibilities of employing strategies which *Tarabai Shinde* had pioneered in our own country.

Another remarkable figure produced by the 19th century social ferment in Maharashtra was *Pandita Ramabai* (1858-1992), who became a legendary figure very early in her life. A.B. Shah, an author known for his preference for understatement, talks of *Ramabai's* achievements in these words.

> *Pandita Ramabai Saraswati* . . . was the greatest woman produced by modern India and one of the greatest Indians in all history . . . She was a *Sanskrit* scholar. She was the first to introduce the kindergarten system of education and also the first to give a vocational bias to school education in India . . . She was the first to rebel against the inhuman slavery to which widows are subjected in Hindu society and to lay the foundations of a movement for women's liberation in India . . . while she accepted, even invited, assistance from all over the world, she never compromised her principles for the sake of pleasing anyone (Shah 1977: xi).

Pandita Ramabai's autobiography *A Testimony* and many other important books including *'The High-Caste Hindu Woman'* and *'Stree Dharma Neeti'* (Morals for Women) written both in English and Marathi stand testimony to her theoretical clarity, analytical vigour and realism.

Pandita Ramabai took the courageous step of accepting Christian faith even though she came from the highest bracket of the Maharashtrian Hindu social order (she was by birth a Chitpavan brahmin). The independence and integrity of her character is clear when we realise that she carried throughout her life a simultaneous battle against both the Hindu and the Christian religious hierarchies as well as against Hindu and Christian masculinist social norms. In a letter to Sister Geraldine, her church supervisor, dated May 12, 1885, she wrote bluntly:

> It seems to me that you are advising me under the WE (authorities of the Sisters of the Community of St Mary the Virgin, Wantage, England) to accept always the will of those who have authority, etc. This, however, I cannot accept. I have a conscience, and a mind and a judgment of my own. I must myself think and do everything which GOD has given me the power of doing . . . Although priests and bishops may have certain authority over the church, yet the church has another Master who is superior even to the bishops. I am, it is true, a member of the church of Christ, but I am not bound to accept every word that falls down from the lips of priests or bishops . . . Obedience to the law and to the word of God is quite different from perfect obedience to priests only. I have just with great effort freed myself from the yoke of the Indian priestly tribe, so I am not at present willing to place myself under another similar yoke by accepting everything which comes from the priests as authorised command of the Most High. (Shah 1977: 59)

The bold and yet balanced attack made by *Ramabai* on the patriarchal order is exemplified in the following passage drawn from her book 'The *High-Caste Hindu Woman'* published in 1887. She writes.

Those who have done their best to keep women in a state of complete dependence and ignorance vehemently deny that this has anything to do with the present degradation of the Hindu religion. I pass over the hundreds of nonsenses which are brought forward as the strongest reasons for keeping women in ignorance and dependence . . . meanwhile it is our duty to take the matter into serious consideration, and to put forth our best endeavours to hasten the glad day for India's daughters, aye, and for her sons also; because in spite of proud assertions of our brethren that they have not suffered from the degradation of women, their own condition betrays but too plainly the contrary (Ramabai 1981: 48).

Anandibai Joshi (1865-89) is another remarkable woman of the last quarter of the 19th century. After her marriage at the age of nine, her husband in a typical colonial reformist fashion compelled her to embark on a course of western-style education. In 1883, she went to the US for advanced medical studies and she graduated in 1886 from Women's Medical College in Philadelphia. She was the first Indian women to study modern medicine. In February 1889, very soon after her return from America, she died at the very young age of 24. Her correspondence with her husband from the US gives us a good idea of the tremendous insights she gained into the Hindu and Christian patriarchal systems. From her letters it is clear that she saw through the strategies employed by the 'modern', 'progressive' Indian educated men in the period of anti-colonial nationalism to mould a 'new' Indian woman to suit their emerging bourgeois needs and tastes. She was able to set forth in clear objective terms the price which men have to pay for enslaving women. Unlike *Ramabai*, whom she knew well, she did not change her religion. In a sketch of her own preferences. *Anandibai* identified slavery and subjugation as the things in the world which she most disliked (Kanitkar 1912).

The record of these three 19th century Marathi women thinkers gives us an idea of the rich heritage of women's protest literature which we have hardly begun to tap for our purposes. Even the treasure of women's writing of our own century is so rich as to justify a long-term programme of collective research.

III. Post-1967 protest literature

For want of space I pass over the women's literature from the beginning of the 20th century to 1967. The writings of these years reflect the perspectives and experiences of women in the environment of the freedom movement, the epoch of *Mahatma Gandhi* and *Pandit Nehru*. By 1967 the good as well as the poor results of the development strategies adopted by Indian decision-makers began to be manifested. Indian society was in the process of shedding its pre-industrial form. Inevitably more cleavages and discontinuities than in the earlier period characterize Indian society today. Women's protest literature of the period since 1967 comprises a wide variety of approaches in terms of both substance and form of expression. *Gauri Deshpande*, for example, expresses creatively the aspirations and the dilemmas of women who have accepted the values and life-styles of progressive individualism. The concerns and woes she depicts are typical of her upper class, highly literate, westernised elite sisters. *Kamal Desai* also adopts liberal, reformist, individualistic world views but betrays her typical middle class upbringing. On the other hand, there are also women writers belonging to both the above mentioned circles who have produced a quite different self-conscious 'women's literature'.

A striking aspect of post-1967 women's literature in Maharashtra is the emergence of Dalit women writers. The dalit movement in Maharashtra represents the revolt of the former untouchable castes against the Hindu/ Indian social order. The movement is based for the most part on the *Mahars* (the largest untouchable caste in Maharashtra) many of whom have given up the Hindu faith and accepted Buddhism as an emancipatory measure. The very term dalit sheds light on the militancy of the movement. It represents a deliberate and deeply felt rejection of the vocabulary employed by the caste Hindus. It refuses equally the designation 'untouchables', the patronising term *'harijan'* proposed by *Mahatma Gandhi* and the official, legalistic version 'scheduled castes'. Dalit implies a secular, egalitarian, emancipative, militant self-identification by the lowest rungs of the Hindu social order. It opens a path for strategies of solidarity on the part of all oppressed humanity including women. The literary and cultural vitality of the dalit protest is amazing. In a number of ways the dalit movement and literature of Maharashtra parallels the Black movement and literature of the US. With the spread of education among the neo-Buddhist women, dalit women writers like *Baby Kamble, Mallika Dhasal, Jyoti Langewar* and *Urmila Pawar* have emerged on the scene. They have slowly begun to articulate not only women's agonies in general, but also the experiences and agonies specific to their caste.

Mallika Dhasal is the wife of *Namdev Dhasal*, a leading figure in Dalit movement. *Namdev* is himself a poet, a creative writer and a militant political leader. *Mallika* was born and brought up in a socialist home. Her father was a Muslim and an active member of the Communist Party. *Mallika* concludes her autobiography *'Mala Uddhvasta Vhaychay'* (I want to be Destroyed) in these words:

> How many times have I gone through an ordeal . . . I have pulled myself to the lowest level . . . My whole life was dragged . . . This is really eating me . . . I had self respect. Instead of calling myself a women's liberationist I would say that I and any other woman in this world is born free and a woman should retain that freedom at any cost. As long us a woman burns her selfness to save her husband and home she will remain a subordinate human being. Man or anyone for that matter will not leave his power easily. Is not it true that we women feed the ego of men? A woman should never tolerate deceit. This is her biggest insult and why? Does woman alone need physical love? The husband who wants his wife to be honest and committed only to him, is it not his duty to observe the same rules? People say that it is very common to have an extra-marital 'affair' and then brush it off. They are bound to justify such things because they are benefited by it. But women's thinking is also very stilted and they refuse to speak. They say 'A man is born that way. He comes back at the end!' and keep quiet for saving the family's honour. This non-speaking is bad . . . as long as you go on tolerating something, the burden of injustice goes on increasing (Amarsheikh 1984: 123-24).

IV Summing up

This overview of women's protest literature in Maharashtra makes clear the irreceivability of any notion that Marathi women took a meek, passive and fatalistic position in the face of the patriarchal order. Once we give up the usual orientalist perspective treating Indian and hence Maharashtrian history as one of stagnation, we can appropriate women's literature through all these centuries as a resource for understanding our own problems and dilemmas. Marathi women's literature from the 13th century onwards gives us a key to the conceptual and practical strategies employed by women to create counter-cultural meanings and spaces. At the same time we should not treat women as a monolithic category. We have seen how their individual voices are concrete and specific, reflecting their own personal, caste and class experiences. We must not be in a hurry to impose on them our own ideological or methodological frameworks. We shall have to make deliberate attempts to develop new canons of literary and social criticism to ensure that a woman's voice is listened to as such and not as a reverberation of something else. In other words, we should try to study the concerns and problems of women which have been actualised in their literature. A sensitive understanding of the visions and utopias entertained by these women can serve as a proper basis for developing a sound historical critique of patriarchy. A knowledge of the multiple strategies of open and guerrilla defence employed by women over the past seven centuries will help us to draw up a concrete programme of action for today and tomorrow.

Original Source

Feminism in India
Chaudhari, Maitrayee (Ed.)
Kali for women and Women Unlimited, New Delhi
2004
(pp: - 296-317)

References

Amarsheikh, Mallika. 1984. *Mala Uddhvasta Vhaychay* (I Want to be Destroyed), Mumbai: Majestic Book Stall.

Bhagwat, Vidyut.1990. 'Man-Woman Relations in the Writings of the Sant Poetesses' *New Quest*, pp. 223-32.

Chakravarti, Uma and Kumkum Roy. 'Breaking Out of Invisibility: *Rewriting the History of Women in Ancient India'* in Retrieving *Women's History : Changing Perceptions of the Role of Women in Politics and Society,* Oxford: Berg/Unesco.

Dandavate, Ganesh Raghunath (eds.).1921. *Marathi Stree Lekhikanchi Suchi* (A List of Marathi Women Writers) 1983-1921, G.R. Dandavate, Baroda Central Library.

Desai, Neera. 1989. 'Women and the Bhakti Movement' in Sangari and Vaid (1989).

————. 1994. *Women and Culture*, Research Centre for Women's Studies, SNDT, Mumbai.

Feldhouse, Ann .1982. 'Bahinabai: Wife and Sant' in *The Journal of the American Academy of Religion.*

Friedhelm, Hardy. 'The Diary of an Unknown Indian Girl.'

Kanitkar, Kashibai. 1912. *Doctor Anandibai Joshi Yanche Charitra* (Dr. Anandibai Joshi's Biography), Pune: Sevasadan.

Kolte, V.B. (ed.). 1982. *Leela Charitre,* Mumbai: Maharashtra Rajya Sahitya Sanskrit! Mandal.

Lele, Jayant. 1989. 'Tradition and Intellectuals in a Third World Society' in Lele and Singh (eds.) *Language and Society: Steps Towards an Integrated Theory,* Leiden: E.J. Brill.

Muktabai Sant. 1978. *Tatiche Abhanga,* Pune: Anmol Prakashan.

O'Hanlon, Rosalind. 1994. *A Comparison between Women and Men: Tarabai Shinde and the Critique of Gender Relations in Colonial India,* Delhi: Oxford University Press.

Ramabai, Pandita. 1867. *Stree-Dharma Niti,* Pune: Sadhana Prakashan, (reprinted in 1982).

————. 1887. *The High-Caste Hindu Woman,* Mumbai: Maharashtra State Board for Literature and Culture, (reprinted 1981).

Ramanujan, A.K. .1973): *Speaking of Shiva,* Baltimore: Penguin Books.

————. 1982. 'On Women Sants' in Hawley and Wulff (eds.) *The Divine Consort: Radha and the Goddess of India,* reprinted, 1986.

Sangari, Kumkum and Sudesh Vaid (eds.). 1989. *Recasting Women: Essays in Colonial History,* New Delhi: Kali for Women.

Sardar, G.B. 1969. *The Sant Poets of Maharashtra: Their Impact on Society,* New Delhi: Orient Longman.

Shah, A.B. 1977. The *Letters and Correspondence of Pandita Ramabai,* Mumbai: Maharashtra State Board for Literature and Culture.

Shevade, Indumati.1989. *Sant Kasayitri: Stree Maharashtratil Paulkhuno,* Mumbai: Popular Prakashan.

Shri Namdev Gatha . 1970, Mumbai: Shasakiya Madhyavarti Mudranalay.

Tulpule, S.G. 1979. *Classical Marathi Literature from the Beginning to AD 1818,* Wiesbaden: Otto Harassowitz.

Zelliot, Eleanor. 1987. 'Eknath's Bharuds: The Sant as Link between Cultures', in Schonckarince and W.H. McLeod (eds.), *The Sants: Studies in a Devotional Tradition of India,* Delhi: Motilal Banarasidass.

Chapter - 3

Man-Woman Relations in the Writings of the Sant Poetesses*

Till very recently Indian women were treated as a silent lot in Indian history. No one had expected them to possess a voice of their own. The motion of recording their alternative conceptions of culture and power simply did not exist. Nor was there any idea of studying Indian women's successive critiques of ideology for the purposes of the present. Almost overnight we are experiencing a sea-change. Anyone who wishes to study Indian women is talking not only about their evergreen creativity but also about the vigour and quality of their expression. We have gone even further. Instead of talking about one monolithic tradition of Indian women's protest and creativity, we acknowledge the immense variety of their projects and voices. We are demanding new research on these differences with the hope that comparisons with other regions and languages may in due course of time yield a coherent and meaningful body of knowledge.

I too was part of this process of growth. I also took an inordinately long time to realize that I was a part of a tradition which I could bank upon; a rich tradition, which opened for me, when in need, new cultural vistas and made available fresh conceptual frameworks in dealing with the problems of the present. Now I think I know something about this tradition in Maharashtra, as available through Marathi literature. I, therefore, need

---

* Extracted from: Vidyut Bhagwat, 'Man-Woman Relationship in the Writings of Sant Poetesses', *New Quest*, July-August, 1990 and 'Marathi Literature as a Source for Contemporary Feminism', *EPW*: April 29, 1995.

to tell you how I made this kind of a theoretical journey. My observations will obviously be rooted in my background and be limited by it. But hopefully they may make some progress in a new direction in women's studies.

I was born and brought up in an urban middle class family in Mumbai. My parental family shared more or less the same values which pervaded families of similar social status. It was neither an orthodox nor a progressive household. The needs and priorities of the male members, namely, of my father and two brothers, always took precedence over the interests and aspirations of my mother and me. But this was taken almost as a natural state of affairs by us all. It wasn't that I did not realize the secondary importance which was given to me in comparison with my brothers. I did express some resentment about it. But no senior woman relative of mine, including my mother, nor anyone in the large circle of my schoolmate girls ever thought it fit or worthwhile to discuss similar experiences of their own. In the final years of my school life, when I was 12-16 years old, I came under the influence of two remarkable teachers - a man and a woman - who introduced me for the first time in my life to the larger universe of social and political thought and practice. I began to take animated and uninhibited interest in all social and political events, which impinged upon my existence. Still no one, even in this new circle, paid any attention to women's problems, predicaments and perspectives. The ill-treatment experienced by women was no doubt noted and talked about. But it was believed that the emancipation of the society as a whole could eventually put an end to all women's problems.

When I left my schooldays behind and entered the realm of collegiate education, I still did not experience much of a change in terms of my experiences as a woman. As a teenager and then as a young woman, I had to take some extra precautions to avoid eve-teasing and occasional male harassment. The need for these additional disciplinary controls was routinely absorbed by me. Again no one in my domestic or public circles made me see these additional burdens as a problem. At the university level, I specialized in Marathi language and literature. My teachers and fellow-students owing loyalties to competing ideologies and political programmes often used to utilize the entire body of Marathi literature to seek support for their positions. The radicals used to unearth and analyze protests against the traditional social order and/or the orthodox literary canons. Interestingly, the differentiations and the specificities related to the case or class of these texts and authors were thoroughly discussed. In this whole game, it was common practice to draw upon relevant material from women writers - ancient and modern. Yet no one took note of the voices of women as women. In sharp contrast to the attention paid to the caste or class dimensions, the gender dimension of the whole literary and social history was not mentioned. In a nutshell, my formal education left me sex-blind in tackling problems of culture and power.

After the first three to five years of my married life, I once again began to participate in contemporary radical movements around me. Both within India and outside, radicalism was in ascendancy. The students, the youth, the blacks, the women and oppressed minorities of all kinds had taken the path of revolt. In India, various kinds of grass roots organizations and movements were coming up in a big way. A major and a very welcome and creative change was .taking place. The young radicals from all quarters were throwing off the shackles of dogmatic versions of Marxism, democratic socialism, and for that matter even liberalism. They were adopting new conceptual frameworks and experimenting with new strategies of action. Problems of the various oppressed sections of the Indian society - the tribals, cultural and religious minorities, slum-dwellers, landless labourers, the non-organized sections of the toiling masses, etc. - were highlighted and discussed in depth. In most cases a conscious attempt was made at the theoretical and practical levels to reappropriate in a dynamic manner the emancipatory content of traditional texts and of the tradition itself within which they are embedded. A creative release of the essential core of tradition into a new context was sought. The Marxists as well as the liberals endeavoured to utilize the revolutionary potential in tradition to justify their new strategies and concerns.

The contemporary feminist movement in Maharashtra also arose in the wake of this development. A number of dedicated women's groups with different ideological perspectives emerged - first in Mumbai, then in Pune and soon in other urban centres and finally even in the countryside. Women's studies programmes were also inaugurated. Yet the feminist movement in Maharashtra differed from other radical movements in one crucial area. The non-feminist radical movements were increasingly refusing to treat tradition as a deadweight opposed to modernity and emancipation. They were trying to develop a critique of tradition which would lay bare its essential emancipatory core. For a long time feminists ignored their own tradition of a succession of women saints and other women writers who had inverted and occasionally even subverted the classic ideals of womanhood embodied in the hegemonic texts. The movement paid a price for this failure. It appeared to be based on dry, upstart ideas lacking roots in the soil. It is only recently, when the movement lost some of its momentum, that I began to worry about this lacuna. In my restlessness and also as a part of my other commitments and interests, I turned to literature for comfort and, honestly, even some kind of an escape from the harsh realities of social life. Suddenly I discovered the tremendous potential of the Marathi tradition which asserted women's right to lead a life of their own. This realization not only provided me with new sources of energy and ideas but opened my eyes to whole areas where women's studies can achieve remarkable progress and tradition.

Accordingly, in this paper, I have tried to probe into the lives and writings of the saint poetesses of Maharashtra in the context of man-woman relations. It is possible that some critics will dub this search as pointless. They will probably say that women like *Mahadaisa, Janabai* and *Muktabai* had already transcended the physiological division of humans into 'man' and 'woman'; that their search for salvation went beyond the limitations of the human body. Freedom meant to them only freedom of the spirit. Men and women craving for spiritual salvation have a total disregard for earthly happiness or unhappiness. They are involved in the broader and deeper problem of determining the relations between humans and the divinity. The joys and sorrows, torments and exultations - all the emotions of such persons have a significance which is unique. It could thus be argued that it is wholly wrong to apply to the writings of these saints - men and women - the contemporary criterion of inequality between men and women.

If this argument is taken to be sound, it leads to another question. If the saintly women like *Janabai* and *Muktabai* were *Mahayoginis*, had acquired the eight *sidhdhis,* conquered the five bodily senses and reached their ultimate goal of spiritual bliss - if all this were true, would it not be pertinent to ask as to how far the greatness of these women sants has gained recognition? Is it adequately and readily acknowledged?

Take the men sants of Maharashtra. There have been controversies as to whether there was one *Dnyaneshwar* or two. The organizational brilliance of *Namdeo* and *Ramdas* has come in for high praise. The spiritual message of *Tukaram's abhangas* has been the subject of many scholarly studies. Then, how is it that the achievement of the women saints has not received any such applauding attention? All these women poetesses are invariably referred in relation to their male mentors. For instance, it is always *Mahadaisa* of *Chakradhar*, *Jani* of *Namya*, little *Muktai* of *Dnyaneshwar*, *Bahenabai* of *Tukaram*, *Venabai* of *Ramdas* and so on. Why does social history have always to mention these women only in male-oriented terms?

Many literary and social scholars feel that the achievements of these women must have been far greater than their literary works, which have come down to us throughout centuries. Why is it then the case that their other accomplishments have been forgotten all these years? Why have these other merits of these noble women suffered non-recognition and oblivion?

There are many similar questions, which can be posed. It is generally accepted that these saintly women having transcended the body, followed the teachings of ancient sages and achieved ultimate bliss. However, their writings are often interspersed with references - direct or indirect - which reveal extremely bitter experiences that must have been their lot, due entirely to their femininity. It is true that all sants, men and women alike, have had to suffer the tribulations of worldly problems. The writings of the women sants, however, reveal to a far greater extent the mental tortures and physical sufferings which they had to bear, just because of their being women.

While a few of these women were gifted with the art of expressing their feelings and sufferings by way of oral or written words, one can only imagine the extent to which innumerable women of those days - girls, married women, widows - leading traditional, routine domestic and social life must have silently suffered, merely in consequence of their being females.

How is it that history does not record the torment of myriads of these utterly helpless, faceless women? In fact, even the male sants who have vividly described various human experiences in every walk of life with the minutest details, have not touched upon, with the same fervour, the sufferings of these women, which was part of the world in which they lived.

Marriage at a very early age, then the annual ritual of delivering a child, the back-breaking daily household chores and the obligation to bear this miserable lot in silence, without a word of protest - that was the fate ordained for women in the past. Sant poetesses represented the contemporary woman in the fullest measure and you can reach this woman, we feel, only through the writings of the women poets of the *Bhakti* period.

In anatomical terms, one may say that the saint movement was connected to the social reality around by an umbilical cord. To put it in Gramsci's words, sants were the organic leaders of the society. It is pertinent to note that no sant considered himself or herself as a person superior to the common people, but associated fully with them. In the compositions of the women sants, particularly, we vividly experience the link which binds us to them.

Janabai belonged to the *Shudra* caste. She was a maidservant of *Sant Namdeo*. But what a giant leap she took! She challenged the elite leaders of the society, the whole community, even God, all alike with pointed questions. She dared to move about in the open market taking off her *sari pallav* from the head down to her shoulder, a thing never done by a woman before. Was this not a trumpet call to all women to defy the shackles of meaningless customs and to assert their freedom?

The godliness of God can have its roots only in your belief in Him. *Janabai* had this perspective, this belief. Does this not have a message for women of today who regard their husbands and other elders as gods?

Muktabai, let us agree, gave up all thoughts of her mortal body and attained eternal bliss. But do we have to forget the torment she had to suffer before she could achieve her goal? Bereft in infancy of parents and destined to lead a life in wilderness with her divinely gifted brethren, *Muktabai*, a genius herself, could not only have enthralling experiences but could express them in words of infinite beauty:

The little ant took a leap to the sky and swallowed the sun itself.

What a gracious heritage for the women's movement of our times!

Mahadaisa (13th Century) and the *Mahanubhava Panth*

The first burst of notable women's protest in the Marathi language took place under the auspices of the heretic *Mahanubhava* sect, which emerged in the second half of the 13th century. A great line of women poetesses and prose-writers including women like *Mahadamba*, *Kamalaisa, Hiraisa, Nagaisa* have left for posterity a rich store of authentic protest literature. *Mahanubhava* was a sect of *Sanyasis* which had no place for ordinary laymen. *Chakradhara* was the founder of this sect and was looked upon as the latest incarnation of God. There were no rituals and no worship of concrete objects. From women's point of view, it should be noted that *Chakradhara's* radical measures included lifting of the ban on the participation of menstruating women in rituals, a common feature of *Brahmanism*.

One can, therefore, imagine the emancipatory space which the *Mahanubhava* women were able to carve out to shape a life of their own nursing, their own forms of life and expressions.

Mahadaisa, for instance, became a widow at an early age. As a matter of conscious choice, she became a *Sanyasini*, a priestess and a poetess of the *Mahanubhava* sect. Her writings as well as life tell us how the heretic sect *Mahanubhava* generated a possibility of transcendence for them.

The *Mahanubhava* cult along with *Leela Charitra* is an important part of the history and culture of Maharashtra.

> A woman is a cluster of intoxicating brews; all brews excite you only when they are sipped but the mere sight of a woman is enough to excite . . . Do not even look at the picture of a woman.

Chakradhar Swami, the founder of this cult said these words, which are clearly derogatory to women. They put a taboo even on looking at the picture of a woman, for fear that it will disrupt the tranquillity of a man. These words might lead us to consider *Chakradhar* as a male chauvinist, a misogynist. The *Leela Charitra* calls upon men to observe strict celibacy; but as far as one can gather, the book does not advocate with the same insistence celibacy for women!

Irrespective of this, the picture of woman and her femininity that one can see in the *Leela Charitra* is full of compassion and intense love for women. Such a viewpoint was rare in those times; it is almost extinct now.

Chakradhar says to *Sarangdhar*, 'In the matter of religion, why can't women be associated? Are they not human beings just like you? Your life may be important; but is a woman's life trivial?'

Chakradhar has also said that there is much that is 'good and fair' in a woman; but since a woman is of service to a man in other ways, he does not care to bring out the 'good and fair' in her. *Chakradhar* was aware that women, much more than men, possess the capacity to develop true friendship. He had a large number of women disciples. But he never took the stance of the 'I command and I demand obedience' type. That certainly was not his attitude with them.

One can find several instances of *Chakradhar* having protested against indignities meted out to women. One anecdote in *Leela Charitra* goes like this: A *Brahman* had five daughters, all of whom were widows. Neighbours used to refer to them as *randas* (widows referred to in a derogatory sense). But *Chakradhar*, when he met the *Brahman*, enquired about the *panchagangas* (five sacred rivers). One can imagine the happiness of the father and daughters at someone speaking about them in kind words.

Chakradhar lived in the 13ᵗʰ century. It is perhaps, not surprising that this liberal-minded preceptor had among his disciples equally liberal-minded persons. What is astonishing is the fact that even today, we find in our society a number of persons who when showering abuses on others deign to utter words and idioms vulgarly referring to the female body. The reference is often to the opponent's mother or sister. What is still more surprising is that no one has the sensitivity or courage to decry such abusive language. The ever-growing instances of eve-teasing and molestation of women too is indicative of a filthy attitude. The writings of *Chakradhar* and *Mahadaisa* clearly suggest that if man-woman relations are to develop on a healthy and equal footing, a fundamental change is essential in all respects, even in our day-to-day speech.

An instance of how the women sants have not received the recognition due to them solely on their own merit may be cited here. *Chakradhar* is known to have defiantly sunk idols of worship in the *Gomati* river. This is one of the counts on which he is recognised as a great thinker, as a heroic founder of a new reformist cult. Ausa, his equally courageous female disciple does not receive such praise when she declared, 'I am the daughter, I am the son too' (when she offered *pinda* to her departed father.)

Pinda-Dan is the ritual offering of food to the soul of the dead; the *shastras* lay down that this is the duty of the son or some other male in the family. Ausa thus defied tradition and in a sense stressed man-woman equality. Why should she not be acknowledged as heroic on her own merit on this count alone? Why is she known as 'just a disciple of a great reformer'?

Chakradhar himself had this broad outlook. The husband of *Gauraisa* forbade her from participating in the meetings of the cult, on the plea that she had to look after the household chores. When *Chakradhar* knew of this, he chastised the husband by saying that, 'It is wrong for a person who seeks salvation to put his wife in shackles.'

It is disconcerting to note that in the *Mahanubhava* sect itself, founded by a man of such catholicity of mind, women, to this day, do not seem to have gained any prominent place of honour. Even followers of the sect as also the scholars delving into its history have glorified only the male saints, paying scant attention to the role of *Mahadaisa* and other women, whose qualities and achievements are not a bit inferior to those of the males. *Chakradhar*, the founder, himself expressed the following sentiment:

> Women trapped in the household are just like cows tied to a post. The more they try to get free, the more are they stifled.

Even in our times, men appear to take fright at the sight of a female's unclad body and its movements. Even men who boast of their 'conquests' when it comes to watching in public the movements of an exposed female body are often embarrassed and appear ashamed, as if with a guilty conscience. Even those men who do not mind to some extent the easy, natural movements and even partial exposure of a woman's body 'in private', are strangely enough shocked at this spectacle in public.

Chakradhar has stated in so many words that a woman has no need to be ashamed when she has to bare her breast to feed her infant nor should she be embarrassed if while bathing her child her legs are exposed up to the thighs. *Leela Charitra* mentions Baisa who used to complete her exercise of two hundred and fifty prostrate *namaskars*, unmindful of the men who might be gazing at parts of her body. It was quite a blow to the misconceived notion that a woman must always be alert and must never expose her body to the stares of men.

Mahadaisa, however, though she was enamoured by *Chakradhar's* handsome features and impressive personality, does not immediately agree to his suggestion that she be his disciple. The noble child-widow replies:

> No sir, please no. My home will be at sixes and sevens without me. It is for me to do all the household chores. When there is a knock at the door, it is for me to open the door. No sir, please no. I cannot stay here.

In those days, it was considered as most improper to forsake one's first *Guru* and to accept another. That may perhaps explain why *Mahadaisa* took quite some time before she could decide to leave *Dadosa*, her first *Guru* and go over to accept *Chakradhar* as her preceptor. To say that she merely respected the conventions of the times does not seem to be quite fair either to her own greatness or even her new *Guru*.

It has generally been observed and emphasised that saintly men and reformers like *Goraknath, Chakradhar, Tukaram, Ramdas* were totally unmindful of the physical charms of their female disciples. They were put to rigorous tests to assess their sense of spiritual vocation and staying power and only those who stood those tests were accepted in the sect. If this quality of the male sants to look beyond the mere physical looks entitle these worthy sants to a place of reverence, then *Mahadaisa* too must receive the same place of pride. She too displayed the same calibre when she was unaffected by the charms of *Chakradhar's* personality, while choosing a new *Guru*.

Mahadaisa, while she held serious discourses on philosophical subjects, was ever aware of the limitations imposed on her by her being a woman, i.e., a soul embodied in a female body. It seems that she had resolved to challenge the male monopoly in the matter of conquest of the senses. She takes to *sanyasasrama* and leads an austere life. It is clear that *Chakradhar* and *Mahadaisa* must have taken an active part in developing and shaping the area of life which she shared with *Chakradhar* which was marked by extreme discipline, and yet was free from tedium. Tradition gives the credit for all this to *Chakradhar*. In justice, it must be said that *Mahadaisa* deserves it in an equal measure. Here too, the *Mahanubhavas* appear to be niggardly in the recognition they have accorded to the contribution which an outstanding woman has made to the achievement which she shared with a man of acknowledged greatness.

Muktabai (1201-1219)

It is not the *Mahanubhava* but the Varkari sect which caught the imagination of the Maharashtrian women of the pre-colonial period. As Deleury, a French Jesuit scholar, has pointed out the *Varkari* movement is not a church but a movement and '. . . there is no centralised organization, no hierarchy, no general councils, no credo, no sacraments' (Deleury 1960: 2). The line of *Varkari* women writers began with *Janabai*, a member of the great *Varkari* sant *Namdev's* household, and *Muktabai*, the younger and the only sister of perhaps the greatest *Varkari* saint thinker, *Dnyandev*. Women writers of note like Gonai, Rajai, Ladai, *Kanhopatra* and *Bahenabai* further enriched the tradition. Another medieval religious-cultural movement viz. the *Ramadasi* sect also produced women I : poetesses of the stature of *Venabai* and *Bayabai* in the 17th century A.D. Very little account is available of *Muktabai*. Her compositions too seem to be very few. Yet her writings are generally held in something akin to almost awe. That she had great spiritual authority is accepted. This high tribute she undoubtedly merits. But it must be noted her *Riddle* [Kutache] *Abhangas* and *Abhangas* of the Closed Door [Tatiche] have not been quite fully studied in depth. It is thus rather difficult to come to any firm conclusions about the details of her life. One can only make surmises.

Right from birth, *Muktabai* was confronted by the social boycott that was the lot of her family. It is possible that it was due to these hardships that she decided to accomplish *sthitaprajnata* or complete tranquillity or balance of mind.

Is there a streak of a feeling of superiority in Muktabai? Her thinking appears to be somewhat on these lines: 'My brothers and myself, we are persons of great authority. Others in the society cannot aspire to reach our heights.' That is why she could comment on subjects like Sublimity of Chanting God's Name, Path of Salvation, Self-Realization – subjects which transcended the mundane problems which the business of living posed before her. That was her way to overcome the thorny world around her.

Like *Dnyaneshwar*, his little sister too does not record any personal matters regarding herself. Perhaps she felt that it would be lowering her spiritual stature to stoop down to put into words her own felt torments. Determined to solve the riddle of the universe, she is also resolute in defence of herself in extremely hostile surroundings. This supreme self-confidence leads her to say:

> Do you desire self-realization? Then do not blindly follow others. Search for the truth in your own self. There lies wisdom.

That is her completely self-assured way of thinking. At the same time, she is modest and broad-minded, for she does not treat the truth and experiences she achieved as the ultimate truth:

> How can I find faults with others?
> I see duality and controversies everywhere.

Muktabai has shown a very simple way for women and men to follow:

> Put yourself to test when you want to verify your experiences.

She herself followed her percept. Her belief in this philosophy is so firm that her self-confidence cannot be dismissed as vanity or false pride.

Bhakti Vijay describes an episode concerning *Muktabai* and *Changdeo*. Once *Muktabai* was having a bath in the nude, *Changdeo* inadvertently approached, but on seeing her, he turned his head back in shame. Addressing him as *Nigura* (one who has no *Guru*) she chastised him:

> If you had been blessed by a *Guru*, you would not have let mean

thoughts enter your mind.
One is not ashamed to stare at the niches in the wall. Do the cows grazing in the fields have any clothes? I too am like the cows. Why are you embarrassed at my sight?

These are very mature words coming as they do from a girl orphaned when she was an infant.

Tradition regards *Muktabai* as *Maha Yogini, Adi Maya, Vishwa Mata*. It is not by being the sister of *Dnyaneshwar* that she earns these tributes. She paid a very high price for it in her very short life. She had purposefully turned her back on earthly life; yet she was fully conscious of the inherent strength of a human being. It has been observed: 'In this process, *Muktabai* had lost all natural attributes of her body. They were stunted. We do not see even a single sign of her being a woman. In short, she strikes us, in a sense, as merely a male person.' I do not quite agree with these comments. It is also said that while *Muktabai's* thinking was not totally unconcerned with society, her quest for self-realisation on an entirely spiritual plane led her to be enmeshed in a passionless inward nook. I venture to disagree with this comment too. As we have already noted, *Muktabai* has emphatically said that one must put everything to the ordeal of a test; one must verify every notion before accepting it. If we interpret her thoughts in the historical and contemporaneous context, is it not possible to discover in them a path eminently suitable to the women's liberation movement of our days?

Janabai (1270-1350)

Janabai, born in a *Shudra* family was brought up in the village Gangakhed on the banks of the Godavari river in the present day Parbhani district of Marathwada. Her parents were the followers of the *Varkari* sect. When she was just five years old, her aged parents handed her over, for reasons not clear, to the family of *Damaji*, the father of the *Varkari* Sant Namdev.

Like many other households belonging to the artisan castes, *Damaji's* family (tailor community) was also full of the *Varkari* ethos. *Janabai's* status in the new family was that of a *dasi*, i.e., that of a bonded domestic servant. She has invariably referred to herself as *Namayachi Dasi - Namdev's* maid-servant:

> I am known to the world as merely *Nama's* maid-servant. I am not learned. I have not listened to discourses, nor have I contemplated. I do not understand proprieties or improprieties of this world.

These are the words of a very modest yet revolutionary soul. The message her words give seems to have gone into oblivion in the course of all these years. The stamp *Namayachi Dasi* has however stuck firmly to this day.

She may call herself by a very humble name, but it is nonetheless true that she had an independent mind. She had firmly resolved to stand up as an independent person. She has in explicit words expressed her anguish at the sufferings of a maid-servant and that too of a *Shudra* caste:

> Rajai and Gonai (women in Namdev's household) are constantly at your (God's) feet; I am low-born and am kept outside.

It is always said that in the gatherings of the *Vaishnavas*, there is no caste or class distinction, that there is complete equality; no one is superior and none inferior. It is a mere myth, as Janabai's words clearly show. The privileges that *Nara, Gonda, Mahada, Vitha* - all members of *Namdev's* family - enjoyed were denied to the maid. She appears to have faced insurmountable hardships.

It is significant here to note that *Janabai* compares herself with *Vidura*, himself the son of a maid, but a man of infinite wisdom, *Janabai* does not beg alms from any human, rich or saintly. She seeks direct dialogue with God - *Viththal*. She asserts that *Chokhamela*, the *Shudra* sant was the only true *Vaishnava*.

Namdev's family was quite well-to-do. But the life that *Jana* had to lead there was far from comfortable. Her *abhangas* are full of references to household work, the numerous chores with which women of those times were burdened. There must have been thousands of such miserable women. *Janabai's* uniqueness was that she made *Viththal* himself come down to earth to help her in her chores.

Her belief was that God derives his godliness from the devotion of the devotee. That is why she is bold enough to say:

> O Lord, what is the point of your getting angry?
> After all, we are the source of your strength.

On the other hand, her own righteous indignation knows no limit. She even pours abuse on Him in choicest words, even threatening Him:

> Vithya, you brat of Adimaya
> You begetter of umpteen kids
> How do you dare forsake me?
> Wages of adultery are burdens of responsibility
> As to myself, I have none else to look up to.

What leads her to this fury? Her hard life has convinced her that she is connected directly to *Viththal* by an umbilical cord. No matter if people around her do not realise this. But *Viththal* himself whom she fondly sees in various intimate forms - as mother, father, brother - why should He too desert her? That is her anguish.

Janabai has said on several occasions that *Viththal* shares her bed. He agrees to take food with her, so that she could sleep contentedly:

> I eat Him, I drink Him;
> He shares my bed, I sleep by Him.

She experiences this state of ecstasy. On one occasion, she even says that *Viththal* embraced her in the presence of *Namdev*.

What are we to do with all these allusions? Is it possible to explain it in terms of union of God with a finite soul? *Janabai* has emphatically said that she was a *Shudra*, yet God himself came down for the sheer joy of touching her.

A woman who declines to lead the humdrum life of hundreds of others, has of necessity to face ignominy even in these days. It must have been infinitely worse, centuries ago. Yet *Janabai*, in no uncertain words says that she will not respect the unjust rules which determine virtue and sin. In justification of what she says, she describes her physical experiences in vivid details. A woman in those days who gave up all domestic ties and craved for God must have been subjected to vile abusive words from others. But, she sustains her morale and never gives up courage. She vowed to move about in the marketplace with the *pallav* of her sari moved from the head down to her shoulder. Others may have called her a prostitute but she didn't care.

There is a lot of difference between a male sant referring to his body and a woman saint alluding to hers. To regard God as superman is certainly a big stride in the feminine thinking. Men are not inclined to treat women with fidelity and respect. Very well. We will identify the real *Purush* of our concept with God himself. We will be happy in constant contemplation of Him. Is that the road to ultimate bliss that the women sants want to follow?

Janabai says, 'I am completely relaxed. I am exulted, happy in all respects. I am indifferent to distinctions of sex or body.'

Bahenabai (1550-1622)

It is said that in traditional India a sense of individuality was absent. Yet traditional India did produce at least one autobiography and that too was written by *Bahenabai* - a woman saint. *Bahenabai's* life falls into an important tumultuous period in the history of Maharashtra. *Bahenabai* was born in the village Devgav in the northern part of Maharashtra. She wrote profusely and quite a lot is known of her life. Her life and writings are researched and studied in various aspects. Yet she merits even further research. Most women will feel a sense of intimacy and affinity with her. Her life may at first glance appear to be just like many others; yet it is very different. When she wanted to get out of a rigid framework, she bent the frame, expanded it and in a sense even broke it.

Bahenabai's parents were poor. At the age of three, she was married to a thirty year old *Vedic pandit* of the *Shakta* cult. The family wandered from place to place - Siddhanath, Mahadevaban, Neera Narsinhapur, Pandhari, Shikar Shinganapur, Rahimatpur. Even in this hectic rush, she could find solace in *katha-kirtans*.

But Bahenabai's mind did not rest with the solace she received by listening to others' *kirtans*. She met *Jayaram Swamy* and pursued the devotional path. Then followed a craving to meet *Tukaram*, the famous sant. One can imagine what a courageous step it must have been in those days for a Brahman woman to seek a *Shudra Guru*. Bahenabai's husband was furious; she was subjected to daily beatings. She endured it all, resolved as she was to secure her goal. It must be noted that this was not an emotional outburst.

Bahenabai translated a Sanskrit book *Vajra-Suchi* a book which attacked Brahmanic privileges derived solely through the accident of being born a *Brahman*. She did this with a critical yet balanced mind. We find her fighting against Brahmanism that had lost its *Brahmatva*. She also protested against the disparagement of womanhood.

In the third month of her pregnancy, the husband threatened to leave her in the wilderness – the fate of many a woman. *Bahenabai* was, however, different from others. On the one hand, she pacified the husband with these words: 'The husband is the God, the ultimate for the wife.' Bur then, she also succeeded in persuading him to take to the path of devotion. This was not a cosmetic change that she brought about. It was no superficial bringing together of the worldly and the spiritual ways of thinking. The husband who previously had nothing but derision for

Tukaram turned into an ardent disciple. And while she achieved this amazing feat, what were her thoughts? She says, 'The changes that have taken place were only inevitable and unavoidable.'

It is only with this full awareness that she revolts and succeeds. She expresses her anguish saying, 'A woman's body is totally dependent on others. The *Vedas* and the *Puranas* have ordained that a woman can bring no good to anyone.'

It is significant to note that *Bahenabai* had transcended the body – the feminine body which tradition had decried as a vicious share. *Bahenabai* did bear children. But as she was suffering the pangs of delivering the children, she was also experiencing the blissful total conquest of the concepts of life and death.

She gave new dimensions to the concept of *pativratadharma* – the duties of a true wife. She did say, 'You cannot approach God if you do not love your husband.' But then she also stressed, 'A true wife is she who is aware of her own self. Being married, she has to fulfil her family duties but she must have the craving for spiritual salvation too. It is possible that the husband, children and others may not approve, but she must not give up her true path.' *Bahenabai* has put all this in a very ingenious way.

In one *abhanga* she has said that all women as also men who live their worldly lives with a sense of *Nijananda Ghana* or supreme self-realization, are all true wives. The path of a true wife is as healthy for a man as it is for a woman.

Who is a Brahman and who is not? *Bahenabai* says that the body, *varna*, caste, community, *Karma or Dharma* – none of these can lead to *Brahmanhood*. The rituals of *Yajna* or sacrificial rituals, charity, ascetism – these also are not the true attributes of a *Brahman*. Here, she appears to take a bold thrust at the caste system itself.

It is a matter of controversy whether *Bahenabai* wrote the *abhangas* describing her twelve previous lives. It is immaterial whether we deny their authorship to her or interpret them in their proper perspective. If these *abhangas* are indeed written by her, it would follow that they must have a much deeper meaning. A woman who spent her entire life in serving the cause of the *Varkari* cult (the *Bhakti* movement) and who missed no occasion to point out the seamy side of the caste system – such a woman is unlikely to indulge in reminiscences of her past lives, as if she was narrating some fanciful tales.

In all these lives she was a woman. In one, she says she was a *Vaishya*, in another a *Gavali* (milkmaid caste) and so on. In the initial lives she was so involved with devotion to God that like *Muktabai* she was either not interested in getting married or like *Meerabai* she was indifferent to married life. In the later lives, however, she was born a *Brahman* and was married. Then while she was always a faithful wife, she also followed the cult of devotion and every time found ultimate salvation.

To me the best way to interpret these *abhangas* seems to be: A woman seeking spiritual emancipation and yet desiring to retain her love for humanity cannot attain significant progress by living a life without the companionship of a man. Since she is born a woman, she has to accept the earthly framework of a family, a household and children. Yet she can certainly make adjustments to this framework. She can bend the frame, or expand its dimensions. If she is resolute enough, she can even persuade and lead the man to the path she herself has chosen. As a woman has a nose, eyes, hands and feet so is she endowed with a husband, household and children. She need not be wholly occupied with all this. But there is no reason why she should totally reject it either.

In the *Parmarthik Fugadi* (parlour game of *Fugadi* in relation to spiritual salvation) *Bahenabai* says, 'If a woman craves for ultimate bliss, she must be prepared to face popular censure. She must defy this censure and must also give up being vainglorious about material possessions like wealth, erudition and children.'

It is possible to cite *Bahenabai's* example and to suggest that it is best for a woman to somehow achieve a compromise between day-to-day life and the spiritual quest. The suggestion would be deceitful. Ramdas fled from the marriage *pandal* when he heard the *Shubha Mangala Savadhan Mantra* and saw a warning in it. For this gesture, he is glorified. Equal praise is due to *Bahenabai* who had so many precious and revealing thoughts to express about *Samsara* or worldliness.

Venabai (1627-1678)

Venabai was the pet student of *Samartha Ramda*s. She had successfully observed hard and fast rules of *Ramdasi Matha* and gained her name. She has written three long *Katha Kavyas viz. Venaswami, Ramayana and Seeta Swayamvar.*

Very little information is available about her personal life. She was born in Kolhapur (South Maharashtra) in a Brahman family, Gopajipanta *Deshpande* being her father. She was a child widow. She was advised to read *Bhakti* literature for her remaining life by her parents. But, fortunately she met *Samartha* Ramdas, asked him some twenty-five pertinent questions and became his disciple. She said, 'My body, my soul/everything is taken away by my *Guruji*.'

She had to face great opposition, but she declared:

> Some praise, some malign,
> I don't wait for them.
> I have held *Guru's* feet to heart,
> I will not leave them till my death.

When her parents discovered her infatuation with her *Guru*, they poisoned her. She lay unconscious. The poison had turned her skin to a deep dark colour. Ramdas touched her and she recovered. He accepted the girl as his disciple. He said to her, 'The path to eternal happiness is not easy. You have to tread the jungles. You have to suffer rigorous heat and cold. It is not for the tender ones to follow this path. Rama himself has put a blue body-armour on you.'

This episode is significant. *Ramdas* gave her succour and guided her on the spiritual path. This speaks for the greatness and courage of *Ramdas*. But *Venabai* could be a great *Sadhak* only after, and perhaps because, she was poisoned and had lost her looks. Otherwise she would have been forever a victim of social censure and boycott. This sort of thing only goes to expose the evils of an unbalanced male-dominated tradition.

Gorakhnath was a handsome person. The charm of his body and features in no way affected, for better or worse, his image as an extraordinary *yogi*. If anything, his looks may have contributed only slightly to his eminence. *Chakradhar* too was very handsome. Irrespective of his charming looks, he achieved eminence as a distinguished seer. His looks had nothing to do with either enhancing or diminishing his image.

In our tradition there are many other saints who were fortunate to be so endowed. But *Venabai* happened to be a woman. She had to pay the high price of losing her looks before she could be in a position to pursue her spiritual path.

Why is it that this question was never posed before, or is not being posed even now?

While studying the lives and writings of the saint poetesses, one must not ignore the context of the times in which they were born, lived and wrote. The spiritual aspect of their achievements certainly deserves to be studied. Yet tribute must also be paid to them for the extraordinary courage which they displayed when they rebelled against several evil traditions and social taboos and misconceptions. To deny them this credit is likely to further corrode our historical and cultural heritage, and secular practices within religion.

Original Source

Feminism in Search of an Identity - The Indian Context
Kelkar, Meena & Gangavane, Deepti (Eds.)
Rawat Publications, New Delhi
2003
(pp: - 192-215)

References

Deleury, G.A. 1960. *The Cult of Vithoba*, Pune: Deccan College Postgraduate and Research Institute.

Javdekar, Shalini (ed.). 1979. *Sant Bahenabaichi Gatha*, Pune: Continental Prakashan.

Joshi, K.V. (ed.). 1967. *Sakal Sant Gatha*, Pune: R.S. Avate.

Kolte, V.B. (ed.). 1982. *Leela Charitra*, Mumbai: Maharashtra Rajya Sahitya Sanskriti Mandal.

Sant Janabai. 1983. *Sant Janabaichi Gatha*, Mumbai: Jagadishwar Book Depot, 11th Edition.

Sant Muktabai. 1978. *Tatiche Abhanga*, Pune: Anmol Prakashan.

Shevade, Indumati. 1989. *Sant Kavayitri: Stree Muktichya Maharashtratil Paulkhuna*, Mumbai: Popular Prakashan.

Chapter - 4

Hindu-Muslim Dialogue:
A Rereading of Sant Eknath
and Sant Shaikh Muhammad

Eknath (1532-99) and *Shaikh Muhammad* (1565-1660) were sixteenth century figures born in the pre-modern Deccan. *Eknath* a Brahman from Paithan is well-known for his scathing criticism of Brahmanism. Paithan was known for its Brahmanic orthodoxy. *Eknath*, right from his young age, kept challenging the orthodoxy by his actions and by choosing to write not only in Marathi, the regional language, but in the people's language which was a mixture of Marathi, Urdu, and at times he used the Dakhni dialect with equal ease. *Eknath* was not alone in this people-oriented effort. There were many sants, their disciples sharing the life world of Eknath: e.g. *Shaikh Muhammad Baba,* who born in Dhanur and had links with *Eknath* as a disciple of *Chand Bodhale* and *Janardan Swami* (Eknath's *guru*). It seems that *Shaikh Muhammad* represented another branch of new thought that was emerging during that period, separated but connected with *Janardan Swami's* as well as Eknath's activities and work. There is ample evidence to show that he was also in touch with *Sant Tukaram* (1608-49). *Shaikh Muhammad* settled in Shrigonde, some 80-90 miles from Dehu. A collection of his writings as *Yogasangram*, edited by historian B. S. Bendre in 1959 notes that not much is known about this poet sant but his writing speaks for itself. His tomb in Shrigonde is worshipped by both Hindu and Muslim devotees separately, but on the same day (Bendre 1959:14). *Yogasangram* consists of 2300 ovis and deals mainly with issues of going beyond this material world while living in it.

Hindu-Turk *Samvad*

In this paper I will try to translate most of the famous *Hindu-Turk Samvad* (Dialogue) of *Eknath* and some narratives from the texts of *Shaikh Muhammad Baba*, to understand and make meaning of the way of dialogue adopted by both these *sants*. How Hindu and Muslim communities and identities were trying to reach the abundance of life by going beyond their given frameworks will be evident through these translations.

Let us first look at the *Hindu-Turk Samvad* as it appears in the *'Shri Sakal Sant Gatha'* (vol. II, 123, 3970, pp. 583-6).

> (Their) goal was one but *marg* was opposite.
> Listen to the dialogue between these two.

> The Turk calls the Hindu a *kafar* (non-believer). Hindu wards him off as a pollutant. This is how their cranky argument went on and a great debate took place.

TURK: Oh Brahman, Listen to my argument. Your religious knowledge deceives everyone. You say god has feet and hands. Is this how you worship him?

HINDU: Listen Oh Turk, you jerk! We look at God as residing in everyone. You ignore this expansive meaning and adopt nothingness or void.

TURK: Listen Oh Brahman. Eternally plunging into water, you are like a water cock. Anyone who reads your philosophy will be fooled. You have many stories which confuse people. Sometimes your god is made to beg, sometimes *Bali* traps him and turns him into a gatekeeper. Your *shastra* is totally slack. You even attack *Allah*. What sort of daring is this! This entire affair is of those with little brains.

HINDU: You do not remember your own texts. You do not read them as a whole. Your *Abdullah* in the beginning preached begging. Begging is advised by your god. He attains salvation by giving up everything and taking pittance from begging. Your god passionately loves this. Every minute you remember *Allah* . . .

> For filling your belly you beg,
> Allah give me *ghee*, bread and sweets,
> Allah give me milk and rice,
> Allah give me varied food,
> Allah give me tasty food.

Brahman at least recites the *shlokas* while begging. His begging is not for collection. You are perpetually unsatiated. You are known to be sinful drunkards. *Bali* is a special disciple of *Khuda*. God is attracted by his devotion. God waits for him always. Why are you criticizing him?

TURK: Your *Brahma* fucks his daughter. He reads all false *Veda*. Your *Vedas* are your *shastra*. *Brahma* easily deceives by taking false form. Thieves can snatch *Khuda's* wife. Monkeys help your god. You have become silly and directionless reading these texts.

HINDU: Look at this *Turk* who finds faults with *Brahman* again and again. How did *Baba Adam* get his Wife? Please read your holy book. You do not have knowledge of your own religion, and you fight with us? For *Baba Adam, Maya* became *Eve*. Since then the whole world became *'Admi'*. You call yourself by that name. You are deceived by your own language. For *Baba Adam Maya* became *Eve*. About her you tell us that she was tempted by the *Satan*. When *Sita* was snatched by *Ravan* why do you ridicule? At that time *Firasta* also took help and rescued *Eve*. Here *Ram* calls his own ancestors for purifying *Sita*.

TURK : Listen Oh *Brahman* whose thinking is on par with a donkey. Whatever you say gets reproduced. Anyone who reads your books will remain ignorant in a big way. Your god was ignorant, and hence brought in jail. Demon *Kauns* came to kill him. Your god was hidden by *Devaki*. This is how your books are a deception. Though he was hidden for a long time, still the god was given poison. Oh what a god! You are cheated by your own words. You call your god a cow herd; one cries listening to this because he calls an animal his God. You *kafar*, you have stopped thinking. You have brought down God. I feel like slapping you . . .

HINDU: Your own people say that God is everywhere. Would he then not be in jail too? You see this dichotomy wrongly. Wherever your mind can imagine, there you can find your God . . . If you imagine god is difficult, your heart will be filled with difficulties. But otherwise all closures will be opened by him. This is what your *Paigambar* says. If you listen carefully to *Shahamodin*, he treats a cow, an elephant and a monkey, all of them as protected by the god. These are the answers you will get from your book, but why don't you accept them? Dog, cow, rat, creatures all are looked after by god. Take your own *shastra* ahead. Why are you fighting with us?

TURK: You Brahmans are experts in spinning yarns. God has shaven your beard and head. You Hindus are purely evil. In your kingdom statues rule. God is given the names of statues. That place becomes a pilgrimage for you. Before these statues, masters become lustreless. Women, men all stand up before him and roll mindlessly. Are they not stupid? That stone which is painted with orange with *sindoor*, women stand before it in naked feet without cover and ask of it a child. Your *Veda* is totally loose. Every word of it is empty. Your god is inadvertent and unaware.

HINDU: God is everywhere; in water, land, woods, stone. This is what your own books say. Why don't you understand it yourself? Turk, you are completely lacking in understanding. Solidified or liquid, ghee is the same. You can see form and formlessness as one. You hate the statue. How mindless you are! God completes what humans leave uncompleted. This is what your own book holds. Why don't you accept this? We have shown your shortcomings. You send your god far away who is so near to you. Every time you call your *Allah* you experience disturbance. You have not met him yet. You need to call loudly one who is far away. To call who is near you, you only need to whisper. Your near one meets you but your *'Maulana'* shouts and wakes you up. You say *'Khuda'* is only to the East. Why are the other directions treated as empty? You must say that god is everywhere, and thus take your thinking ahead. You pray five times a day as these are god's times. What happens to all other times? Do they belong to a thief? You have deceived your own *shastra* by making it unidimensional. You accuse us of worshipping stones; why then do you keep stones on your dead bodies? You worship *'Haji'* with stones and treat him as *'pir'*. You save the bones of a mere corpse; you dedicate sheets and flowers on stones and burn incense before it.

TURK: If all of you could purify yourselves by bathing in the Ganges, then why do you cook at separate hearths? You shout about 'pollution' and classify most people as 'impure'. You talk of god in every human being, yet you eat separately, you do not touch fellow human beings and keep human groups separated. You wish to throttle the one who grows grain for your food. You refuse to give up old habits and are left crying within your isolated communities. You declare as impure your own woman, whose cooking you eat. You sleep with her at night but banish her from the kitchen. Does this not make you 'impure'? You do not eat in homes where your daughter is married but delivers a girl child. You like the daughter but not the food in her house? So much for your great Brahman texts! You think your cooked food is the ultimate commitment but their food is the ultimate falsity! How come purity-impurity enters even father-daughter relationship? In building new relations you do not make people your own. Your *shastras* are fables. Therefore your religious texts will be reduced to ashes; rites and rituals will go to hell. You will have to shake this world, Oh Brahman.

HINDU: You Turks are the height of stupidity! You have no sense of right and wrong. Despite being a living being yourself, you harm other living beings. The death conferred by *'Khuda'* makes the victim non-edible, but when you kill it you treat it as pure and edible. You treat yourselves as purer than *'Khuda'* himself. You *Yavans* have been proven to be of lowly order in both the worlds. You fall prey to the *maulana's* directives and follow the rituals of slaughtering the cock that flutters and struggles to escape. If salvation is in slaughtering the goat, then why do you pretend to do *namaaz* and keep the *roza*? The *maulana* who gives you directives is considered great while your sins keep growing and all your efforts are wasted. Oh Brother, God created both Hindus and Muslims. But if your commitment is only to the Turks, then you want to forcibly convert the Hindu to a Musalman. You think *Khuda* has made a mistake in creating a Hindu. What a brain you are! By converting a Hindu into a Musalman, you commit a crime to none other than your own *Khuda*!

TURK: Without *Khuda* humans cannot operate. Turk and Brahman both have only partial truth on their side but if they cut each other's throats then God is sure to punish them.

HINDU: We are all basically one. We fight in the name of caste and religion here but death does not recognize the discrimination.

TURK: God does not have a caste; *Khuda* does not discriminate us.

HINDU : I am delighted.

Interpreting Samvad

Let us see how this *Samvad* was received and interpreted by scholars. Romila Thapar has underlined in this imagined dialogue an undercurrent of satire, in the treatment of both the Brahman and the Muslim who seems to have been a *maulana*. 'The language used by each for the other would today probably cause a riot. The crux of the debate states, "You and I are alike, the confrontation is over *jati* and *dharma*." The attempt is at pointing out the differences between facets of what were seen as Hindu and Muslim beliefs and worship, but arguing for adjustment' (Thapar 2000: 1008).

In her opinion, if we move away from the notion of monolithic communities, we will be able to see the historical potential of understanding how identities may actually have been perceived at points in time and their multiple manifestations and functions. Identities in history were neither stable nor permanent, hence the dialogue between Islam and other religions must always have been an ongoing process.

Shashi Joshi points out that the historical analysis of 'religion' as a motif and 'religious conflict' as a category for medieval India is focused on a wrong problem. These were not religious conflicts but very worldly confrontations, negotiating power relationships in culture and society, employing religion but more often, cultural symbolism. She sees *sufi bhakti* mixing and merging of cultures as a cultural contest for hegemony. The *sufis* were effectively the channels through which Islamic cultural hegemony penetrated the mass. The *bhakti sants* were the conduit forcing hegemonic ties (as opposed to dominant/subordinate) between Brahmanical culture and people. Though internal contest of *sufis* (who expressed knowledge as power), the *ulamas* (who expressed power as knowledge) and Sanskrit *pandits and bhaktas* was not insignificant, Joshi declares: 'The anti-caste, anti-Brahman rhetoric of the *bhakti sants* was, in effect, a readjustment of relationships of power within non-Islamic caste society...' (Joshi 1994; 39-40). She concludes that though the form and content of both Islamic *sufi* and Brahmanic ideologues changed and adjusted accordingly, changing the nature but not the fact of power relations in society. *Sufi bhakti* adopted cultural strategies as modes of cultural integration and at the same time as channels of hegemony integral to the ideological influence of Islam and Brahmanism. This helped in locating them in the interplay of power between them.

Since 1980, Eleanor Zelliot has been writing on *sant* poets, translating their texts highlighting mainly caste and occasionally gender issues, explaining contemporary relevance of *bhakti* for the Dalit movement in India, particularly Maharashtra. She treats *Eknath's* writing as a mode of legitimacy for modern change. *Eknath* was not only a Brahman, but one from a famous family and lived in Paithan which was an ancient capital and a trading centre of great importance even in the sixteenth century. *Eknath's* massive volume of work, varied influence on his writing, his training in the mainstream shastric tradition, his visit to Kashi but conscious choice of *bhakti* and devotion to Pandharpur, his knowledge of a very heterogeneous world in a religious centre and market city crossed by several trade routes are noted in details by her. *Eknath* by birth experienced a highly orthodox and closed Brahmanical world but in his adult life he was in contact with common struggling people from both

Hindu and Islamic communities. Zelliot points out how *Eknath's bharuds* as a dialogue and performance are appreciated by many Dalit, *Bahujan* scholars (Zelliot 1981). In a way *Eknath* is seen by her as a model of modernization in relation to *bhakti*.

We need to address the question of how *bhakti* tradition was received and interpreted in the colonial period in Maharashtra. The arrival of colonialism marked the rise of print culture and in consequence, a new intelligentsia. The new rulers (Elphinstone for example) as well as a band of Christian missionaries needed to learn Marathi for the implementation of their desired projects. The evangelical missionaries began to distribute translated scriptures on a massive scale. The new intelligentsia's response appeared in the form of printed texts of the key *sants* like *Dnyaneshwar* and *Tukaram*. The process began in full vitality from 1844. *Sadanand More* points out that *Tukaram's* writings appealed to the religious as well as literary taste of the missionaries and colonial officials as his writings were direct and simple, lucid and trenchant in its critique of Brahmanism. A leading liberal British official like Alexander Grant confessed in the *Royal Asiatic Journal* that *Tukaram's* poetry revealed a high sense of morality and authentic spirituality based on *bhakti* (devotion) (More 1996: 225).

Missionaries treated *bhakti* as a bridge to Christ for commoners in Maharashtra. Eminent social thinkers like Justice *M.G. Ranade* turned to *bhakti* as an alternative to utilitarianism. He also argued that bhakti provided the energies which resulted in the rise of *Maratha* power under *Shivaji*. His own *Prarthana Samaj* initiative drew its sustenance from the *bhakti* tradition, and above all from *Tukaram*.

Mahatma Jotirao Phule had a complex relationship with *Varkari Sampraday*. He founded *Satyashodhak Samaj* (1873) as an alternative to *Prarthana Samaj*. But he knew the potential of *Varkari Sampraday* in resisting casteism and untouchability. More has demonstrated that while *Phule* kept himself aloof from the *varkari* tradition for reasons of his own, his *abhangas* are in fact organically linked with *Tukaram's* abhangas. *Lokmanya Tilak's* interpretation of *Geeta* is a confluence of *bhakti* and *karma*. Tilak stood against the rituals of *Varkari Sampraday* and followed Sant Tukaram in his forthright critique of hypocrisy.

Anthropologist *Iravati Karve* countered Rajwade's and Ketkar's denigration of the *varkari* endeavor as unscientific and backward. She in fact participated in the *vari* or pilgrimage to Pandharpur and then defined Maharashtra as that region where people visit Pandhari. *G.B. Sardar* refuted the charge of the *Varkari Sampraday* being non-intellectual and praised *Tukaram* for his honesty and transparent self-expression. *D.K. Bedekar*, an eminent and creative Marxist scholar, read *Tukaram* and *Varkari Sampraday* in a democratic, secular framework.

Jayant Lele argues that in order to understand the revolutionary potential of *Varkari Sampraday* one must enter the world-view of the peasant with gentle humility and alertness. He sees *Varkari Sampraday* as an example of an immanent critique of Brahmanism. 'It rejects both counter culturalism and ritualism. As a discourse of the underprivileged, it penetrates the falsehood of an ideology through the eyes of suspicion but it does so in order to extract and expose the encrusted truth of that ideology through the sensitive ears of a believer' (Lele 1995: 80). For him the *sant* poets of medieval Maharashtra offer a most important methodological lesson of unmasking the hypocrisy and falsehood of the beliefs, and also developing the art of listening. *Sadanand More* considers the *varkari* tradition as the core of Maharashtrian culture and sees *Tukaram* as a social critic and a poet of a high order with matchless clarity of expression and an utter fidelity to his own integrity as a free and radical human being and *bhakta*.

Scholars and activists in Maharashtra have for several years sought to challenge the *Ramdas*-centric hegemonic discourse of *bhakti* and in doing so a *Tukaram*-centric counter hegemonic discourse on the *Varkari Sampraday* has emerged. This *Tukaram* discourse no doubt has been extremely significant to the rewriting of the history of Maharashtra culture and society. However this paper, by highlighting the rather sidelined discourse of *Eknath*, suggests opening up of plural voices and the connections between them in the counter hegemonic discourse.

The *Hindu-Turk Samvad* provides ample evidence of how local Hindu and Islamic traditions interacted and strengthened each other; how *bhakti* and *sufi sants*, despite their trenchant criticism of people's everyday life practices, were popular amongst them; how they created a new dialogical *marga* for India in combining varied traditions, particularly Hindu-Islamic confluence and how they make it possible for us to search for the gray areas between the communal and the secular.

Situating *Eknath*

In this context a brief review of Marathi reception of *Eknath* may help us in making meaning of the texts translated in this paper. *Eknath's* writings were studied mainly as literary expression. Many scholars studied *Eknath's* life, work and writing emphasizing the many genres he adapted. I will stick only to one study which was used as a textbook by many generations of students of Marathi literature since the 1950s.

N. R. Phatak's book *Shri Eknath: Vangmay ani Karya* (Shri Eknath's Literature and Work) was first published in 1950 and was revised several times. While contextualizing the *Hindu-Turk Samvad*, *Phatak* mentions *Narsi Mehta* from Junagadh and uses *Meerabai* from Udaipur. He uses the term 'Hindu Community' and its efforts to organize itself through stories of *Ram, Krishna* from fourteenth-fifteenth century. *Phatak* notes that both the Hindu and Muslim communities were in a mood to rethink about the aggression around the sixteenth century. *Phatak* narrates a story. Under the rule of *Sikandar Lodi* (r. 1489-1517), a Brahman made a claim that Hindu and Islam, both these religions have claims towards truth and have equal merit. Sikandar Lodi then asked the Brahman to convert to Islam and of course after the Brahman's refusal, killed him. This story is narrated by the author to prove how the Brahmans were open and ready to give equal status to Islam. *Phatak*, while reporting the dialogue omits an extremely crucial part of the dialogue where the Turk points out sharply the injustice and irrationality that was inherent in Brahmanical patriarchal practices. While reporting *Eknath's* Hindu-Turk dialogue Phatak gives two examples of Muslim religious leaders (*dharma pracharaks*) *Sayyad Shah Muhammad Sadik Sir Mastan Hussaini* (1568) and *Khusuja Khunmir Hussaini* (1520) who travelled from Madina to Paithan to Nasik, and who forcibly converted Hindus to Islam. This is mentioned as necessary background for *Eknath's* Hindu-Turk dialogue, but we find no reference to *Shaikh Muhammad Baba's Yogasangram* in *Phatak's* writing.

Phatak has historically reviewed *Eknath's* period and admitted that local Muslims in southern India were neither dogmatic nor aggressive. *Eknath* had been born in an affluent family and left his comfortable home in his young age. He was made to return home to marry and to accept family life. *Phatak* has noted that *Eknath* went beyond his caste and challenged all those conservatives who tried to outcast him. *Eknath's* son Hari Pandit was unhappy with his father's popularity and people-orientedness. But *Eknath's* time was such that under Islamic rule Hindus had space to bring about a change in their plight. In *Phatak's* opinion *sufis* were also outwardly Islamic but had seeds of Hindu philosophy in them. Islam had in it freedom of thought and *sufi sants* were prompt enough to criticize rigidity and conservatism of both Hindus and Muslims. Hindu *bhakti* borrowed a lot from *sufis*. But *Phatak*, while summing up the dialogue between Hindu and Turk tells us that Hindu's sharp question 'Does god have caste?' was immediately accepted by the Turk, saying '*Khuda* does not have caste, he does not need to discriminate.'

N.R. Phatak has also noted that Islam and Hindu religions in *Eknath's* time were becoming more people-oriented and less rigid. But Hindu caste system was turning out to be more tight as a self-defence. Brahmans taking lead in torturing other religious groups made *Eknath* to be so openly harsh on Brahman community. Huge, well-known Hindu temples were attacked by Muslim rulers for tremendous wealth but small villages had *Bhairav*, *Vetal* (folk deities) and pir supporting each other. In *Phatak's* view neither *sufis* nor *sants* were successful in stopping their practices and rituals. *Eknath* was good in writing Sanskritized Marathi as well as using Persian Arabic language. *Phatak* noted many dialogues written by *Eknath* like 'Child and an adult Brahman', 'Dog and a Brahman', 'A Mahar and Brahman', etc. Every dialogue tells us about how the so-called power-lessness of these figures was compensated by their real knowledge. While ending his book on *Eknath*, *Phatak* appreciatively highlights some part of *Eknath's* dialogue between a dog and a Brahman.

> BRAHMAN: How do you call a Brahman as devoid of knowledge?
> DOG: Can anyone be a Brahman only as a body?
> BRAHMAN: *Vedas* tell us that by birth Brahman is superior.
> DOG: If Brahmans are so great why do they also die? Why *bhaktas* become immortal?
> BRAHMAN: How to make meaning of it?
> DOG: One must become like them. *Bhakta* has no caste or kinship.
> BRAHMAN: How did you achieve this knowledge?
> DOG: I was blessed by *Guru Eka* and *Janardan*.

The translated texts written in a mixed form of Marathi and Dakhni suggest that in the Deccan region during the sixteenth century there was an official patronage to the production of vernacular literatures and encouragement and space for people's language.

Phatak has noted that the languages used by both *Eknath* and *Shaikh Muhammad* exhibit confidence of their own language without seeking any sanction from outside authority, without feeling the need to fall back upon either Sanskrit or Arabic expressions.

Hindus during this period were practicing diverse kinds of worships and rituals in *Vedic*, Non-*vedic*, *Purana* traditions. But they were all bound by the caste system which basically provided them with their specific occupation and skill. There are many stories about *Eknath* which tell us that *Eknath* did not observe rules and restrictions of purity-pollution but the stories also tell us that even *Eknath* had to go through penance for feeding *Mahars* at the occasion of his father's *shradha*.

Phatak also tells us about *Eknath* writing nearly 300 *bharuds* which reflect his close association with people from *Dhangar*, *Gosavi* communities who were of course a part of the village economy and culture. *Eknath* wrote sometimes becoming *Marie aie, Satwai* or *Khandoba* leaving consciously his caste and his Brahmanic training. This is how he was able to become people's organic representative. Historians like *Mate, G.T. Kulkarni* note that we do not get any information of ruling *Sultans*, their officials, their behaviour or overall torture suffered by people, issues of conversion wars, truce in *Eknath's* writing. *Janardan Swami* was employed in Devgiri as an inspector, *Eknath* himself was well versed with trade and accounts but he has not at all directly addressed the political issues of his time. Instead he preached a life world where every human being had to go beyond self or body but every day hard work had to continue with commitment. In this period *Burhan Nizamshah* organized open discussion of philosophers from different religious background. Shah Tahir presented his view on the *'Shia'* sect and *Nizam* accepted to convert to the Shia sect. *Phatak* notes that this must have produced intellectual openness amongst Maharashtrian Muslim thinkers. *Mrutyunjay* (1565-1650), and *Shaikh Muhammad* (1560-1660) were two prominent Muslim sant poets and many others like *Hussein Amberkhan, Muntoji, Latif Shah* also wrote on similar themes. *Eknath's bharuds* are particularly appreciated by many contemporary scholars like *Dr. Dhande* and highlighted *Eknath's* specificity as writing for and becoming marginalized (Dhande 2003).

Dialogue As a Form of Expression

Eknath wrote several dialogues. These dialogues were invariably written between two polar opposite existences or beings, e.g. a child and a Brahman or a *Mahar* and a *Brahman* or a dog and a Brahman and a Hindu-Turk dialogue. What was he trying to achieve through these dialogues? *Eknath* had observed his people and society around him all through his life. He saw them fragmenting, suffering and searching for answers to their crisis by creating their own small gods and their own small answers. *Eknath* learnt a lot from these toiling people. His method of reaching people was by internally examining, critically looking at himself, his own location, his training. *Eknath* gave up many privileges as a Brahman who was trained properly in *Veda, Vedanta, Upanishad, Geeta,*

Bhagvat. He faced wrath from his own community. There are many stories about him of being excommunicated, hated by his community even by his son as noted earlier.

Eknath's choice of writing in the form of a dialogue needs a sensitive understanding. He was trying to capture many worlds of experience and knowledge through it. His language in these dialogues at one level was disclosing world around him and also making sense of things, e.g. a dialogue between 'Hindu-Turk' begins with confrontations, they accuse each other but this debate historically makes sense when both of them realize that their seeing each other was at once superfluous but pertinent. *Eknath* in a way adopts a genre of play or game. The dialogue has a performative quality. *Eknath* himself is outside this dialogue. Hindu and Turk are imagined characters. Turk is an outsider who looks at the Hindu scrutinisingly as a dominating Brahman; Hindu also has skepticism about Turk and his knowledge. Through this imaginary dialogue many things are said harshly, mockingly. Points, counterpoints carried out in their dialogue reveal normative structures disclosing worlds which were forming their self, e.g. rituals which were making them blind towards the larger reality and goal. All dialogues written by *Eknath* make all speaking subjects capable of knowing and acting, taking responsibility for their knowledge and action, e.g. Hindu and Turk both raise truth claims, pursue their truths and at the end when they accept a common ground they create validity of each other. Tey reach a consensual agreement but avoid power or coercion and reach an agreement on truth as part of its meaning. In every dialogue *Eknath* makes the speaker raise claims to validity. Turk when accuses Hindu texts, *Purana* stories as a deception; gives concrete examples and proves his point. The Hindu partially has to accept it in order to create shared meaning. Slowly they in the course of dialogue create the life world, the social space inhabited in common. Both Hindu-Turk are made to represent the dogmas initially but both of them are depicted to be in search of a real cooperative truth which is capable of self-criticism and criticism of others. The language as is evident even in the English translation as is used by Hindu-Turk is dynamic. It flows like a stream, carries many possibilities and it is not a standard sophisticated expression. It has its own power rooted in its context, circumstance and its specific cultural, social context in which it operates.

In short I would like to suggest that *sufis* and *sants* both were very much a part of the early modernity of India. *Eknath* and *Shaikh Muhammad*, were struggling, negotiating within their context. We must see, understand and interpret them as part of the emancipatory cultural histories. Drawing them out solely as '*sant poets*' often excludes their agency in challenging the political priesthood of their times and blurs their historical relevance as early voices against violence, power and coercion. These voices are expressions of freedom and equality emerging from their lived experiences as members of specific communities. These texts are a demand for a new world to be realized not in the next life through karma but in their empirical world. This nascent modernity has several clues for today. The Hindu-Turk dialogue was not only a plea for adjustment but an attempt to locate unity and commonality between the two religious groups.

Shaikh Muhammad

Let us now turn to *Shaikh Muhammad Baba* and read some select texts in translation. *Shaikh Muhammad* writes as a local Musalman. He is not an outsider in his region. He does not adopt a dramatic mode of dialogue, but his writing is in tune with what *Eknath* was trying to achieve. In a way there is an unsaid dialogic relationship between *Eknath* and *Shaikh Muhammad*. Both of them belonged to one and the same guru-disciple tradition. In this text *Shaikh Muhammad* has redefined and conceptualised in a new emancipatory way all the basic terms used by both the communities.

(Why the need of a *guru*?)

One who has the skill of singing is known as a singer.

One who knows dancing may have the capacity to hypnotize the whole world.

But they (the experts) help you go beyond this world. For that you need a real *guru*.

Who is a real *qazi, maulana, fakir*?

The *qazi* is one who understands everything without telling, while practicing justice he will not allow his mind to be unstable.

'Equal' and 'unequal' both will be weighed by him in a perfect balance.

As a principle he will not take a bribe.

He will blame or reward a person as he deserves it.

He becomes one with God and cleanses his mind from inside and expresses it from the outside.

One must recognize such a person as *qazi*.

Maulana is the one who knows his roots. He treats others' pains as his own.

His silent prayer creates a bang in the world.

He is one with the ultimate spirit.

He cuts with the knife of wisdom the buffalo of ego and eats it.

His *namaz in the masjid* is done in a trance. This is what a *maulana* is like,

A *fakir* is one whose sensory pleasure splits.

With every breath he remembers Allah.

He runs away from vulgar gossip and enjoys solitude.

He does not boast about being a *fakir*.

His natural meditative posture is ruled by love.

This is how the true live *fakir* is. (Bendre 1959: 88-9)

Who is a Musalman?

Only one feature allows anyone to be called a Musalman.

Everyone resides in the womb for nine months. If you markedly recognize where you were, you are a real 'pure' being.

But when you take birth by detaching yourself from the womb, I do not know anyone remembering this process. Everyone holds onto their opinion desperately.

See as many people as you want—they have all been nurtured in a womb. Without the womb this animate/inanimate world cannot have occurred. *Sants* and *bhaktas* alike must experience this truth. All had a Sunni Musalman name. But hiding it as *Vaishya* (trader), *Kshatriya* (warrior), *Brahman* (priest - highest in the *varna* hierarchy) they identify themselves by different surnames and talk loosely, giving untrue ideas. If you call a Brahman a Sunni Musalman, he will be furious. This is how he hides the truth and celebrates falsity. It is like hiding your body by exhibiting clothes. Those who hide the weapon by brandishing only the scabbard. This is the ritual of *Vedas* which hides the original birth place. (Bendre l959: 93).

. . . while you utter the word *Allah* if you also call him *Hari*, what do you lose?

Those who do not talk about either *Allah* or *Hari* are to be recognized as barbarians, rouges. Listen, if *Allah* and *Hari* were two, they would have fought and finished each other. They would not have kept trace of each other. (Bendre 1959: 142)

Creatures residing in water never thank water, until they are out of it and are tormented by lack of it. The same happens to people towards the end of their life.

Sunlight keeps the animate and inanimate world going, but never gets thanked or saluted. But when the sun sets (in the twilight) all crazy people become perplexed (Bendre 1959: 180-1).

Shaikh Muhammad's Request

Shaikh Muhammad has answered with love. He says:

I do not know etymology. I am unskilled. Those learned sages (*pundits*) laugh at me because I do not speak a pure language. I was born a 'Mlechha'. I am not socialized in Marathi. This is how all these knowledgeables criticize our language. I have not learnt the old texts (*shastra-puranas*). I have also not learnt to use pure language. I have taught myself with the help of God. Then Goddess *Saraswati* told me that I am at the root, fallen from *yoga*. But that is how God has decided to reside in my speech (Bendre 1959: 195).

In short both *Eknath* and *Shaikh Muhammad Baba* were trying to democratize the social discourse around them and empower people to go beyond their caste community boundaries, e.g. *Eknath's* dialogue between a *Brahman* and a *Mahar* shows how a *Mahar* has the strength, wisdom, knowledge making capacity when he redefines *nirguna* (abstraction-formlessness) and spells out a new theory of 'selfhood' in the *bhakti marga*. *Eknath* redefines his own identity along with the *Mahar* identity and suggests that rebirth was a problem only for those who lived the life of conservation and pseudo purity.

One needs to note that this text *Yogasangram* was selected as an important signpost of Muslim Marathi writing by the Muslim Other Backward Classes organization in Maharashtra as a secular, democratic voice immediately after the Babri Masjid and the riots that followed (1993). The last two decades, Mandal, Masjid and the World Bank years, have created a need for a new language, new visions to address the complexity faced by the intellectual and political world of India. Different camps - socialist, Marxist, radicals - are not so certain about their standpoint. Post-modernism which challenged all meta or grand narratives has also rejected the 'dialectic of spirit'. Some scholars suggest a *marg* of secularization of cultural common-sense as an answer to Hindu nationalist bigotry in contemporary India. They suggest that this would help in avoiding falling in the trap of populist movements, which contribute to reactionary modernism. Many look at the gloomy presence of the twenty-first century as a result of our being in the transitional period of experiment and exploration. If the dream of a secular, democratic modern India is to be realized, a re-reading of the pre-modern medieval *bhakti* texts with more sensitivity seems to be one of the possible *margs*.

Primary Texts

'Hindu-Turk Samvad'. 2000. In R.R. Gosavi, ed., *Shri Sakal Sant Gatha*, vol. II, Pune: Sarathi Prakashan,.

Bendre, B.S. 1959. *Yogasangram, Shaikh Muhammad Baba Krut*. Pune: PPH Bookstall.

Original Source

Marga: Ways of Liberation, Empowerment and Social Change in Maharashtra
M. Naito; I. Shima & H. Kotani (Eds.)
Manohar Publication,
2008
(pp: - 77-94)

Reference0s

Dhande, Chandrakant. 2003. '*Sant Eknath ani Dalit Samvedan*' (Sant Eknath and Dalit Sensitivity), in R.T. Bhagat, ed., *Sant Sahitya ani Dalit Samvedan*, Kolhapur: Chaitanya Prakashan.

Joshi, Shashi. 1994. *Composite Culture and Cultural Fault Line*. Nehru Memorial Monograph Second Series, No. LXXXVIII.

Lele, Jayant. 1995. *Hindutva: The Emergence of the Right*, Madras: Earthworm Books.

More, Sadanand. 1996. *Tukaram Darshan*, Pune: Gaaj Prakashan.

——. 2004. '*Varkari Sahitya: Bhumika ani Swarup*' (Varkari Literature: Content and Form) in Special Issue of *Varkari Tradition and Marathi Culture*. Pune: Satyashodhak Sanghatak, November 2004, pp. 32-39.

Phatak, N.R. 1950. *Shri Eknath: Vangmay ani Karya* (Shri Eknath: Literature and Work), Mumbai: Manoj Printing.

Thapar, Romila. 2000. 'The Tyranny of Labels', in Romila Thapar, *Cultural Pasts: Essays in Early Indian History*, New Delhi: Oxford University Press.

Tulpule, S.C. 1962. *Pach Sant Kavi* (Five Sant Poets). Pune: Sangam Anand.

Zelliot, Eleanor. 1981. 'Chokhamela and Eknath: Two Bhakti Modes of Legitimacy for Modern Change', in Jayant Lele, ed., *Tradition and Modernity in Bhakti Movements*, Leiden: E.J. Brill.

Chapter - 5

Patriarchal Discourse : Construction and Subversion – A Case Study of the Nineteenth Century Maharashtra*

Over the last two decades and more, feminist scholarship in India has engaged itself with women's writings; both of the colonial period and the contemporary. The project of 'Women Writing in India' (Tharu & Lalita 1991) was engaged in tracing a lineage of women writers; as a regional editor, one was involved in tracing the lineage of women's writings in Maharashtra. Scholars engaged in this project were convinced that women's expressions were to be read as more than those of either purely 'Victims' or as 'free agents'. As Tharu and Lalita point out in the introduction, all the participants of our project soon learnt to '. . . read them not for the moments in which they collude with or reinforce dominant ideologies of gender, class, nation or empire, but for the gestures of defiance or subversion implicit in them' (Tharu & Lalita 1991: 35). Women's writings were documents that showed women's struggle for making the world habitable. A struggle at the margins of patriarchies that were being doubly enforced by the dominant colonialists and the emerging bourgeoisie in India. This paper is an attempt to further explore the themes in the patriarchal constructions and subversions in 19th century Maharashtra. How were women's worlds shaped in colonial Maharashtra? What were the strategies of subversion and modes of resistance against patriarchies?

* I am thankful to Ram Bapat, Sharmila Rege and other colleagues in the women studies centre for discussions on this paper.

I

The *Mahanubhav* (c.1194-1276) and *Varkari* literatures (c.1275-1690) in Maharashtra provide us with ample and valuable information about the everyday life of Marathi women in the pre-colonial period. We can begin with consulting the writings of the heretic *Mahanubhav* sect which emerged around the thirteenth century. A succession of *Mahanubhav* women writers including *Mahadamba, Kamalaisa, Hiraisa, Nagaisa* have left for posterity a rich store of authentic protest literature. As G.B. Sardar has noted, '. . . It was the *Mahanubhav* and the *Varkaris* who first wrote in Marathi for the common people of Maharashtra. They reinforced the religious sentiment of *shudras* and of women with spiritual instruction. They created in the common people a desire for a different and higher level of life.' (Sardar 1969: 59)

The *Varkari* movement produced a long line of women *sants* of all castes and regions in Maharashtra. *Muktabai, Janabai, Soyrabai, Gonai, Rajai, Ladai, Kanhopatra, Bahenabai* and many more have left a rich body of literature. It was a part of the larger *bhakti* movement, which arose first in the Tamil region around the 6th century and later spread from there to encompass Kannada, Marathi, Hindi and other linguistic areas. *A. K. Ramanujan* has made it clear that '. . . *bhakti* movements are also social movements. We should not forget that here all sorts of crucial human experiences are cast in religious idiom. In *bhakti* 'man is a man for all that' and women are very much a part of the scene. Feelings are more important than learning, status and privilege. In fact, status, panditry, even maleness and the pride that goes with such things are seen as obstacles to a true experience of God' (Ramanujan 1973:10).

One can make some general observations about women's life in pre-colonial Maharashtra based on this history:

a. While women's literacy rate was much lower as compared with the present, they did possess a considerable degree of knowledge and skills.
b. Women's contribution to oral literature was noteworthy.

c. The joint family system though hierarchical in nature, did grant to women some spaces of their own.

d. Motherhood must have played an unusually big role. Mother–child relation seems crucial and intimate,

e. Guilt ridden notions of sexuality are relatively absent. For instance, in the different texts coming from *Varkari* tradition, inhibitions in this respect were not so pervading and oppressive.

The arrival of colonialism in Maharashtra in 1818 and the end of the Brahmanical *Peshwa* dynasty marks the beginning of a new epoch. New configurations of power emerged in the strategic areas of social life.

The colonial rule ushered a period of decay and disintegration of national life as also, creation of room for departures of a new kind. The twin processes of deindustrialisation and deskilling led to a loss of productive employment for both men and women. Most of the brunt of this situation was borne by women. The contestations and collusions between the colonial state and the Brahmanical ruling circles opened unforeseen opportunities for those sections of the society who had suffered from powerlessness in the earlier scheme of things. A demand for a new distribution of power soon appeared on the scene from the oppressed castes, classes and women as well. As Sumit Sarkar points out that in Maharashtra some signs of an inversion of a more fundamental kind were seen during this period. 'In Maharashtra . . . in the wake of powerful lower caste movements, alternative versions of history were constructed . . . and [they] projected a counter-myth of Northern. Brahmanical foreign conquest and tyranny over the indigenous *"bahujan samaj"* of intermediate and lower castes' (Sarkar 1998: 33).

The colonial order also led to the breakdown of the earlier systems of knowledge set up by both the Brahmanical and non-Brahmanical ruling elites. The various modes of self understanding achieved by the diverse sections of the society in the previous contexts experienced shock and rupture. The search for new identities followed in their wake. English soon replaced Sanskrit as the vehicle of the scholarly discourses. New cultural norms set up by the Colonial administrators generally with a utilitarian bend of mind or by the missionaries began to percolate and to influence all sections of the society. Culture inevitably emerged as the main battlefield. Colonialism, first and foremost, gave rise to a new class of English educated intellectuals.

The new intellectuals had to carry out as Lele puts it '. . . the task of justifying not only their own subaltern existence but also an alien regime, looked upon with suspicion both by the indigenous ruling class and the common people' (Lele 1986; 14). The new intelligentsia began appropriating some of the ideas of the philosophical radicals to build new system of knowledge capable of sustaining its newly gained vision, norms and interests. The new middle class in Maharashtra, drawn mostly from the Brahmans, gained access to the colonial lower administration through English education. Imbibing the cultural models set up by the colonialists, it began to initiate reforms in order to overcome what they considered to be a gulf between the 'advanced' West and the 'backward' Indian society.

The colonial ideology, in particular, constantly advertised its moral superiority in the areas of gender relations. As Uma Chakravarti points out, 'The "higher" morality of imperial masters could be effectively established by highlighting the low status of women among the subject population as it was an issue by which the moral "inferiority" of the subject population could simultaneously be demonstrated. The women's question thus became a colonial tool in the colonial ideology' (Chakravarti 1989: 34). The new regime glorified family based on the conjugal love and 'culture' - women's patient and supportive understanding sense of sacrifice. The coloniser began to set up the traditions in tune with their interests and in line with their Victorian mind-set. In general, they desired to shape a new Indian society on the values and programmes of possessive individualism.

In the face of the coloniser's attempt to set up a new understanding of Indian history, the new middle class made equally determined endeavours to rediscover tradition. In the process certain texts, norms and ideal types were valorized by both the sides at the cost of others. A series of articles, pamphlets and books offering guidelines to women both for their moral uplift and for their housewifely roles appeared in print one after the other. As a part of this project an interest in women's education emerged and focussed its attention in particular on problems and miseries of women. As a result considerable literature concerning women produced by men is available in Marathi right from the inception of the colonial rule to the beginnings of Gandhi-led freedom movement since 1920.

The first major text was published by *Gangadharshastri Phadke* on *Widow Remarriage and Women's Education* in 1841. The text begins with four problems concerning the child widows: illegitimate sexual relations, abortions, infanticide and mixture of varna (Varna Sankara). All of them are termed as a 'sinful acts'. The text argues that 'if intelligent and balanced men do not have the capacity to control their senses (*indriyas*) how can women have that control? Since nature has treated men and women equally, it follows that men and women are endowed with similar kinds of passion and desire.' The text quotes a story from *Shrimad Bhagvat* to attack prevailing notions which held education responsible for either causing women's moral downfall or early widowhood. The publication of *Phadke's* text was a part and parcel of the joint attempts made by Indian reformers under the leadership of *Jagannath Shankarsheth* and the top officials of the colonial regime to secure a law legitimising the high-caste widow remarriage. As such it did not miss the opportunity to make a strong case for women's education. The whole case is argued in a low key, balanced and persuasive manner. Among other points *Phadke* interestingly argues that women now need to be educated 'as in the company of the European women they appear as a goose in the presence of a swan' (Phadke 1841: Preface, Ch. 3).

Another debate about the 'moral improvement' of women through education was going on almost side by side with the earlier one. The first generation of Mumbai-based reformers had initiated a series of measures to encourage 'female' education both for their secular and spiritual enrichment. A series of texts appeared making a case for women's education and offering a new moral guide for women in tackling their worldly affairs. As early as in 1842, both *Dnyanoday* and *Dnyanadarsh*, representing respectively the missionary and the liberal Hindu worldviews, were publishing articles arguing a case for education of women so as to make them capable bearers of the *Streedharma* defined in terms of service to parents, care and nurture of the children and observation of *Pativratya. Govind Narayan Shenavi (Madgaonkar)* published on behalf of the Deccan Vernacular Society a book related to this theme in 1850 carrying the title *Runanishedhak Bodh* [A Precept on the Evils of Debt]. The text challenges the stereotype male arguments holding women responsible for the dissipation of wealth arising out of their alleged passion for display, pomp and ceremony; egoistic; self centeredness and their general inclination towards deceit, misadventure and temptation. Far ahead of his times, *Madgaonkar* argues that properly educated woman alone would be equipped not only to bring up well their children and take care of their spouses but more importantly to avoid non-productive and vain employment of wealth. Though, he still places the argument in the framework of strategies making women more amenable to educated men's needs and commands, his presentation represents an interesting combination of patriarchal interests and emancipating concerns (Shenvi [*Madgaonkar*] 1850: Ch. 3, pp. 28-32).

Before we look into the debate about women's responsibility in dissipation of the domestic wealth, which occupied both the conservative and reformist camps for the next four decades, we must have some idea about its historical background. Much earlier than the rise of the famous drain theory of *R. C. Dutt, Dadabhai Naoroji* and others explaining the problem of Indian poverty as developed by Mumbai-based intellectuals like *Bhaskar Tarkhad, Bhau Mahajan* and *Ramkrishna Vishwanath* were taking a public position throughout the period of 1840 to 1850 to declare that there was no such thing as a beneficial alien domination. They called the British Rule as a vile curse on India and pointed out that India's surplus was the base of England's prosperity. The destruction of indigenous manufacturers and high duty on indigenous textiles offered notable examples of political and economic cruelty practiced by the British Rule (Sunthankar 1988: pp. 434-41). All the texts of the period dealing with the woman question therefore reflect the conditions of a disturbed family life resulting from this economic trauma. But unlike the above two texts, the new middle class patriarchal texts exploited this fact as one more handle to browbeat women for their so called 'natural' inclination for wasteful expenditure of all sorts and to justify their traditional pre-colonial prejudice that women were by nature careless free spenders. They continued to be depicted in the contemporary male literature as illiterate – *'adivasi'*, animal-like and gossiping, but in the context of the economic drain as also financially irresponsible and short sighted. It is however in this context that men like Madgaonkar and later women like *Tarabai Shinde* ridiculed this trail of thought and used the opportunity for pushing the cause of women's education.

II

A good way of understanding the nature of confrontations between those who tried to handle the woman question within a patriarchal reformist framework on the one hand and those who, while in outward agreement with the general programme of reform, sought to expose the double standards inherent in patriarchal constructions would be to compare relevant texts produced by *Bal Gangadhar Tilak, Narayan Bapuji Kanitkar* and *Mahadev Shivram Gole* and by *Tarabai Shinde, Pandita Ramabai* and *Anandibai Joshi.*

These confrontations are of great significance in understanding women's subversive consciousness and activities in the first hundred years of colonial rule in Western India. All these texts had achieved certain renown even at the time of their publications. More importantly, they also give us a good understanding of all the complexities and contradictions, which governed the actualities in the domain of gender relations. Interestingly, these texts also tell us about the elite character of these discourses if we note that with the exception of one [i.e. *Tarabai Shinde*] all other participants come from the urban *Chittapavan Brahman* caste that constituted the new colonial middle class, the administrative intelligentsia. *Tarabai Shinde*, a top bracket *Maratha*, represents the *Satyashodhak* body of thought, which challenged the Brahmanical hegemony. But otherwise she too shared a similar background in terms of educational upbringing, financial status and secular activities. These texts belonging to the two warring campus (the 'patriarchal reformist' vs. the emancipatory) constituted the core public discourse in Maharashtra on gender-related issues.

Tilak, Kanitkar, Gole produced the first set of texts under our consideration. *Lokmanya Tilak* needs no introduction. A leader of the nationalist movement in an epoch named after him, *Tilak* was a preeminent thinker, and possessed in *Kesari* and *Maratha* two outstanding instruments of communication to reach a large audience on matters of contemporary significance. As liberal as his rival reformers in terms of his own day to day life and personal conduct, he quite self-consciously had undertaken the role of reconciling tradition with modernity in his single minded attack on all forms of imperialism. *Narayan Bapuji Kanitkar* came from a well-known affluent family with a high social prestige and was a true representative of the first generation of English educated graduates. His farcical writing, titled *'Taruni Shikshan Natika'* (A Satire on Educated Modern Young Women) was published and staged in 1886 and thereafter had achieved a considerable degree of reputation and even notoriety. *M. S. Gole* was the principal of the famous Fergusson College in Pune founded among others by great liberals like G. G. Agarkar and later on developed by *Gopal Krishna Gokhale*. All the three authors and all the texts before us authored by them do not take an openly hostile stand against women or the reforms. In fact, all of them claim that they support the cause of enlightened reform to improve and enhance the status of women. Instead of a negative, reactionary and an outright statusquoist attitude, they adopt a forward looking, supportive and rather patronising stance in the name of a realistic, practical orientation towards the problem of historical change. In other words, through their redefinitions of gender relations they reformulate patriarchies and do not intend a programme for their annihilation. They seek to pursue reforms in the domain of gender relations not for subverting patriarchy but for securing its readjustment in the face of changing social realities.

The fifth volume of *The Collected Works of Lokmanya Tilak* published by *Kesari Prakashan*, Pune, brings together his writings on the public debate about the character and contents of 'the female education', the famous '*Rakhamabai* Trial', 'the Age of Consent Bill' and the issue of 'Widow Remarriage'. This paper concerns itself mainly with *Tilak's* views on female education.

A series of articles which *Tilak* wrote on the syllabus adopted by the female high school in Pune provide us with further clues about the patriarchal appropriation of the woman question in the nineteenth century. As we expect, Tilak notes that his position differs from the other camp not in terms of their institutionalisation given the context of time and situation, stressing the crucial difference between the adventures and the realistic ways of tackling the problem of social change, *Tilak* questions the logic of the wholesale and mechanical application of the colonialist modernising doctrine to the social reality of female education under the Indian conditions. Noting a further distinction between imitation and creative application he challenges the relevance of educating the Indian women as if they belonged to the same social structure, which supported the life style of the highly educated English ladies of the British middle classes. *Tilak* therefore challenges the idea of floating a separate female high school when already primary and secondary schools for girls on the one hand and the female training college for producing female instructors for female primary schools were in existence. He questions the need for floating institutes of higher education of alien character for the perusal of a fraction of high status women. *Tilak* declares that the genuine women's education would truly begin only if and when we would perceive the whole issue in terms of the bulk of our married women.

In his concluding remarks on the series of four essays which he devoted to the ritual of celebrating the arrival of menstruation (*nhanavali*), *Tilak* bluntly points out that he would always abide by the concern for truth and in no case would allow religious customs, conventions and traditions to overrun the quest for truth. He further asserts that any number of so called religious practices have nothing to do with religion as such and that most of them are indeed in that context superficial and practically absurd. *Tilak* further states that while he would not go out of the way to antagonise popular opinion as the followers of *Brahmo, Prarthana, Arya Samaj* movements usually do, he would not hesitate to attack such so called norms, values and practices which are wasteful, vulgar and absurd which, worse still, would go by the name of religion (Tilak 1976: 38).

At the same time *Tilak* was always critical of taking a prudish, sanctimonious and elitist high moral stand on various kinds of social practices. He was in his personal life style and values almost a classic exemplar of the Victorian code of 'simple living and high thinking' and yet was a realist enough to take objection to the fact that some high minded liberal social reformers refused to accept funds from a class of courtesans in the name of moral purity. *Tilak* argues that all courtesans must have rights like any common citizen, and he points out how many reformers who were claiming moral superiority were getting caught into alcoholism themselves (Tilak 1976: 180).

Tilak's position on the issue of women's education is defined by him in the third article which he wrote on the problem of curriculum for a female high school. He observes that:

some women as in England admittedly entertain the goal of securing professional capabilities in their pursuit of higher education and later on they do work as either advocates or doctors or editors or as administrators. We do not want to say at all that women should not secure emancipation from male bondage, by pursuing various professions on equal terms with men. But so far as our women are concerned we foresee given our social reality a protracted educational process running perhaps into hundreds of years or even millenniums. We also note that the establishment of female colleges and women's access to male educational institutions are matters of very recent innovations even in western societies where the adult marriage and conjugal relations based on consent or contract have come to stay . . . But our situation is such that it would take a long time for our women to set aside the household work in favour of public and professional work . . . [It is therefore that] our middle class educated men desire to promote female education for acquiring skills in reading and writing necessary for a better discharge of their household work and for securing self-reliant moral upliftment through a perusal of various scriptures in their leisure time and for supporting the men folk in running a smooth domestic life. As in the case of artisans for whom vocational interests take the first place and liberal education necessarily the next one, so also for our women household activities come first and education as such a secondary one . . . In-law's household is a perennial workshop for female education. We are all for the facilities for practical, applied and appropriate (at: *'Swadharma'* oriented) liberal education for women so long as it does not mean their withdrawal from the above workshop (Tilak 1976: 219).

In a nutshell, *Tilak's* approach to the issue of female education is based on two positions. He insists that most or almost all our women find themselves in a marital status at a very young age and, therefore, the key to female education in India lies in developing and identifying appropriate syllabi and procedures to enhance the scope and quality of married women's education.

Tilak's overall worldview was of course anchored in his patriarchal understanding of the whole issue of the sexual division of labour. He is of the opinion that the truth of the matter consists in recognising that in the given and appointed natural order of things women have been invested with the responsibility of managing a household and therefore, they must be given education appropriate to this scheme of things (*Tilak* 1976; 230). The heart of the matter, in his opinion is that so long as our marriages are not based on adult consent, our educational system will have to approximate this stark fact of social life. *Tilak*, in our opinion was certainly not what was then called a liberal reformer or not as it is termed now a progressive thinker. He was rather a conservative thinker in Burkien sense of the term. The difference, is underlined, when we consider, the two texts by *Narayan Bapuji Kanitkar* and Principal *M. S. Gole* were certainly supporters of the orthodox order, taking pride in its total patriarchal character.

N. B. Kanitkar came from an elite Brahman family in Pune. His position represents the uncertainties, ambiguities and tensions entertained by the new University graduates towards the new value system that was emerging in the wake of the colonial order. His play *'Taruni Shikshan*

Natika' (hence referred to as TSN) was a sensation in those days. The play received popular acclaim and the book itself ran into a second edition within a period of four years. His book had a longish preface running into some 14 pages followed by 2 page quotations respectively from *'Manusmruti'* and *'Mahabharata'*. We are saved from a trouble of interpreting the text as the playwright's position is spelt out so carefully at the beginning. The preface as expected has long quotations from the contemporary British periodicals and book like John Bull's *Womankind* and the British daily *Spectator* to underline the point that the patriarchal norms and expectations held by the Indian men were no different from those entertained by their colonial counterparts. The patriarchal assertions made by the British men to legitimise the claims, the arguments, the excuses of the Indian men. In addition, *Kanitkar* also relies upon certain celebrated Indian public figures of his days, viz. Bhagwant Singhji *Thakursaheb*, the chief of Gondol Principality in *Kathiawad* and to boot even the famous *Mr. Behramji Malbari*. The quotations are first given in their original English and followed by Marathi translation to invest greater authority in the statement made. *Kanitkar* has also woven a secondary theme both as a matter of dramatic technique and more importantly, to have a look at another contemporary popular concern viz. the increasing social acceptability of drinking among the new university intelligentsia. The portrayal of the social reformist as drunkards no doubt helps the playwriter to poke fun and take pot shots against the overall reformist positions and perspectives. In fact the strategy of thus killing two birds in one throw enhanced the bite and the satire of this farce in terms of its popular appeal.

An idea of *Kanitkar's* views about women's education and the general issue of the emancipation of women can be gathered by the kind of quotations, which he has collected, from European writing. Thus a French Historian is quoted to say that 'England made all her great conquests at a time when her women were treated with about as much consideration as the inmates of an Eastern harem and it is to this masculine independence, this indifference towards women, that the success of the English may partly be ascribed' (*Kanitkar* 1889: 8). The quotation from John Bull's *Womankind* runs as follows:

'Take care, friend John, you are on a downward and dangerous path. I see you presiding over meetings of blue-stockings and hear you adding your voice to theirs in their demand for women's rights. It seems to me that it is your future happiness that you stake. You will have a wife who will know the differential and integral calculus but will be all unskilled in the art of those nice puddings and pies you like so much. No more warm slippers awaiting you by the fender; instead of the song of kettle on the hob, that sweet household melody, you will hear the litany of the Rights of Women' (Kanitkar 1889: 9).

Kanitkar in fact is so enchanted by John Bull's *Womankind's* positing that he has cited a quotation on a frontis piece of the first edition of the play viz. 'The Rights of women! What a fine phrase! What a pretty farce! What a sonorous platitude!' (*Kanitkar* 1889: 1)

He has not missed the opportunity to quote the well-known reformist leader *Behramji Malbari* who in his letter dated 14th March 1886 made the following statement in relation to the news of an elopement of two Parsi girls.

'The recent case of elopement which have caused such a flutter in the Parsee Community may be traced chiefly to want of honest occupation and spiritual decay, if we may use the phrase. With the spread of education, so called more ornamental than useful, there has sprung a sort of distaste for work at home, so essential to the happiness of domestic life. Parsee girls, not many of them we hope are becoming strangers to the dignity of labour and its saving grace' . . . 'More than sixty percent of the children of well to do Parsis at Mumbai are, we believe, nursed and tended by *Goanese* women and we should not at all be surprised if two of the three girls, who have run away with these Goanese boys, are found to be practically Goanese girls themselves. This is the result of high living amid questionable associations. Leaders of the community will do well to see to this in time Indian Spectators' (10,11).

Kanitkar has invoked further the authority of *The Maratha* dated 28th March 1886 which maintains 'Mr. Justice Scott's remark on the occasion of the distribution of prizes to the students of the Indo-British Institution at Mumbai embody valuable criticism on the sort of education given to girls in departmental schools. It is very fortunate that Lady Ray was present on the occasion. Hindu mothers have been heard complaining that the education their daughters receive in schools is worse than useless for it incapacitates the young girls to become good housewives. Since the new notorious case of the restitution of conjugal rights pending decision of the High Court was instituted they have begun pointing out to the unfortunate but civilized daughter of *Dr. Sakharam* as a typical lady, they produce of female education. We trust Justice Scott's remarks will produce their desired effect and turn the tendency of female education from academial to practical training' (*Kanitkar* 1889: 12).

Kanitkar follows the familiar strategy of equating the cause of Women's education and emancipation with Anglophil, loyalist, imitationist, opportunist, self centric, and alienated modernist world view of the 'upstart' new university educated intelligentsia. The play written in 1886 is placed in terms of its narrative setting at the end of the year 1895. It claims to be a projection of the future state of affairs following the introduction of an anglicist and alien female education. The play in fact carries a subtitle 'A prophecy concerning the modern education for girls and liberty for women.' He wants to make it clear that he is not someone who hates women's education or the cause of women's liberty. In his opinion, his objection is to the kind of impractical, unrealistic and particularly ornamental syllabi which was being adopted and preached in the name of an appropriate education for a new Indian woman. He fully supports the chief of Gondal State when the later asserts in his book regarding his travels in England that

> Indian women should be educated in the old fashion. I am not in favour of sending grown up girls and young women to schools. In former times we had no girls schools or female colleges; but our women were none the less educated for all that. A woman used to receive the necessary education from her father, brother, mother,

husband or some other relations and this education passed from mother to daughter as a sort of inheritance. A mother was the real mistress of her daughter. She taught her to read and write the vernacular and Sanskrit characters to make her pious, chaste and modest, taught her to sing hymns, gurbas and nuptial songs, taught her sewing-cooking, worshipping and managing the household affairs. Elementary arithmetic was also a part of her curriculum. An implicit obedience to the husband's order was the first duty impressed on her mind. This sort of female education is not yet defunct. It prevails even now in certain families. I should like to see this revived to a great extent (Kanitkar 1889: 1).

Kanitkar uses the setting of his play in a manner whereby the nouveau rich affluence gained by the educated reformists through the colonial patronage, and the consequential Westernized style of living, glamour and etiquette is contrasted with the culture of poverty, apathy, tradition and overall lack of sense of style and grace of an impoverished lower middle class *brahman shastri's* household. Such a setting helps the playwright to project caricatures of *Pandita Ramabai, Rakhmabai* and two or three other equally well known educated women of his times. A neglect of considerations related to place, time and the context in relation to the cause of female education is shown to lead to such practices as women taking to ballroom dancing, social drinking with men that too including strangers; indulgence in reading cheap and populist Western literature such as Renaulds and Boccassio. And finally a pompous but ridiculous admixture of English slang with traditional Marathi idiom. In short, female education is made to stand for all kinds of imitative, licentious behaviour in terms of apperal, bodily gestures, other manners etc.

The play including the preface celebrates the following image of a woman who is a classic model of patriarchal othering of the woman:

'The Word "woman" denotes many qualities. Beauty, tenderness, courtesy, companionship, humility . . . Imagine such a virtuous woman is yours, she has submitted all herself to you, it is only you who have to provide total protection to her, who will not feel blessed by this? The quality of generating pleasure and happiness is innate to women. It is therefore no accident that not only the Hindus but rest of all the human beings all over the world have set them as goddesses of the households and have accepted a position of dedicated divoties to them. Keeping in mind their delicate bodies and natural powerlessness men have allotted them light and congeneal types of duties. They are ornaments, they are our life givers, they are our welfare, pleasure, joy . . . keeping this place of women in mind, men have accepted all these burdensome works outside the households to save women from arduous labour . . . If men adopt such an attitude towards women and behave accordingly how strange it is that they are making a hue and cry about the emancipation from the male bondage? Your rights are superior to men. Men are always in your feasts, they bend as you wish. They are bound to you by mystery, love, temptation and affection . . . they have sacrificed and will continue to sacrifice their estates, states, merits and standing in life but then why raise such hullabaloo? Women don't be envious of men. If you see men as enjoying more happiness then it is an absolute misconception (*Kanitkar* 1889: 7).'

Kanitkar then paints a rather lucid picture of what would happen, to them if they buy the trap which reformist men were setting for them. He declares

'. . . once for all if you become equal to men, fearless and tough like them and start wandering like them on roads then men will not have any feelings for you. This will destroy all the pleasures, pride, and honour that you have. Indian men are not free as much as you are today. You must forever endeavor to gain such education as befitted Arya Woman . . . . as was available to our ancients' (Kanitkar 1889: 8).

The text published in 1898 by *M. S. Gole*, titled, as *Hindu Dharma ani Sudharana* (Hindu Religion and Reform) is different in many ways. It is as if written by one *Mr. Vidhyadhar Pandit* - a fictitious character - who travelled through the positions of 'reformism' 'conservation' to a complete, nuanced understanding of the contemporary Indian society. Hence, *Gole* suggests that the book should have been titled as 'A Real Story of Soul Searching' (Gole 1898: 8).

After taking an extensive review of reformist arguments and conservative arguments the text pleads mainly for gradual reforms (Gole 1898: 331). The text accepts that Indian society was going through a change but it argues that the change in the social conditions is always very slow. Some old habits, which hamper the steadiness and continuing of the changing society, are replaced by the new habits and the new codes of conduct or reforms. This text sets three principles as the basis for deciding which reforms should be carried out are: Truth, happiness and beauty or in other words proper thinking, convenience and good taste. The reforms should cater to the needs of the whole society and not only to an elite section. Hence one has to take care that all the people in the society will accept those reforms which would help change their thinking, everyday life practices, customs, etc. *Gole's* text written by the *'Pandit'* warns against immature reforms and worries about the ridicule that we may have to face from the foreigners (Gole 1898: 6).

The text is deeply worried about the permanence of the society. In this context, it gives women an agency in reality a burden and the responsibility of keeping the society's health and lineage intact. At this point the *'Pativrata'* (dedicated wifely) role is treated as crucial. Hence there is a declaration that -

> All those social projects which are against breaking the norms of *'Pativratya'* (purity/chastity and dedication), are helpful to the society. Hence without bringing down the strength of those projects women must be granted freedom as much as possible (*Gole* 1898: 293).

In the context of widow remarriage the text starts arguing about the meaning of 'motherhood' itself and expresses a need for a broader meaning of motherhood. If men through their profession or through philanthropy can achieve dignity on par with their dignity achieved through fatherhood why couldn't women do it? Here the text is talking to us almost in the modern framework of equality for women. In order to achieve greatness and eternal fame or reputation, women should be encouraged to carry out their 'specific' social duties in the best possible manner. The honour of motherhood should not be linked to biological reality and in fact, marriage was an extremely degraded path to achieve greatness of motherhood (Gole 1898: 326-27).

Widows can nurture their society by extending their immediate 'self' through the 'affection of their son' and achieve larger goals through *'Dharma'*. The text juxtaposes the issues of 'conjugality' against the concept of an eternal love. It appears that any love in marriage in reality is based on childhood familiarity and practical benefits. Women's education will entirely depend on the economic condition of every family. Hence *Gole* insists that the debates about education for women should pay attention to this reality.

The text now takes an important turn. The argument comes in the following words:

> Those who really wish to do something good for widows, they must direct them towards the path of knowledge, towards religious actions, towards altruism. Give widows an opportunity for travels, for visiting pilgrimages, seeing different places. Do spend as much as possible for such activities. Widows will gain knowledge in this process and this will help all women. Remarriage should be prescribed only for those widows who have no intelligence, no higher goals, no pure ambition - in short for those widows who only understand animal level instincts (Gole 1898: 328-29).

We can conclude this section with some observations. As many historians have observed this period was in fact one of 'traditionalisation' and 'rigidification' of caste boundaries. Since caste, customs and family were treated as changeless and private and outside the normal purview of the State, increasingly political representation, access to education and other forms of privilege came to depend on the assertion of clear and bounded caste identities. Women as gate keepers of caste purity had to fit in the model of *'bhadramahila'*. As O'Hanlon (1991), Uma Chakravarti (1989), Lata Mani have observed, this model was a fusion of older brahmanical Pativrata and Victorian enlightened mothers and companions to men in their own sphere of the home. Rigidification of caste boundaries had led towards increased control over women. All the texts introduced in this section are engaged in redefining *'Pativratya'* (chaste wife's devotion to husband). These texts apparently seem to be discussing education and women's entry into the public domain. Yet a feminist reading of the same suggests that redefinitions of *'Pativratya'* are employed in the milieu of intensifying public scrutiny of women's behaviour and in practice pushes them out of the public domain. It is therefore important to note the voices of subversion of women who had access to this much debated education.

III

1857 onwards we witness a spread of women's education at different levels in Maharashtra. According to one authority, some 300 women produced creative literature during the years 1873 to 1920. They produced books, pamphlets, occasional papers, poems, short stories, novels and essays devoted to variety of topics (Dandavate 1921: 2-3).

The two major streams of thought and expression in this period are represented by the national awakening, led by dominant upper caste men and the 'cultural revolt in Colonial Society' (Omvedt 1976) staged by the non-brahman castes and the subaltern elements of the Indian Social Formation. This stream is associated primarily with the name of *Jotirao Phule* (1827-1890) or the *'Satyashodhak Samaj'*, which he founded in 1873. *Phule*, deeply aware of the social history of India from the ancient times, being a *Shudra* himself, appreciated some aspects of Western influences that came in the wake of the British Rule. He tried to create a new life and a new society for all those also suffered under social slavery of the caste ridden Hindu Society. *Jotirao* and *Savitribai* opened the first school for women as early as 1848. He looked at education especially for the low caste women as a means towards emancipation.

The two streams, it is apparent had different views on the education of women. This also seems to have had a differential impact on the strategies employed by women in the two streams. The following three subsections seek to reread the texts of three educated women thereby underlining their different strategies of subversion.

III-A *Tarabai Shinde*

In 1882, *Tarabai Shinde* brought up in the milieu of *Satyashodhak Samaj*, offered in her *'Stree-Purush Tulana'* (A Comparison between Women and Men) an acute analysis of women's issues from a perspective far ahead of her times. *Tarabai* was the daughter of *Bapuji Hari Shinde*, a founding member of *Satyashodhak Samaj* and lived in the small provincial town of Buldhana between 1850 to 1910. Born in a high caste Maratha family her radical father taught her to read and write not only Marathi but to some extent Sanskrit as well. The *Vijayalaxmi* episode drove *Tarabai* to offer a critical between women and men. Widow *Vijayalaxmi's* trial involving infanticide took place in 1881 in Surat. The case became a centre of public debate. The Brahmanic, patriarchal perspectives shared with each other a common concern over women's so called immorality. Women's conduct was treated as the central and sensitive barometer of the moral health of Indian tradition. As O'Hanlon has remarked 'In slightly different ways, both perspectives (orthodox and liberal reformist) created a position for women in public discourse at once of acute responsibility and of powerlessness, confined within an essentialized nature and deprived of any recognised presence of power or agency on their own account' (O'Hanlon 1991: 92).

Tarabai Shinde offered the first fully worked out analysis of the ideological fabric of Hindu patriarchal society. Her waiting could be taken as the first major feminist expression in the colonial Indian context. Her text is written on behalf of whole humanity. Her narrative is thus the narrative of the community and persistently invokes the rhetoric of love and kinship. Her text is complex in its expression and deeply rooted in the social history of Maharashtra. *Tarabai* made a frontal attack on the patriarchal culture, making use of *Vijayalaxmi* case. With a good deal of strategic cunning she identified two very widely read texts glorified by the mainstream canon to depict 'female stereotypes' set up by the patriarchal hegemony for subverting the patriarchal value system. *Shridhar's* work *Harivijay, Ramvijay, Pandavpratap* was read in every upper caste Marathi household. *Bhartruhari* was a classical author known all over in India. His three *shatakas Niti* (morality), *Shrungar* (Eros) and *Vairagya* (Asceticism) were quite popular.

The texts in question read as follows:

> Woman is only the axe that cuts down trees of virtue. Creatures through thousands of births know her to be the temptress and embodiment of pain in this world.
>
> A whirlpool of changing whims, a house of vice, a city of shamelessness.
>
> A mine of faults, a region of deceit, a field of distrust obstacles at heaven's door, mouth of hell's city, well of evil magic.
>
> Who made this woman device, sweet poison and trap of all creatures?

Tarabai Shinde rebels against this defamation. She makes it clear in the opening section of her essay that she wrote it to defend the honour of *all* her country women. She says 'I pay no attention to particular jati or families in it. It is a comparison between men and women'. The subtitle of her book namely 'Who is adventurous - women or men?' sums up her problematic in blunt terms. *Tarabai* presents her argument point by point in an extremely robust, down-to-earth, powerful and satirical manner. Her language is peculiarly 'feminine' revealing the subversive linguistic skills. She states:

> If a woman is an axe why do you spend whole of your life in her control? Why do you slog in day to day life like a bull? Even a bull is better because being an animal bull lives for himself, you can't

even do that.

If woman-device is so powerful why do you not use your strength of brain to overpower her?

Women are suspicious but it is because they have no education and exposure to the outside world. Women's suspicion is limited but you men are confused by your complex ways of life have all kinds of treacherous plans in your minds. Not a single man is exception to this way of life.

You say women are impudent - men are more and more impudent.

Women are called as magapolis of inadvertent acts - men are known for cutting somebody's throat, immediately after winning their confidence.

Women are accused as the treasure houses of transgressions but men are more fit for this description - Men do not like a bad, ugly, cruel, uneducated wife, full of vices, why should women like such a husband. But women do not run off with another man.

Women are believed to be enveloped in a hundred guised of fraud and deceit. Men are incarnation of this - they have evil in their mind and like a crow they roam around looking for the weaknesses of others. Women never behave this way.

A woman is a temptation incarnate. If even sanyasi men run after women how can you hold her responsible for it? Men do not have any inherent knowledge in them, they get a chance to roam around the world that they are able to get out of difficulties. Women's world is limited – 'from stove to the door step'.

You call women destroyers of the path to heaven, the gate to Yama's city. The same women are your mothers, sisters, wife. If you give them such names then we will call you mother-haters, slanderers of your own mothers.

Are we fitting vessels for all the sorts of deceit? It is you who kill each other every day over *jagirs, vatans, deshmukhis*, just over some scrap of a patil's office, even poison each other.

At the end of the essay *Tarabai* urges men that they should function like a strong tree-trunk and should take a vow to behave like *Bhishma*; clarifying that she was not propagating unlimited freedom for women. She expects women to be as pure as Agni so as to put men to shame and to make them cast down their eyes. *Tarabai* was quite aware of the context within which she was operating. British rule and its impact on Indian economy was quite evident. She points out in her introduction that

> . . . the fine circumstances we used to have in our country are all gone now. Those beautiful saris from Paithan which used to sell at five hundred rupees each they have all gone now. (Malshe 1975: 26)

She mentions towns like Dhanwad, Nagpur as once prospering markets. She also declares that men in India will have to find out *Swadharma* once again. Within this framework *Tarabai* also exposes patriarchal values doled out by the popular literature like *Mukta-mala, Manjughosha* which flourished with the advent of the printing press. She has ridiculed the play *Manorama* which was published in Mumbai in 1871. This play written by *Chitale* was introduced as a plea for the remarriage of widows but had sensational accounts of brothels, adultery, infanticide, and an ethos of *Pativrata* in danger. As Rosalind O'Hanlon has pointed out, a virtual genre in itself of Stricharitra 'Lives of Women' were published from the 1850s onwards. The first text was by Ramjee Gunnojee which was titled in English as '*Streecharitra* or Female Narration, comprising their course of Life, Behaviour and under-taking in four parts with moral reprimands checking Obscenity to secure Chastity' (O'Hanlon 1994: 40). *Tarabai* was not only aware but annoyed by these popular texts and its patriarchal ethos. *Tarabai* not only refuses to be homogenised as morally weak creatures but she mentions prostitutes and asks forthright questions like 'who are these prostitutes? Are they made by some other god?' She holds men responsible for creating prostitutes through their double standards. *Tarabai* time and again exposes the patriarchal nature of Indian family and society. She is aware of the reality that the ban on widow remarriage was practiced not only by the Brahman castes but also by other high castes. She identifies some high caste *Maratha* families and declares, 'In these people's houses you can wait till the end of your life but they will never ever allow remarriage' (Malshe 1975: 25). Her argument about *pativrata-dharma* is very logical. If women are expected to become *Pativrata*, men have to be like gods and here she even makes fun of Hindu gods who have complex life stories in this context. It would be worthwhile to follow her critique of *'Streedharma'*. 'By shaving heads and wiping off the *kumkum* you cannot save *Streedharma'* she argues.

> Women's heart, mind and faculty of thinking cannot be wiped off this way. They will not accept partiality, which is implied by the terms *Pativratadharma* or *Streedharama*. A man kicks/drinks, keeps prostitutes, squeezes people and then expects his wife to observe *Streedharma*. Woman have the capacity to differentiate between good and evil so how will she have faith in such ideals?

Tarabai locates her critique of patriarchy within a certain conception of the ideal relationship between men and women. Her project woven around the recognition of their mutuality and of the utter and ever-present need for maintaining the practical day to day equality of this relationship governs her critique. O'Hanlon's translation of *'Stree-Purush Tulana'* has a longish introductory essay explaining what she understood by different themes used in this text and its wider significance. Her suggestion that in the process of traditionalisation of colonial society, gender relations emerged as a powerful new means for the consolidation of social hierarchy and the expression of caste exclusively is evident in the texts that we reviewed in the earlier section. But her observation that *Tarabai* had ambivalence about women's proper rights and duties is more important. *Tarabai* while seeking answer to such a question that why and how women get blamed for every kind of evil and suffering in Indian society, bitterly denounces all men who were priests, religious leaders, reformers, politicians, journalists, writers. In fact because she is aware of the new form of patriarchy in Colonial India monopolising all rights and freedoms for men, she adopts negotiating strategies with the Hindu patriarchy. At one level *Tarabai's* text tells us about how the construction of a housewife and a prostitute was interlinked. But being a high caste Hindu woman she has to use the language of complementarity between men and women and women as essential *Pativratas*. But she dares to analyse the powerlessness of women in these words – '. . . Can't a woman have the power to speak even one word, or have a pinch of grain to call her own ?' (*Malshe* 1975: 16). This is how *Tarabai* points out the structural powerlessness of women in colonial India. At one level she has challenged and subverted Hindu patriarchy's 'purity' 'chastity' framework at another level she is asking men to become pure like fire for bringing in reality the much needed sanctity in man-woman relationship.

III-B *Pandita Ramabai*

Ramabai belonged at least until she was 13 years of age to a high status *Chitpavan* family of good means and a strong tradition of learning. She also had an unusual exposure to social realities all over the country through her journeys over a long period of time; she moved in high *Brahmo* circles in Bengal and Assam and in *Prarthana Samaj* circles in Mumbai and Pune.

Her father, *Anantshastri Dongre*, had decided to teach classical Sanskrit texts to the women members of his family. In her book *A Testimony* of 1907, *Ramabai* stated : 'He (*Anantshastri*) could not see why women and people of *Shudra* caste should not learn to read and write the Sanskrit language and learn sacred literature other than the *Vedas*' (*Ramabai* 1977:10-11). It is no wonder that in her testimony before the Hunter Education Commission she made clear her resolve to consider it her duty to the very end of her life to advocate women's education for achieving the proper position of women in her land.

Her lectures in Calcutta, delivered in Sanskrit, attracted considerable curiosity and recognition. She was given entry to the highest circles of *Brahmo Samaj* men and women. Her personality and achievements exactly suited the colonizers and the colonized in their search for a model of a new Hindu woman. She was acclaimed as *Pandita Sarasvati* both by the British administrators like Sir W. W. Hunter and by the leaders of the *Brahmo Samaj*. The *Brahmos* were busy pursuing the bourgeois nationalist project of rationality and reforming the 'traditional' culture of their people, and of achieving, in this context, both emancipation and self-emancipation of women. During her four years' stay in Bengal and Assam from 1878-1882, *Ramabai* was exposed in turn to the *Brahmo* ideas and to missionary Christianity. At the same time, her nationalist pride in Sanskrit and in the ancient past ran equally strong, along with her doubts about the truth of Hinduism. She spent most of her time in Bengal delivering lectures on female emancipation. The tragic death of her husband, her consequent loneliness, her quest for medical education, and the sincere and urgent requests from the leaders of the *Prarthana Samaj* persuaded her to leave Bengal for Maharashtra.

Mumbai, Pune, and the adjacent areas of Western Maharashtra showered high praise on her. We also note, in her writings from this period, an undercurrent of anxiety about her future course of action. Her stay in Maharashtra from May 1882 to April 1883 was quite eventful, and various interests played a part in it. She moved among *Prarthana Samaj* reformers, Arya Samajists, and also the Anglican Church circles represented by the Cowley Fathers and the Wontage Sisters. *Ramabai* visited all parts of the Mumbai Presidency, organizing branches for the Arya *Mahila Samaj*, the women's branch of the *Arya Samaj*. Finally, she took the important decision to pursue her higher education in England.

Throughout her life, *Ramabai* insisted on maintaining independence in financial matters, in order to protect the integrity of her ideas and projects. She therefore decided to raise the funds for her foreign journey by publishing a book in Marathi addressed to women in Maharashtra. Written when she was 24, the book was first published in June 1882 and ran into a second edition within six months. She also secured patronage from official quarters. On the strong recommendation of *Dadoba Pandurang*, the government of Mumbai purchased 50 percent of the first edition (Tilak 1960:115-16).

'Strī-Dharma Nitī' is *Ramabai's* first book in Marathi. In the preface to the first edition of the book, *Ramabai* makes a reference to the distressing situation of women trapped in the fallen state of the society. She is hurt by the helpless and abject condition of women who were totally devoid

of any kind of knowledge. She notes with gratitude the endeavours undertaken by the enlightened sections of society to promote education among women as a necessary condition for national regeneration. She laments that almost all the texts capable of transmitting moral knowledge and conduct on religion, ethics and philosophy were available only in abstruse and rare Sanskrit, and were thus simply out of the reach of illiterate women. She states that she could not identify even a single text in Marathi for conveying the essence of moral teaching.

'*Strī-Dharma Nitī*' is divided into eight chapters. The construction of the text reveals a good deal of deliberation and narrative cunningness on *Ramabai's* part. In the first chapter, *Ramabai* identifies knowledge, self-reliance, self-advancement and self-help as the basic resources for individual, social and national development. Drawing a careful distinction between the necessary interdependent relationship between human beings and a bonded dependence on others, *Ramabai* denies the common prejudice held by both men and women as to women's so-called natural and innate weakness and lack of interest in cultivation of the intellect. Making another crucial distinction between license and freedom, *Ramabai* urges that self-reliance, discipline and industry are the only trustworthy instruments for the welfare of womankind.

The next chapter, on knowledge, defines knowledge as the immortal wealth, authentic seeing - an inward eye - and the very core of human life. Drawing a distinction between knowledge and learning, and treating the first as the base of the second, *Ramabai* lays down a series of regulations to govern the cultivation of knowledge. Her set of regulations reveals both her minute observations of the learning process and her attachment to Brahmanical and Victorian values and methods. Emphasizing the need for moderation, punctuality, physical fitness, respect for teachers, a sense of modesty and character practice, *Ramabai* then offers a concrete program. It stresses the need for learning grammar, history, the *dharmasastras*, physics, geography, economics, ethics, health, hygiene, culinary skills, tailoring, embroidery, music and some arithmetic.

The third chapter, on self-discipline, celebrates the virtues of self-restraint, a sense of proper limits, and modesty.

The fourth chapter is the culmination of *Ramabai's* overall approach to the whole problem of social and moral degeneration, inclusive of the sad state of women. She identifies religion as the most fundamental duty and also the sole foundation of all human ends and purposes. *Ramabai* treats religion as the fountainhead of sanctity, as a true path, guide, companion and friend in life.

Chapters five and six cover *Ramabai's* ideas on the duties and concerns of a wife. Demonstrating the injury caused by child marriages, she prescribes the age of 20 as the proper age for marriage for both men and women.

Ramabai then identifies the roots of discord between husband and wife leading to male violation of the sacred code abiding in the institution of marriage and points out the absence of any kind of political or social deterrent to control male license in such matters. She explains that some women react by deciding to spend a lonely but holy life, or by taking to suicide, or by resorting to adultery. We should not overlook the fact that, although *Ramabai* holds men primarily responsible for familial discord, she imposes the burden of maintaining a peaceful environment within the household almost totally on women.

Ramabai opens the seventh chapter with a frontal attack on the selfish, self-centered, and short-sighted behaviour of contemporary Indian men, who followed a double standard in denying women access to knowledge and thereby independence of mind and character along with the means for gaining sound health. She also denounces the *dharmashastras* for their partisan and opportunistic prescriptions against women, based on negative images of women as full of malice, misadventure (sahasi) and guile. In *Ramabai's* opinion, the denial of the right to education is at the root of the anaemic health of Indian women and the consequent degradation of childcare and children's health. *Ramabai* takes this opportunity to expose the empty rhetoric of the modernized, English-educated, so-called leaders of contemporary public opinion who mouth patriotic and high moral rhetoric imitative of their English masters, and yet lack the courage to put it into practice. She traces the moral failure of these leaders to their weak constitution and character. She argues that ignorant mothers and lack of proper child care create this problem. The *Pandita* recommends a comprehensive and detailed plan of child care, and offers it in the name of the great and wise mothers of the ancient past: *Sumitra, Vidula, Kunti* and others.

The concluding chapter invokes the laws of eternal change and cyclical history to request women and men to maintain and develop a spirit of fortitude in the face of adversity. She defines the role of religion as the rock and the path, which offers an honorable resolution of the critical situation. She cites the examples of the sage Mandavya and Jesus Christ to demonstrate how great men of high moral character do not hold gold or religion responsible for the downturns in their life, but face adversity with a spirit of dedication, sacrifice and peace of mind.

In the text *Stri-Dharma Niti*, although *Ramabai* was looking critically at the Hindu fundamentals evoked by the 'modernizing' Hindu elites, she herself participated in the same discourse. As a result, she not only frequently valorizes the *Vedas* and the *Smrtis* as authoritative texts, but also sees Indian women as *satis* and *sadhvis*. Although *Ramabai* was increasingly uneasy about having no religious consolation through the Shastras, she used their framework in writing *'Stri-Dharma Niti'*. She wrote this book because, as a self-reliant person she wanted to earn her fare to England. As *Ram Bapat* points out, *Stri Dharma Niti*, '. . . while aimed ... at assisting women in all ranks of society to build the home called happiness on the firm foundation of knowledge, the typical atmosphere pervading is that of high caste, patrician households. It must have appealed . . . to modernizing elites and officials' (Bapat 1995:233).

We must note here that, in negotiating with the modernizing elites and officials, *Ramabai*, accepting at one level the deeper meaning of the interdependence between men and women, tells her women readers in clear and simple terms to avoid total surrender or subjection. She pleads for 'unpolluted' self-reliance and urges women to take responsibility in the matters that concern their vital interests. *Ramabai* advises women to become industrious individuals who seek knowledge, and warns them against the patriarchal trap that tries, even with benevolent intentions, to capture women. Here she skilfully takes support from *Vyasa Muni*, the classical Hindu sage: 'One who does not help you to dispel your ignorance, do not call him your father, mother, kin, teacher, husband or god' (*Ramabai* 1967:51).

The second major text relevant in this context, written by *Ramabai*, is in fact *The High Caste Hindu Woman*. But as Kosambi has pointed out '. . . the major influence that shaped the evolution of *Ramabai's* feminist consciousness, as reflected in *The High Caste Hindu Woman* was her exposure to the more progressive and less asymmetrical gender relations that prevailed in England and America' (Kosambi 2000: 18). *Ramabai's* travelogue of United States and especially her description of 'The condition of women' in it, published in 1889, provides us with a concrete proof of how she was seeing the linkages between women's education, knowledge and creation of an overall egalitarian progressive nation state.

From March 1886 to end of November 1888, *Ramabai* travelled about 30,000 miles around the United States. She tells us why she wrote this book in these words:

> The joy that I felt in the United States in seeing the wonderful things there would be incomplete if I did not share some portion of it with my Indian brothers and sisters; and that is why I am publishing this small volume...

Her intention of writing this travel account was to create at least 'a little more love of hard work and good will in the service of our mother - India in the hearts of her dear Indian fellow citizens'. She accepted the invitation to go to America because she was inspired by a woman called Bodley who in spite of being a foreigner and non-Hindu had a compassion for Hindu women. Dr. Rachel Bodley was the Dean of the Women's Medical College in Philadelphia. *Ramabai* also was keen on attending *Anandibai*

Joshi's graduation. In her words, '*Anandibai Joshi* is the first instance of a Hindu Woman studying a science as difficult as medicine and acquiring degree in it'. We must note here that *Ramabai* in 1883 had expressed her opinions before the Education Commission on the changes and improvements needed in the system of women's education. She had recommended that women should be allowed to receive education in medicine. *Ramabai* tells us about how she was surprised to see some reformers who had claimed to wish for the progress of women were against offering medical education for women. Reformists like *Keshab Chandra Sen*, the Bengali leader of the Indian *Brahmo Samaj* had expressed his fear that University Education would end up destroying women's femininity or women were naturally not fit for such studies. *Ramabai* notes

> Women doctors are badly needed in India. Our shy Indian women feel great shame about letting men know their condition when they are suffering from many kinds of women's diseases and especially during child birth . . . But men continue to be obstinate no matter which country they belong to. Some oppose medical education for women out of ignorance, some out of jealousy, and some out of simple selfish interest (Engblom & Gomez Trans. Manuscript: 1-3).

Ramabai is keen on women's education not only because she was a woman who was benefitted by having an access to education but as a knowledge-making citizen of India. While travelling in the United States she was constantly comparing America with Britain, India and even China. She was impressed by the United States because of its democratic governance. She has argued in this context that America had not accepted the King's rule and also avoided the misrule or anarchy only by granting all human beings a status of a free, equal and creative being (*Ramabai* 1889: 41).

Ramabai's praise for the Statue of Liberty is noteworthy when she highlights that the lady of liberty stands with a torch in one hand to shed the light of freedom upon the whole world and a book in her other hand to eradicate the ignorance of humankind by giving it knowledge. *Ramabai* was aware of the possible criticism that she would invite of being blinded by the richness of the American Life. *Ramabai* is neither judging critically nor appreciating blindly the world of United States. She is critical about their discrimination and bigotry in the context of racism but she is also critical about the Indian system where all privileges and services were available only for a certain class. In America *Ramabai* saw ordinary people having access to privileges and services. She was especially impressed by the facilities like free education for all children. She saw that one's social group was not the determining basis for acquiring a certain position. An individual could freely attain excellence or inferiority. This was in a way *Ramabai's* utopia. She had seen *Tilak* declaring that the self-rule was his birthright but was sceptical about bringing in reality the self-rule without giving away the sahib-orientedness. She had observed that in her own country common ordinary people did not receive the benefits of cleanliness and good health and the services that they should. *Ramabai* sarcastically points out that the more bellicose and socially conservative nationalists of her time were using the term '*Swarajya*' without having thought about the real meaning of the equality principle (*Ramabai* 1889: 949-95). She has also pointed out that the Indian government was spending more money on martial army than on education. She tells us that self-governance, local governments, self-reliant families, self-respect, politeness all these qualities are there in the American society because they have a superior system of governance. Time and again *Ramabai* compares her own homeland and points out how in Hindustan girls suffer because of child marriage and how they are discriminated right from their birth as girls. *Ramabai* in her sixth chapter talks to us, about 'the pursuit of learning'. She declares in these words – 'Where there is learning there can no longer be any social discrimination'. She repeatedly underlines the importance of women's education while comparing Europe and United States. She observes :

> . . . the very life of the monarchies of Europe resides in their armies, whereas the strength and life-breath of the democracy of the United States resides in education. This is only one nation in the entire world that spends more on its system of education than

on its department of war and this is none other than this democratic nation (Engblom & Gomez Trans. Manuscript: 1-3).

Ramabai was obviously aware of the spaces created by the colonial intervention especially for women. While in the United States, she saw women teachers carrying their teaching profession creatively and standing against the practices such as cruel punishments to deviating students. In fact this was the time she must have come to a firm conclusion that combating women's subjugation was possible through higher education which would give them a status of 'knowledge-makers'.

This is evident in the eighth chapter titled as 'The Condition of Women'. *Ramabai* in this chapter has reviewed the progress made by the women in the United States and its impact on the larger society. This chapter begins with giving us information about how Harriet Martineaue in 1840 had written about American women's plight and compared it with slavery, in her book *Society in America*. *Ramabai*, tracing the progress of American women from slavery to becoming an independent individual, points out that those who essentialize women as powerless are at a barbaric stage of development. In her opinion, one can judge the progress of any nation by examining women's condition in it. *Ramabai* was aware of the fact that if women in England or America had any higher status it was not the credit of the prevalent Christian religion but the dynamism that was shown by many thinkers who were truly reforming the Christian religion in the context of slavery and women's condition. *Ramabai* has argued here that women are made to work hard when they enter the public domain but are always denied a legitimate space in it (*Ramabai* 1889: 220-221). She also points out how women made spaces for themselves in the anti-slavery movement. This chapter has different sections like (a) Education (b) Employment (c) Legal Rights (d) Collective Efforts and Nationalist Society (e) Women's Solidarity (f) Women's Crusade (g) Women's National Anti-Liquor Association. We will take brief review of some of these sections highlighting *Ramabai's* vision and insights about the possible direction that Indian women's education would adopt.

a. Education -

In this section she declares that 'fundamental root of progress is Education'. By using the term *'Vidya'* she suggests 'education' was another name of 'knowledge'. While giving us a brief history of Western women's education, from 1789 to 1809, she highlights the efforts of Mary Wollstonecraft (1789), More (1799) and Sidney Smith (1809) and calls this period as the 'preface to the History of Western Women's Education'. *Ramabai* carefully notes that though the discussion about higher education for women began in the US in 1819 with the efforts of Ema Willard, up to 1831 those who were supporting women's education were against their entry into the higher education. She also points out that Oberlin was the first College for Women and Boston city, which was known for its educational quality, especially the well known Harvard University took 125 years to grant women's entry even at the primary level. *Ramabai's* argument time and again revolves around the point that women do not lose their femininity, break homes just because they have higher education.

b. Employment -

In this section *Ramabai* enumerates different professions adopted by educated women in the US, such as Teachers, Professors, Organisers of Kindergarten, Public Schools, Journalists, independent Editors of different Journals, Doctors, Women Medical Doctors, writings about Women's Health, Lawyers, Priests, Stenography, Scientists, Sculpture, etc. What she was really trying to achieve was to highlight how creating spaces for women's development was the only answer for achieving a progressive industrious society. Women who worked in the anti-liquor campaigns or who initiated campaigns for achieving political rights for women are the examples given by her. In the field of medical science she tells us that women's entry changed the male perception of human body and anatomy. The vulgarity of male medical practitioners was stopped by women entering into it. *Ramabai* like many feminists of our time has argued against women taking up marginal jobs. Primary teaching, serving, running boarding houses, domestic services, typesetting, folding, stitching papers, unskilled work in factories - such spaces were open for women in the period when Harriet Martineau wrote her text (1840). But *Ramabai's* effort is towards women taking higher positions, they becoming decision makers, using their imagination. She demonstrates through Beethoven's sister's example or Caroline Herschell's -the sister of astronomer William Herschell – examples of how women's imagination was subsumed by the patriarchal structures. These brothers became famous forever but their sisters and their contribution remained invisible. The inventions like underwater telescope, life jackets, rafts, steam making machine, improvements in the locomotive engines, reducing noise of the inner city trains, preventing standing crops due to flooding, were all women's contributions (*Ramabai* 1889: 245-56).

In short, *Ramabai's* text is in a way rooted in the liberal philosophy which endorses human being's superiority over the rest of the animal kingdom and legitimizes existing forms of social order in Western Capitalism. *Ramabai* like Wollstonecraft is many times into a framework, which can be put forth, as 'if man can transcend his animalistic, instinctual origins to create a world of reason, culture and social order, the woman also can do the same'. *Ramabai* is pleading for the chance for women to fulfil their socially endowed functions with self-control. Her properly educated women will be able to curb men's unbridled and corrupt practices. She shares with the nineteenth century liberals the conviction that it is the duty of women to be moral conscience of male sexuality.

In 1888 through *'The High Caste Hindu Woman Ramabai'* launched her devastating critique of Hindu patriarchy. She goes much beyond the first wave western feminists like Wollstonecraft. As *Gauri Vishwanath* has pointed out *Ramabai* '. . . meticulously takes apart the various philosophical underpinnings of Hinduism and shows how they have succeeded in mainstreaming the low status of women in Indian Society' (Vishwanathan 1998:124). For eg. *Ramabai* points out that the high caste women were threatened by the popular belief that their husbands would die if they should read or should hold a pen in their fingers.

It is necessary to avoid seeing gender oppression as a context free universal phenomenon. *Tarabai Shinde, Pandita Ramabai, Anandibai Joshi* were part of the collective challenges to structures of power.

Ramabai in her writing has critically looked at western modernity's claims as well as claims of her own tradition. *Ramabai* was a person who interrogated both Hinduism and Christianity. It seems she was different from *Tilak* when she rejects to seek answers from the 'community' framework and chooses to be an individual in the enlightenment framework. Her modernity gives her strength to attack the hypocrisy of Brahmans and the irrationality of Brahmanism and to reject the hegemony of *Varnashvamdharma.* She also was puzzled, repelled and saddened by the sectarianism prevailing in the Christian world. *Ramabai's* refusal to let any authority take decisions on her behalf and her declaration that 'I have a conscience, and mind and a judgement of my own' (*Vishwanathan* 1998: 126) is crucial in understanding her position as a woman - a marginalised category in the world.

III-C *Anandibai Joshi* (1865-89)

Anandibai Joshi is another remarkable woman who is noted as the first woman from Western India to qualify as a medical doctor as early as in 1886. She had an extremely coercive childhood at the hands of her own mother. After her marriage at the age of nine, her husband in a typical colonial reformist fashion compelled her to embark on a course of western style education. In 1883, she went to the US for advanced medical studies and graduated in 1886 from the 'Women's Medical College of Pennsylvania' located in Philadelphia. In February 1889, very soon after her return from America, she died at the very young age of 24. Her correspondence with her husband from the US gives us a good idea of the tremendous insights she gained into the Hindu and the Christian patriarchal systems. From her letters it is clear that she saw through the strategies employed by the 'modern' 'progressive' Indian educated men in the period of anti-colonial nationalism to mould a 'new' Indian woman to suit their emerging bourgeois needs and tastes. She was able to set forth in clear objective terms the price which even men have to pay for enslaving women. Unlike *Ramabai*, whom she knew well, *Anandi* did not change her religion. In her sketch of her own preferences, *Anandibai* identified slavery and subjugation as the things in the world, which she most disliked.

In order to understand *Anandi's* views on women's education and an overall changing situation in Indian and world over we have to depend heavily on her personal correspondence and on some of her public speeches. After her death, two biographies of *Anandibai* were published within two year's time. The first one was published in the US in 1888, written by Caroline H. Dall, an American journalist and womanist writer, titled as *'The Life of Dr. Anandibai Joshee'*. The second one was written by *Kashibai Kanitkar* (1861-1948), the first major novelist in Marathi, in 1889, titled as *'Kai. Sau. Anandibai Joshi Yanche Charitra'* (Late Mrs. Anandibai Joshi's biography). Both these biographies tell us about how *Anandibai* struggled hard for achieving educational excellence and how her brahmanical socialisation, her physical tiredness made it ultimately impossible for her to make use of her medical science knowledge. Her life story also reveals to us how the condition of her mother's generation, which neither had the protection and harmony of the traditional joint family nor an access to the opportunities opened up by modernity, was caught up into the trap. Hence her mother, full of fears and anxieties about *Anandi's* possible transgression of patriarchal rules, took to beating her own daughter coercively. The institution of education came in *Anandi's* life not for gaining knowledge but for refraining her from playing and for engaging her in some activities.

Gopalrao Joshi, Anandi's husband is described by many scholars as an eccentric and a whimsical person, but keeping in view his time and his context, I see him as a norm and not as an exception but a typical male reformist of 17th century India. In his childhood he had witnessed his sister's sharp memory, her picking up of reading, writing skills. It seems that he was even jealous of her. *Kanitkar's* biography tells us that *Gopalrao* was convinced that '. . . women have a sharp intellectual capacity. If they get an opportunity for education, they can perform on par with men' (*Kanitkar* 1889: 19). *Gopalrao's* letter written in 1878, from the local post of Kolhapur to Reverend Wilder of Princeton is pertinent in this context. He wrote 'Ever since I began to think independently for myself, female education has been my favourite subject . . . to raise the nation to eminence among civilized countries. It is the source of happiness in a family' (*Kirtane* 1997: 435). *Gopalrao* taught *Anandi* to read and write both *Modi* and *Balbodh* script. He also made it sure to teach her good English. She was taught arithmetic up to decimal fractions and was taught to read the world map. She was also good in translations from Marathi into English. *Gopalrao* tells Rev. Wilder 'I should like to see her follow any profession, namely medicine or education so that she may be of immense use to her country sisters' (Kirtane 1997: 435).

It was *Gopalrao*, as a reformist who became first uneasy about the marital scene in the Indian families. He saw the mother-in-law, daughter-in-law as a power relation and in-law's home as a prison. His ambition was to set up an example before the world of a wise educated 'Indian' woman. He was even ready to give education to a woman who was drawn into prostitution in those days (*Kanitkar* 1889: 20). *Gopalrao* was radical in his views about women's education. It seems he was annoyed by those fellow beings who supported women's education but were afraid of its consequences. The typical fear that women's education would empower them to leave their husbands was answered by *Gopalrao* in a radical mode. He said :

> it is good to free oneself than accept lifetime imprisonment. Man can leave his wife anytime if she makes any mistakes. It doesn't harm him. If women themselves take this initiative and free themselves, it is so much better for them (*Kanitkar* 1889: 25).

Gopalrao after marriage changed the structure of his household and created a space for *Anandi's* education. Her grandmother formed a part of this new nuclearised home. He even fought with his father and got estranged from him on this issue of women's education 'how far and how much'.

Anandibai, thus trained by her husband, of course, goes much beyond him. Her letter to Mrs. Carpenter in 1880 is an eloquent proof of this, she wrote:

> 'We Hindu women are backwards in all respects. I want to learn from you a lot but I don't have much to give to you . . . We do not have a custom of calling our husbands by name. It is believed that

by doing so we lessen their lives. *But I don't believe in such things*. My husband's name is . . .'

Anandi in this letter also talks about her own ill health and relates it to the Indians custom of a child marriage. Her perception of her caste framework is also revealing. In this letter, she sees the Brahman caste as controlled and restricted by many dos and don'ts (*Kanitkar* 1889: 55-6). Her letters to Mrs. Carpenter are in a way a guide for the foreigners on how to understand the diversity in India especially the different languages, behavioural patterns and various rituals in every group. But *Anandi* was convinced about the modernity that came through education. She says in one of her letters to Mrs. Carpenter - 'Women in India suffer immensely ever . . . Western education would provide them with "light" .. "rescue".' Men and women must be made able to protect themselves, they should not depend on each other for survival as well as for any other thing . . . this would reduce the conflicts and slavery in our society' (*Kanitkar* 1889: 59).

In 1883 *Anandi* spoke about her future visit to America and public inquiries regarding it. In this speech she posed six questions to herself and systematically answered every question. The questions were:

Why I go to America?
Are there no means to study in India?
Why do I go alone?
Shall I not be excommunicated when I return to India?
What will I do if misfortune befalls me?
Why should I do what is not done by any of my sex?

Answers to these questions reveal the complexity and multi-dimensionality of *Anandibai's* life. She was convinced that there was no other alternative for her than to visit the most civilized part of the world for achieving medical knowledge. She openly criticised the patriarchal practices of the Indian missionary and the subordinate knowledge that was available for women. She declared openly that she would remain unchanged as far as customs, manners, food or dress were concerned. Was the observing of

Hindu patriarchal rules to its extreme a strategy on her part? Or was this a reaction to the imitative, westernized middle class that she saw around her? One can conclude from her speech that *Anandibai* wanted to claim for herself a legitimate membership of human society. Her ideals were Manu, Shibi and even Jesus Christ. Her decision was to live for a wider cause at any cost.

One more text that is crucial for our purposes is her letter to her brother in law from New Jersey written on 2nd January, 1886. *Gopalrao's* brother was about to accept the clerical employment offered by the British government. This letter is full of *Anandi's* new personality which was benefitted by the exposure to different situations in the US and by the new skill that she had achieved through learning. She writes:

> . . . among three of us (me, my husband and you) I have experienced the world more . . .this may be the reason why I am not able to understand your decision . . .I do not think that I am superior to you by age or intelligence . . . but have you forgotten our own thinking? Where is your earlier heartfelt passion about independence? (*Kanitkar* 1889: 75)

Anandi herself had rejected a clerical job in the post office when she had needed it badly. She was not ready to compete with her own people and sell her autonomy for the sake of a monthly salary. Here she does not one-sidedly glorify her own decision but also reflexively says 'But now I feel sad about that decision because if I had taken up that job I would have set an example for many other women who were in a similar situation. At least they would have got an entry into that world, but that did not happen'. She further notes in her letter that though she was a powerless backward woman, she chose to become doctor by avoiding falling into the trap of competition set by the colonial rulers. '. . . That is how I was in search of a small profession, which would help my motherland and its powerless women' (*Kanitkar* 1889: 75). *Anandi* is in fact advising the young generation of India to take up modern professions. Her concern is about how education in India was becoming trivial, a symbol of hypocrisy and a means of heavy expenditure. She points out

'. . . We must imitate what is good in Westerners and must achieve knowledge and gain profit and then must show the rulers our real worth' (*Kanitkar* 1889; 76).

In short, like all other nationalists of her time, *Anandi* was pained by the degeneration and decay of the Indian people. No doubt she nurtures the dream of bringing back 'tradition', but was also aware of the possibilities of modernity.

Anandi's letters to *Gopalrao* though apparently written in the '*Pativrata*' mode, adopts a subversive mode when she makes such statements as

> 'Quiescence is the best path that every Hindu husband must learn from his wife' (*Kanitkar* 1889:189) or 'Every nation must learn pain-bearing capacity from the Indian women. They may have religious naïveté or ignorance or wrong beliefs, but we cannot hold them responsible for it. This is because all laws, regulations, practices are congeneal to men . . . we must know for what, when, in what way men did protect our dignity or did release us from enemies or how they snatched rights from us instead of lamenting about the present day situation . . . we must concentrate upon how to get rid of ignorance.'

Anandi was against publishing her own writings and letters. She was against any kind of exhibitionism. She wanted to lead a responsible life, taking her decision and acting upon it accordingly. Her letter written in the year of 1884 tells us about her presentation on 'child marriage' before missionaries. *Anandi*, who had once accepted child marriage as hazardous to health in her letter to Mrs. Carpenter before visiting the US, defends it in the US before the gathering of missionaries. Does *Anandi* surrender to the conditionalities of female reformism by publicly defending it as suggested by *Sangari* and *Chakravarti*? (*Sangari* 1999: xxiv) Or could we understand this in the light of her statements about her own perception of self as a 'cool' and 'decision-making' individual. *Anandi* defended child marriage when she was abroad and when she perceived herself as a representative of her nation and more so when she knew about missionary politics. She subverted the hidden agenda of the missionary politics by giving positive points of child marriage. *Anandi* thus grew into a mature person. One can vouch this in her letters advising her husband in every realm, be it religion or domesticity, during this period. She writes to *Gopalrao* about how to behave with the domestic servant at home. She says,

> I want to request you to have compassion about the woman who cooks for us. You yourself say that she is good and is better than me in the upkeep of the house. Remember, she also has pain and pleasure like you. Hence for my sake, please try to adjust and do good to her as far as possible... (*Kanitkar* 1889: 81)

Anandibai, like *Tarabai Shinde* and *Ramabai*, is very much aware of the male chauvinism that was prevalent in her time. She points out that the general ethos of women's victimisation is aggravated by male deviance and women pay a very heavy price. But it is easier to be deviants. They

> '. . . marry one woman, lure the other with promises, bring the third one . . . in the home and have a need for the fourth one' (*Kanitkar* 1889: 82)

Her conclusion in this matter can be summed up in these words – 'men's irresponsible behaviour is painful. They have such a powerful lust that they cannot control it. Thus those trapped in the prison of desire are ignorant and silly men'.

In November 1886 *Anandi* came back to India in February, 1887. She died in Pune. During her illness when she was sure of death she had asked her ashes to be sent to Aunt Theo. Her ashes were later buried in the cemetery at Poghkeepsie, where she had spent very meaningful years of her life.

Anandi's untimely death, her fears and anxieties, her dreams and premonitions, her faith in good and bad omens, her belief in astrology, particularly at the end - her insistence of taking *Ayurvedic* medicine - all these need nuanced complex understanding. One can neither paint her as a total victim or as an individual who resisted, struggled and was victorious even when she died untimely.

Anandi's text of her thesis submitted in 1886 for the degree of Doctor of Medicine was rescued in 1963 and is now available in *Kirtane's* book on *Anandi's* life. This was titled as '*Obstetrics Among the Aryan Hindoos*' which was to introduce gynaecology as practiced in India. It seems that she had through this text made an effort to prove that the Indian obstetrics had its path of-making knowledge. In explaining her objectives in writing this thesis, she has noted that

> As the importance of obstetrics can be measured only by the value of life and health, and both being of paramount consequence it is deserving of most careful study. When we realize how difficult and vast the subject is, it is not surprising to find so many great minds thoroughly absorbed in its magnitude, from the time immortal. Since our study naturally embraces the cause and effect, race, habits, climate, influences and means of assisting Nature in her operations, we must not entirely overlook the history of past ages and consider the superior minds which laboured, with marked success, in the same field of investigation, under promptings of the same motives, as far back as 15 century BC. They may enable us to the better appreciation of the science and pay due respect to the discoveries, thesis and mode of application of remedies of minds of different nations at different times. I therefore need not apologise for choosing the subject (*Kirtane* 1997: 460).

One must analyse this text and raise many critical questions about its content. But for our purpose, this proves that *Anandi* was trying to represent India as she understood it while she was confronted by developed Western world of the US and was also keen to bring new knowledge to her world which was in her opinion decaying rapidly.

IV

This extensive review of the patriarchal discourse in the context of women's education through a case study of the nineteenth century Maharashtra brings out many important issues and underlines complexities involved around gender politics.

We must, first of all note that *Tilak, Kanitkar, Gole* and *Tarabai, Ramabai, Anandibai* were not read here as binary opposites. They were contemporaries, and in fact shared many ideas. All of them were genuinely concerned about the degeneration of their society and were convinced about the modernity that came not only along with the colonial rule, but through the churning in their own society. As feminist researchers while challenging other disciplines and opening new ways of questions and interpretation of social life, we must be context sensitive. Hence this case study is especially trying to understand what were the constructions of the patriarchal discourse which were looking at women's education with suspicion and caution. At the same time the concern is to outline the ways in which these constructions were subverted through individual resistances.

Tilak's self conscious undertaking of the role of reconciling tradition with modernity and his single minded attack on imperialism in all its guises is the context within which he differentiates between common Indian women and professional English women. His insistence on women's education for enhancing the scope and the quality of married women's life became ultimately problematic. In other words, *Tilak* presents a case of the nineteenth century reformer who had recognised the potential of education for women but the compulsion of the 'political' or the 'nation' in a sense did not allow him to recognise the potential of women as knowledge makers, as nation builders. Obviously, history of feminism in India is very much a part of anti feminism. The real question we should ask is how in the face of open support to women's education by political leader like Tilak, it was constantly contested through the strategies of ridicule as in the case of *Kanitkar* and through the instrumental approach for building up Hindu Religion and Nation as in the case of *Gole*.

Women's education came to be framed by 'Nation' and 'Conjugality'. Even the resistance to patriarchy was circumscribed by concerns of 'nation'. There were no two polar opposite camps one for women's education and the other against it. For women's education was intrinsically linked to tradition and the definitions of boundaries of castes and classes. But still the individual resistances of these three women studied here present to us some insightful modes of subversions. It would be limiting to have simplistic formulation of women's space, women's voices while attempting to theorize the historical transitions. Gender roles are not static and fully formed, there are discontinuities. Hence readings of the texts must go beyond the notion of gender as a dichotomous and as an exclusively hierarchically structured realm. The lives and works of the three women are more than individual case histories. *Tarabai, Ramabai* and *Anandibai* are studied here because historically, women in India like low caste were denied an access to those texts which relegated them to subordinate positions. Women's resistances to their enforced destinies were almost absent in the written domain. All the three women studied here have broken this rule. Their life and their writing foreground the issues of justice, equality and human dignity. Their narratives are not at all a linear narration of victimization. All of them have challenged essentialized notion of complimentarily between men and women and at the same time they do not glorify the antagonism between them. *Tarabai's* critique of colonial rupture - deindustrialisation, deskilling and its implications for women's lives or *Ramabai's* critique of Hindu-Brahmanic patriarchy and her faith in liberal democratic nation or Anandibai's critical understanding of the need of expanding Hindu patriarchal structures from within need nuanced, complex understanding than just 'women's voices' framework. A complex understanding of how education for women was tied to processes of caste and class formulations and distinctions and to nation making itself need to be underlined. These women's demand of full rights to higher education for women without challenging the 'better motherhood' or 'better home making' framework was in fact a crucial strategy. We must also note that *Tarabai* ended her life as a lonely widow; though *Ramabai* was active till the end, in her last days she lived, in a way, in isolation in Kedgaon and *Anandibai's* life ended untimely. It would be erroneous to fit these women into pre-constructed moulds of resisting heroines or as always and already victims or worse still, in a psychologised reading of feminine imbalance. This would be disrespectful towards the rich and complex developments of feminist historiography that have spanned the last 25 years. In this tradition of feminist research the present paper seeks to make comparisons, connections and distinctions between women who entered colonial education at different levels. It traces the hostility to education as well as underlines the gap between what their education was designed for and the way in which they used it. This paper therefore, works towards in the final analysis understanding the persistence of the structures of patriarchies in colonial India.

Original Source

Feminism, Tradition and Modernity
Padia, Chandrakala (Ed.)
Indian Institute of Advance Study, Shimla
2002
(pp: - 316-358)

References

Bapat, Ram. 1995. 'Pandita Ramabai Faith and Reason in the Shadow of the East and West' in Dalmia Vasudha and Steitencorn [Eds.] *Representing Hinduism: The Construction of Religious Traditions and National Identity,* New Delhi: Sage Publications.

Bhagwat, Vidyut, 'Negotiating Strategies with Hindu Patriarchy', *The Book Review* Vol. XVIII Number 10 (pp. 14-15).

_____. 1995. Marathi Literature as a Source for Contemporary Feminism, *EPW* Vol. XXX No. 17, April 29, 1995 WS 24-29.

_____. 1990. 'Man-Woman Relations in the Writings of the Saint Poetesses', *New Quest:* pp. 223-32

Chakravarti, Uma. 1989. 'Whatever Happened to the Vedic Dasi? Orientalism, Nationalism and a Script for the Past' in Sangari and Vaid [eds.] *Recasting Women: Essays in Colonial History,* New Delhi: Kali for Women.

Dandavate, Ganesh Raghunath [Ed.]. 1983 (1921). *Marathi Stri Lekhikanchi Suchi* (A list of Marathi Women writers), Baroda Central Library.

Engblom, Philip and Kshitija Gomez, *United Stateschi Lokasthiti ani Pravasvrutta,* Translation Manuscript (unpublished)

Gole, Mahadev Shivaram. 1898. *Hindu Dharma ani Sudharana,* Pune: Jagathitechchu Press:.

Kanitkar, Bapuji Narayan. 1890. *Taruni Shikshan Natika,* Pune: Shri Shivaji Press.

Kanitkar, Kashibai. 1912. *Kai. Sau. Anandibai Joshi Yanche Charitra,* Pune: Sevasadan.

Kirtane, Anjali. 1997. *Dr. Anandibai Joshi: Kalani Kartrutva,* Mumbai: Majestic Prakashan.

Kolte, V. B. [Ed.]. 1982. *Leela Charitra*, Mumbai: Maharashtra Rajya Sahitya Sanskriti Mandal.

Kosambi, Meera [Ed.]. 2000. *Pandita Ramabai: Through Her Own Words*, New Delhi: OUP.

Lele, Jayant. 1989. 'Tradition and Intellectual in a Third World Society' Lele and Singh [Eds.], *Language and Society: Steps Towards an Integrated Theory*, Leiden: E.J. Bill.

Malshe, S. G. [Ed.]. 1975 (1882). *Kai. Tarabai Shinde Krut Stree Purush Tulana*, Mumbai: Mumbai Marathi Granthasangrahalay.

O'Hanlon, Rosalind. 1991. 'Issues of Widowhood: Gender and Resistance in Colonial Western India' in Haynes and Prakash, *Contesting Power Resistance and Everyday Social Relations in South*, New Delhi: OUP.

Omvedt, Gail. 1976. *Cultural Revolt in a Colonial Society, The Non-Brahman Movement in Western India: 1873 to 1930*, Mumbai: Scientific Socialist Education Trust.

Pandita Ramabai. 1889. *United Stateschi Lokasthiti ani Pravasvrutta*, Mumbai: Nirnaysagar Press.

Pandita Ramabai. 1967 (1882). *Stree - Dharma niti*, Kedgaon (Plow): Ramabai Mukti Mission.

Parchure, Atre and Omkar [Eds.]. 1997. *Anandi - Gopal: New Profiles from Unpublished Sources*, Pune: Maharashtra Prakashan.

Phadke, Gangadhar Shastri. 1841. *Stree Vidyabhyas Prakaran Punarvivaha Prakaran*, Pune: Ganapat Krushnaji Press.

Ramanujan, A. K. 1986 (1982). *Speaking of Shiva*, Penguine Books: Baltimore; 1973, 'On Women Saints' in Hawley and Wulff [Eds.], *The Divine Consort: Radha and the Goddess of India.*

Samagra, Tilak. 1976. Vol. V, Pune: Kesari Prakashan.

Sardar, G. B. 1969. *The Sant Poets of Maharashtra: Their Impact on Society*, New Delhi: Orient Longman.

Sarkar, Sumit. 1997. *Writing Social History*, New Delhi: OUP.

Shenvi, (Madgaonkar) Govind Narayan. 1850. *Runa Nishedhak Bodh*, Mumbai: Deccan Vernacular Society.

Sunthankar, B. R. 1988. *Nineteenth Century History of Maharashtra, Vol. 1 1818 -1557,* Pune: Shubhada Saraswat Prakashan.

Tharu, Susie and K. Lalita. 1991. *Women Writing In India, Vol.1 and 2*, New York: The Feminist Press.

Vishwanathan, Gauri. 1998. *Outside the Fold, Conversion, Modernity And Belief,* New Jersey: Princeton University Press.

Chapter - 6

Pandita Ramabai's *Strī-Dharma Nīti* and Tarabai Shinde's *Strī-Puru Tulanā*: The Inner Unity of the Texts

The year 1818 marks the end of the Brahmanical *Peśvā* dynasty in Maharashtra. The advent of the East India Company's rule soon led to fundamental changes in all walks of social life and to new configurations of power in the vital spheres of economics, politics, administration, education, and culture in general.

The arrival of the colonial regime led to the collapse of state support of all varieties to the Hindu religious tradition as determined and practiced by the Brahmans. The Brahmans' loss of secular power in the form of the state generated a novel kind of social situation. To be sure, colonial rule meant the total loss—or at least decisive erosion—of freedom for all sections of society. But it also opened new and fresh opportunities for those sections that had experienced powerlessness in the earlier scheme of things. The changing equations of power gave the oppressed sections room for creative manoeuvre. The new situation was bound to produce a new distribution of power among the various castes of the Hindu social order.

Company rule produced a trauma which sapped the institutional fabric, the ideological texture, and the will of the conquered. A correct understanding of the rupture caused by the new, alien regime is necessary in order properly to grasp the social conditions at that time. The colonial order meant that the earlier systems of knowledge and the disciplines handed down from generation to generation, among both Brahmans and non-Brahmans, and in a tradition that was literate as well as primarily oral, suddenly lost patronage. The new order also caused discontinuity with earlier experiences and made them meaningless in the eyes of both the colonizers and, soon, the colonized. It meant primarily that the various sets of self-understanding entered upon by the different sections of society according to their station in life were shattered. As a result, every section of the society began to search for new identities and new sets of criteria by which to judge themselves and others. In other words, the situation became open for reshuffling of texts, signs, and symbols used to demarcate all kinds of boundaries, inclusive of the boundaries of the self.

As the days passed, the medium of the new discourses began to change even in narrow linguistic terms. The English language with its privileged position replaced both Marathi and Sanskrit as the vehicle of the discourses generated by free people. In the course of time, both Marathi and Sanskrit seem to have entered a period of rapid development in terms of their prose forms and the print-based tradition. In reality this growth, with all its achievements, reflected the world of the objects of colonial rule.

The rupture in the sphere of knowledge was accompanied by a profound rupture in the domain of culture. The cultural norms of the colonizers, as defined and practiced through administrators, missionaries, or other agents, began to percolate down and to influence all sections of society. The coexistence of two parallel sets of culture systems, that of the colonizers and that of the colonized, was bound to generate a wide variety of permutations and combinations. Culture soon emerged as a battlefield.

The onset of the colonial regime gave rise to a new group of people variously termed nowadays a new middle class or classes, a new intelligentsia, or a nascent bourgeoisie. As is well known, in Western India this class was mostly drawn from the Brahmans. The Brahmans soon occupied all available clerical and professional positions in the lower reaches of the colonial administration. This was not an accident. Indeed, under the colonial regime, Maharashtrian Brahmans lost their prominent political and administrative positions along with the role they had shared as the makers of the dominant canons in various disciplines. But both the Brahmans' mental makeup, as moulded by tradition, and the material decline they experienced, led them to turn to English education as institutionalized by the colonial order. Their virtual monopoly in gaining access to colonial administration gathered tremendous power in their hands.

This created a peculiar situation. The Brahmans began to claim a natural role of leadership over the rest of Hindu society. They took for granted their superiority over others, and began to behave with a certain sense of pride and superciliousness. But, on the other hand, they stood in a subjugated role before the colonial power and at heart suffered from a feeling of inferiority vis-à-vis the culture of the rulers. As a result, they began to imbibe the cultural models of the west and to transmit them to the various orders of society. The self-demeaning comparison between British and Indian ways of life assumed the built-in superiority of Western culture in matters related to liberty, social justice, and so on, in comparison with the hierarchical values of Hindu or Indian social structures. This state of mind was a logical culmination of the kinds of knowledge that had been set up and were being spread by the newly-established colonial schools, institutions, and, later, universities. The establishment of this order led to the phenomenon that Edward Said has called 'Orientalism.' The question of women was a part of these developments.

Uma Chakravarti has identified the working of orientalism in the matter of gender construction in the following words (Chakravarti 1989: 34):

In seeking a psychological advantage over their subjects, colonial ideology felt compelled to assert the moral superiority of the rulers in many subtle and not so subtle ways. One of the not so subtle ways was in the area of gender relations. The 'higher' morality of the imperial masters could be effectively established by highlighting the low status of women among the subject population as it was an issue by which the moral 'inferiority' of the subject population could simultaneously be demonstrated. The women's question thus became a crucial tool in the colonial ideology.

Orientalism also built the myth of an Aryan golden age wherein the men were modelled after the Victorian male of the ruling classes in England and the women after the Victorian ladies strutting everywhere in the contemporary novels of the Victorian age. The model treated family as based on conjugal love, sustained and nourished by the 'cultured' woman's patient, understanding sense of sacrifice. A series of articles and books offering guidelines to women were published. These were meant for their moral upliftment and also prescribed rules for their role as the ideal housewife. These texts provide us with insights into the process of modernistic gender construction throughout the greater part of the nineteenth century.

The colonialist articulation of gender was part of a larger project taken up by the colonizers to recover and set up the traditions as required by the colonial interest in line with their Victorian mindset. It was matched by an equally-determined process of rediscovering tradition on the part of the new middle classes. The legal system introduced by the colonial regime was based on Whig political ideology and the values of a market economy. It aimed to shape a new Indian society based on modern possessive individualism. The formulation of the required personal law was to be achieved by discovering suitable customary and religious norms in the past. In the process, certain texts, traditions, and ways of life were valorized at the cost of others. This new legal system replaced the diverse customs, conventions, and ideological formations embedding the rich variety of historical experiences of the various sections of Indian society with a homogenizing, regimented set of legal norms and social practices within the framework of upper-caste values and images. Privileging of certain so-called 'core' and 'representative' texts in place of the concrete plethora of social practices helped both the apologists and the rebels in the 'Hindu tradition' that was now imbibed by the Western-educated classes. This paper presents an analysis and comparison of two texts that are anchored in this kind of discourse: *'Strī-Dharma Nīti'* by *Pandita Ramabai*, and *'Strī-Puruṣ Tulanā'* by *Tarabai Shinde*.

Both these texts appeared in 1882. They arrived at the end of a long line of Marathi texts highlighting both the ideals and the experiences of women as 'individuals.' The texts are significant for several reasons. The writers were personalities with a strong sense of identity of their own. In addition, the texts reveal their authors' outstanding skill in organizing them. The quality of their prose is a product of the authors' immediate personal and political attainments. And finally, to read the texts against the grain is a challenge for contemporary feminist scholars: although outwardly using the language of male reformists, the texts challenged the male hegemony of their times in subtle and not-so-subtle ways.

Pandita Ramabai

Pandita Ramabai belonged to a Citpavan family of high standing that had migrated to South Canara in what is now the state of Karnataka. She was brought up in the milieu of *Citpavan* tradition as it existed at the end of the *Peśvā* dynasty. She was a rebel by birth. Her father, *Anantshastri Dongre*, had decided to teach classical Sanskrit texts to the women members of his family. Although he was following the example of the wife of one of the Peśvās, who had studied the *Raghuvamsa* under the guidance of her husband's guru, the act was nevertheless heretical and was bound to provoke *Anantshastri's* Brahman neighbours and the higher authorities of the *Mādhava* and *Vaiṣṇva* sects. His determination to educate his second wife, *Laxmibai, Ramabai's* mother, led to his being tried before the religious assembly (*dharmasabha*), and to his voluntary self-exile. In her book A *Testimony* of 1907, *Ramabai* stated: 'He [*Anantshastri*] could not see why women and people of *Shudra* caste should not learn to read and write the Sanskrit language and learn sacred literature other than the *Vedas*' (*Ramabai* 1977:10-11). *Anantshastri's* endeavours to educate *Ramabai's* elder sister led to a domestic tragedy that made a lasting impact on *Ramabai's* mind, making her realize the injustice that social, religious, and state laws did to women (*Ramabai* 1977:33-34). It is no wonder that in her testimony before the Hunter Education Commission she made clear her resolve to consider it her duty to the very end of her life to advocate women's education for achieving the proper position of women in her land.

The *Pandita's* mother, *Laxmibai Dongre*, played an equally outstanding part in her life. In the dedication to The *High-Caste Hindu Woman*, *Ramabai* acknowledges her mother's role. The quality of *Laxmibai's* scholarly achievements was reflected in the fact that she trained *Ramabai* single-handedly. *Laxmibai* taught her daughter elementary Sanskrit grammar and vocabulary, as well as the entire *Bhagavata Purana* and the *Bhagavadgita*—in all, more than 20,000 verses! *Ramabai's* writings give the impression that her early life was spent in a comfortable, prosperous, lively, affectionate, and industrious household that reflected the virtues and traditions of high-status Citpavans. This atmosphere must have shaped the basic core of *Ramabai's* personality before the total decline of the family fortunes that began in 1871.

Given her affection and gratitude towards her parents, some things must be borne in mind in order to understand *Ramabai's* personality. As she made clear in *A Testimony*, *Ramabai* was not given any kind of secular education, and she was brought up in isolation from the outside world. Her father's background and preferences led to a concentration on the study of classical *Sanskrit* texts at the cost of the *Prakrit* literatures. Thus her universe was primarily rooted in the tradition handed down by the classical Brahmanical lore wedded to *dharmaśāstra* literature.

Between 1872 and 1878, *Ramabai* went through a harrowing phase of her life. She lost her parents in the great Madras famine of 1871-1874, witnessed the untimely death of her sister, and, along with her brother, travelled on foot all over the country in a condition of near total destitution. It was with these complex experiences behind her that *Ramabai* arrived in Calcutta in 1878. She was at the point of losing her faith in the rituals and the Hindu 'scriptures.'

Her lectures in Calcutta, delivered in Sanskrit, attracted considerable curiosity and recognition. She was given entry to the highest circles of *Brahmo Samaj* men and women. Her personality and achievements exactly suited the colonizers and the colonized in their search for a model of a new Hindu woman. She was acclaimed as *Pandita Sarasvati* both by British administrators like Sir W. W. Hunter and by the leaders of the *Brahmo Samaj*. The *Brahmos* were busy pursuing, in the words of Partha

Chatterjee, 'the bourgeois nationalist project of rationality and reforming the "traditional" culture of their people, and of achieving in this context both emancipation and self-emancipation of women' (Chatterjee 1989: 233-53). During her four years' stay in Bengal and Assam, from 1878-1882, *Ramabai* was exposed in turn to the *Brahmo* ideas and to missionary Christianity. At the same time, her nationalist pride in Sanskrit and in the ancient past ran equally strong, along with her doubts about the truth of Hinduism. She spent most of her time in Bengal delivering lectures on female emancipation. The tragic death of her husband, her consequent loneliness, her quest for medical education, and the sincere and urgent requests from the leaders of the *Prarthana Samaj* persuaded her to leave Bengal for Maharashtra.

Mumbai, Pune, and the adjacent areas of Western Maharashtra showered high praise on her. We also note, in her writings from this period, an undercurrent of anxiety about her future course of action. Her stay in Maharashtra from May 1882 to April 1883 was quite eventful, and various interests played a part in it. She moved among *Prarthana Samaj* reformers, Arya Samajists, and also the Anglican church circles represented by the Cowley Fathers and the Wontage sisters. *Ramabai* visited all parts of the Mumbai Presidency, organizing branches for the Arya *Mahila Samaj*, the women's branch of the Arya Samaj. Finally, she took the important decision to pursue her higher education in England. In the face of contrary advice rendered both by some missionaries for denominational reasons and by Hindu friends out of fear for the loss of her religion, she decided to face the unknown for the sake of her soul and for the sake of her sisters in India.

Throughout her life, *Ramabai* insisted on maintaining independence in financial matters, in order to protect the integrity of her ideas and projects. She therefore decided to raise the funds for her foreign journey by publishing a book in Marathi addressed to women in Maharashtra. Written when she was 24, the book was first published in June 1882 and ran into a second edition within six months. She also secured patronage from official quarters. On the strong recommendation of *Dadoba Pandurang*, the government of Mumbai purchased 50 percent of the first edition (Tilak 1960: 115-16).

Her potential readership, the purposes for which the book was written, and the climate of thought which governed the educated and particularly the *Prarthana Samajist* circles moulded the text in its present form. The audience consisted of upper-class, upper-caste, primarily Hindu men and women in need of guidelines to promote the rise of a new woman in tune with the times. *Ramabai's* immediate purposes precluded her from causing immediate offence to her readers' Hindu susceptibilities. At the same time, *Ramabai* was not going to miss the opportunity to state the ideas about womanhood that she had gained at the cost of so much personal suffering! The book reveals an extremely fascinating play of ideas drawn from the *dharmasastric*, Brahmo and *Prarthana Samajist* canons, with faint suggestions of her developing interest in the message of the Gospel.

A close look at the reports of her lectures, talks, *kīrtans*, and sermons in Bengal, Assam, and Maharashtra tells us that the *Pandita* was adopting similar strategies in addressing women to those of the leading social reformers of her times. She highlighted the high status and honour enjoyed by the Hindu women of the hoary Aryan past, singled out *Sītā, Draupadī, Kuntī, Damayantī, Sāvitrī* and such others as model figures, and dwelt upon the patriotic need to secure the upliftment of women. The previous emphasis was on the urgent need for practical, secular education and cultivation of a high moral code for personal and social action. A sound and healthy man-woman relationship was seen by her in terms of companionship and not subordination. Virtues of proper deference to authorities, decorum, modesty, and all-round balanced development of personality were highlighted. The domestic atmosphere which was evoked in these presentations was that of high Brahmanical families of good means and education.

'Strī-Dharma Nitī' is Ramabai's first book in Marathi. As she had been brought up in a household where Sanskrit was the primary vehicle of even domestic conversations, *Ramabai's* Marathi in the text sometimes betrays a rather quaint and involved diction. Later on she became one of the masters of Marathi prose. She addressed this first book primarily to women. Underlining the prescriptive and non-literary character of her

text, the *Pandita* acknowledges her own experiences, the discourses of eminent scholars, and a study of texts. In the preface to the first edition of the book, *Ramabai* makes a reference to the distressing situation of women trapped in the fallen state of the society. She is hurt by the helpless and abject condition of women who are totally devoid of any kind of knowledge. She notes with gratitude the endeavours undertaken by the enlightened sections of society to promote education among women as a necessary condition for national regeneration. She laments that almost all the texts capable of transmitting moral knowledge and conduct on religion, ethics, and philosophy were available only in abstruse and rare Sanskrit, and were thus simply out of the reach of illiterate women. She states that she could not identify even a single text in Marathi that could convey to women the essence of proper moral teachings in a simple and lucid manner.

'Strī-Dharma Nīti' is divided into eight chapters and takes up 142 pages. The construction of the text reveals a good deal of deliberation and narrative cunning on *Ramabai's* part.

In the first chapter, *Ramabai* identifies knowledge, self-reliance, self-advancement, and self-help as the basic resources for individual, social, and national development. Drawing a careful distinction between the necessary interdependent relationship between human beings and a bonded dependence on others, *Ramabai* denies the common prejudice held by both men and women as to women's so-called natural and innate weakness and lack of interest in cultivation of the intellect. Making another crucial distinction between license and freedom, *Ramabai* urges that self-reliance, discipline, and industry are the only trustworthy instruments for the welfare of womankind. She has no doubt whatsoever that the above course of action, combined with a constant concern for each other, would secure for women equal and in fact superior eminence in social affairs. Stressing patriotism, unity, a sense of solidarity and industriousness as the key to the rule of the numerically small yet powerful British over the numerically vast but feeble Indian society, *Ramabai* deplores the moral decay of the community due to indulgence, jealousy, and a lack of patriotic responsibility.

Saying that women's laziness makes them vulnerable to male charges of indolence, stupidity, and obstinate behaviour, *Ramabai* urges women to undertake work appropriate to their delicate and somewhat weaker constitution. But, with an equal degree of emphasis, she tells them that God has created them not only to spend their whole life looking after domestic chores full of drudgery, but to act as co-sharers with men in all earthly endeavours (*samsāra*). Pointing out that the pursuit of self-interest has been linked in a divine design with mutuality of needs and reciprocity of actions, she highlights the need for men and women to share all common concerns.

But *Ramabai* considers dependence to be the root of all evils. She considers liberty the root of happiness and welfare, clearly holding women themselves responsible for their bondage and unequal relationship with men. She appeals to women to cultivate self-reliance and industriousness.

The next chapter, on knowledge, defines knowledge as the immortal wealth, authentic seeing—an inward eye—and the very core of human life. Drawing a distinction between knowledge and learning, and treating the first as the base of the second, *Ramabai* lays down a series of regulations to govern the cultivation of knowledge. Her set of regulations reveals both her minute observation of the learning process and her attachment to Brahmanical and Victorian values and methods. In an autobiographical passage, she takes the opportunity to tell us how wasteful it is to spend one's valuable time, health, and financial resources on empty and blinding rituals instead of securing true knowledge and learning. She also demonstrates the folly of treating ornaments as the sign of individual refinement. Emphasizing the need for moderation, punctuality, physical fitness, respect for teachers, a sense of modesty, and character practice, *Ramabai* then offers a concrete program. It stresses the need for learning grammar, history, the *dharmaśāstras*, physics, geography, economics, ethics, health, hygiene, culinary skills, tailoring, embroidery, music, and some arithmetic.

The third chapter, on self-discipline, celebrates the virtues of self-restraint, a sense of proper limits, and modesty. *Ramabai* identifies religion and good conduct not as impediments to happiness but as its necessary conditions. She urges women to choose the path of moral action instead of the path of temptation. She asks women to respect god, parents, teachers, and other respectable persons. Finally she tells women to cultivate manners and an etiquette appropriate to their high station in social life. *Ramabai* describes how the various types of sermon-performances—*purān, harikathā, kīrtan,* and *pravacan*—which were thought of as the appropriate media for learning propriety, had instead become arenas of vice and moral corruption. She even requests that women pick up a working knowledge of Sanskrit in order to gain first-hand knowledge of their Hindu religion, and suggests that, as far as possible, they listen to *purān* recitals from woman *purāniks*[1]. *Ramabai's* firsthand observation of the decay and corruption in the Hindu religious sphere, and her anger, find very pertinent and poignant expression here. She ends the chapter by applauding the virtue of the right kind of company for developing and protecting one's own character.

The fourth chapter is the culmination of *Ramabai's* overall approach to the whole problem of social and moral degeneration, inclusive of the sad state of women. She identifies religion as the most fundamental duty and also the sole foundation of all human ends and purposes. Religion keeps the world free from sin, discontent, and anarchy. *Ramabai* then identifies and explains ten basic properties of religion. She argues that these properties are common to all religions in the world, and that their cultivation secures—opens the high road to—honour and rectitude. *Ramabai* treats religion as the fountainhead of sanctity, as a true path, guide, companion, and friend in life.

Chapters five and six cover *Ramabai's* ideas of the duties and concerns of a wife. Treating the mutuality and interdependence of men and women as a divine mission, and marriage as the most happy and desirable relationship true to the religious and divine order, *Ramabai* considers the proper form and time for marriage. Demonstrating the injury caused by child marriages, she prescribes the age of 20 as the proper age for marriage for both men and women. She requests women to treat not wealth and beauty but moral conduct, learning, charity, and love as the proper standard in seeking an alliance with a man. Arguing that a union of manly virtues arising out of masculine strength, and womanly virtues arising out of feminine delicacy, is necessary for personal and social well-being, *Ramabai* insists that the proper fruits of such a combination will be available only within the framework of marriage, and certainly not through any other kind of man-woman relationship. Considering the varieties and multiple meanings of love—parental love (*vātsalya*) towards children; devotion (*bhakti*) towards parents, *gurus*, and God; affection (*sneha*) between brothers and sisters and between friends; and compassion towards the meek and the sufferers (*dīn*) shown by good people—*Ramabai* considers the love between wife and husband as not only true love in every sense of the term but also the highest and most complete form of love. She argues that marriage is essential to realizing this last form of love in practice. Marriage, in her opinion, is the answer to the utter need for companionship in the various trials of life.

Ramabai then identifies the roots of discord between husband and wife leading to male violation of the sacred code abiding in the institution of marriage. Men begin to insult and demean their wives; or they marry another woman, discarding the first; or they engage in adultery. *Ramabai* points out the absence of any kind of political or social deterrent to control male license in such matters. She explains that some women react by deciding to spend a lonely but holy life, or by taking to suicide, or by resorting to adultery. But, whatever happens, *Ramabai* holds men responsible for the initial discord.

Next *Ramabai* warns women about the dangers involved in resorting to stupid, ignorant, and superstitious solutions. She demonstrates how such solutions are exploited by all kinds of charlatans in the name of magic, religion, or ritual. She then prescribes secular, moral equivalents of these false gim-micks. In her opinion, devotion, deference, loyalty and service towards one's husband, apathy towards superficial finery and ornamentation, honest and open conduct toward one's husband—leaving no room for suspicion on the part of the husband, the mother-in-law, or other senior members of the family—and all-round moderate and disciplined behaviour will lead to moral and secure domestic happiness.

We should not overlook the fact that, although *Ramabai* holds men primarily responsible for familial discord, she imposes the burden of maintaining a peaceful environment within the household almost totally on women.

In outlining the domestic duties of the wife, *Ramabai* once again sermonizes against indolence, pride, jealousy, anger, hatred, and violence. She lays down a schedule of work for the housewife, designed to achieve health, grace, economy of effort and the resultant efficiency, beautification of the household, proper management of domestic servants, a function-oriented organization of household articles, and a careful account of income and expenditure. We are struck by *Ramabai's* minute observation, her deep understanding of the smallest details of the daily and occasional chores of household work, and her strong common sense, accompanied by faith in reason as the true guide for taking decisions. But we are equally struck by her typically Victorian outlook, bordering on prudishness, in matters involving women's costume, appearance, social etiquette, and behaviour.

Given the even, quiet, and non-confrontational approach, tone, and language of the book up to this point, the opening passages of the seventh chapter take a surprising turn. *Ramabai* opens this chapter with a frontal attack on the selfish, self-centered, and short-sighted behaviour of contemporary Indian men, who followed a double standard in denying women access to knowledge and thereby independence of mind and character along with the means for gaining sound health. She also denounces the *dharmaśāstras* for their partisan and opportunistic prescriptions against women, based on negative images of women as full of malice, misadventure (*sāhasī*), and guile. In *Ramabai's* opinion, the denial of the right to education is at the root of the anaemic health of Indian women and the consequent degradation of child care and children's health. *Ramabai* takes this opportunity to expose the empty rhetoric of the modernized, English-educated, so-called leaders of contemporary public opinion who mouth patriotic and high moral rhetoric imitative of their English masters, and yet lack the courage to put it into practice. She traces these leaders' moral failure to their weak constitution and character.

She argues that ignorant mothers and lack of proper child care create this problem. The *Pandita* recommends a comprehensive and detailed plan of child care, and offers it in the name of the great and wise mothers of the ancient past: *Sumitrā, Vidulā, Kuntī*, and others.

The concluding chapter, devoted to the true ends of *'strī-dharma-nīti'*, invokes the laws of eternal change and cyclical history to request women and men to maintain and develop a spirit of fortitude in the face of adversity. She defines the role of religion as the rock and the path which offer an honorable resolution of the critical situation. She cites the examples of the sage Mandavya and Jesus Christ to demonstrate how great men of high moral character do not hold gold or religion responsible for the downturns in their life, but face adversity with a spirit of dedication, sacrifice, and peace of mind. All the dimensions of *Ramabai's* essentially religious personality find graphic expression in this chapter. *Ramabai* urges all women, and men as well, to place their trust in the ever-merciful lord who is the only solace of all beings full of sorrow.

In the text *'Strī-Dharma-Nīti'*, it is quite evident that we do not see *Ramabai* expressing her ideas in a unified feminist framework. Moreover, although *Ramabai* was looking critically at the Hindu fundamentals evoked by the 'modernizing' Hindu elites, she herself participated in the same discourse. As a result, she not only frequently valorizes the *Vedas* and the *Smrtis* as authoritative texts, but also sees Indian women as *satīs* and *sādhvīs*. Although *Ramabai* was increasingly uneasy about having no religious consolation through the *Sāstras,* she used their framework in writing *Strī-Dharma-Nīti.* She wrote this book because, as a self-reliant person, she wanted to earn her fare to England. As *Ram Bapat* points out, *Strī-Dharma-Nīti* '. . . while aimed . . . at assisting women in all ranks of society to build the home called happiness on the firm foundation of knowledge, the typical atmosphere pervading is that of high caste, patrician households. It must have appealed . . . to modernizing elites and officials' (*Bapat* 1995: 233).

We must note here that, in negotiating with the modernizing elites and officials, *Ramabai*, accepting at one level the deeper meaning of the interde-pendence between men and women, tells her women readers in clear and simple terms to avoid total surrender or subjection. She pleads for 'unpolluted' self-reliance and urges women to take responsibility in the matters that concern their vital interests. Women should not rely on anyone, she says, particularly on men, to carry out required social change. *Ramabai* advises women to become industrious individuals who seek knowledge, and warns them against the patriarchal trap that tries, even with benevolent intentions, to capture women. Here she skilfully takes support from *Vyasa Muni*, the classical Hindu sage: 'One who does not help you to dispel your ignorance, do not call him your father, mother, kin, teacher, husband or god' (*Ramabai* 1967: 51).

Ramabai sees the realm of religion in a broad framework and as an essential foundation of human life. For women, in her view, religion was a possible space for gaining true selfless friendship and protection. She points out that women's lonely journey toward selfhood will be impossible without an intimate friend. But, because of the patriarchal context within which *Ramabai* was operating, she could not see the possibility that men could become real friends to women. *Ramabai* thus suggests the realm of religion and spirituality as the one in which women can gain fearlessness to stand by their truth (*Ramabai* 1967: 64-66).

Writing about women's crucial role as mothers, *Ramabai* reviews the man-woman relationship in her times. She states, 'In this country, men's minds are always filled with contemptuous thoughts about women. They do not have open minds towards women but show superfluous hypocritical affection. They take for granted their own superiority and then rule women as they wish. All this leads to unhappiness in women's minds' (*Ramabai* 1967:111). This distorted relationship between men and women results in their giving birth to children who have defeatist tendencies. *Ramabai's* advice to women is to achieve independence and thus take control of their motherhood. Doing this will give them the strength to spell out their own truth to their husbands as well as to society as a whole (*Ramabai* 1967: 80). *Ramabai* advises women to stand up against the common, stereotypical opinions and beliefs.

In his otherwise sensitive understanding of *Pandita Ramabai's* life, *Bapat* sees her as a religious revolutionary but not as a social revolutionary. In his view, 'Her one-sided emphasis on the spiritual domain at the cost of its material counterpart resulted in the failure to develop a new and distinct conception of gender roles in contrast to the existing models available in various patriarchal traditions' (*Bapat* 1995: 250). But this way of dichotomizing the spiritual and material domains does not help us much in understanding *Ramabai's* struggle historically. Whether *Ramabai* can be labelled a feminist in the contemporary sense or not is not really the issue at stake. What is crucial at this juncture is to understand the complex process through which she was trying desperately to fight for the cause of women, to make meaning of their lives in the context of colonial rupture and the overall degraded situation of women in India.

Pandita Ramabai, having seen through both Hindu and Christian religious frameworks, tried only as a last resort to build up an alternative world for women at the Kedgaon Mission. She obviously did not want to shut herself into a ghetto. However, her time and situation did not allow her to take a leadership role in the larger society around her. The dead end that *Ramabai* experienced at the Kedgaon Mission in the last stage of her life prompts us to give serious attention to the limited discursive space that was available to women of her times. This is more significant than labelling her a religious or social revolutionary.

Tarabai Shinde

The second text under consideration is *Strī-Puruṣ Tulanā* by *Tarabai Shinde*. This text was published in 1882, the same year as *Ramabai's* text. Born into a *Maratha* family of some standing, *Tarabai* was a daughter of Bapuji Hari Shinde, a founding member of the *Satyashodhak Samaj*. Her father worked as a head clerk at the office of the Deputy Commissioner of Revenues in various places, including perhaps Pune and Mumbai. He was the author of a book called '*Hints to the Educated Natives*', which was published in 1871. He must have been a man of some social standing, as the Government of Mumbai took the trouble to seek his response in relation to *Mr. B. M. Malbari's* well-known notes dated 15 August 1884[2]. Her radical father taught *Tarabai* to read and write not only Marathi, but also elementary Sanskrit. Her diction and style of argumentation suggest that she must have been very familiar with the *Satyashodhak* discourse. As pointed out by Tharu and K. Lalita (1991: 222):

> *Stri Purush Tulana* is probably the first full-fledged and extant feminist argument after the poetry of the *bhakti* period. But *Tarabai's* work is also significant because, at a time when intellectuals and activists alike were primarily concerned with the hardships of a Hindu widow's life and other easily identifiable atrocities perpetrated on women, *Tarabai* was able to broaden the scope of the analysis to include the ideological fabric of patriarchal society.

When *Strī-Puruṣ Tulanā* was written, the widow *Vijayalaxmi's* infanticide trial in 1881 in Surat had become a focus of violent public debate. Almost all the men who fought over the matter shared a common concern about women's alleged immorality, and treated women's conduct as the central and crucial barometer of the moral health of society. These writings provoked *Tarabai* to make a frontal attack on the patriarchal stereotypes about women. *Tarabai* writes :

> The Almighty God who created this fantastic world is the one who has created men and women. Is it true that only women have internalized the reckless values bordering on vices, or do men also have the same faults? I am writing this small essay in order to make this absolutely clear, keeping in mind the pride for my countrywomen who are my sisters. I am not talking on behalf of a particular caste or lineage. This is only a comparison between women and men (*Malshe* 1975: preface; my translation).

With a great deal of strategic cunning, *Tarabai* identifies two texts by *Srīdhar* and *Bhartrhari* that were glorified by mainstream literary and religious authorities and had a wide following among literate Hindus. *Tarabai* identifies one stereotype after another and subverts each of them in a highly polemical style, demonstrating how they fit the accusers rather than the accused. In the face of every binary opposition relegating women to a position as the 'other' of men, *Tarabai* retains the division but treats men as the embodiment and the root cause of the 'other'. Her strategy is far ahead of her times. Her technique of writing is in some ways similar to that adopted by Simone de Beauvoir in *'The Second Sex'* in 1939.

Tarabai's language is robust, down-to-earth, powerful, highly allusive, and biting. She reveals all the subversive linguistic skills of Indian women brought up in an oral tradition. Her imagery is highly pictorial and her language is full of slang and idiom drawn from daily life. For example, in her introduction she states:

> In fact, it is you men and these beggarly fads and fancies of yours that have wrecked all our own native ways of making a living, so our trades-men and skilled craft people are all perishing of hunger. Our glory has all been driven away, and *Laxmi* . . . she has seen these fads, these dirty defiling habits of yours, and she's taken herself away now, on the road to a distant country. So I place this little book before you, so you might have some pity for women who are widows, and for the wives and children of these poor working folk ... I am doing it out of the hope that you might stop treating all women as though they had committed crime and making their lives a hell for it' (O'Hanlon 1994: 76).

Tarabai opens her argument by highlighting the one-sided, partisan code of conduct of *pātivratya³*. She argues that women were bound to follow the evil ways of their so-called exemplars—that is, men, who themselves violate each and every canon of *pativratya*. She states, 'If every husband is to be treated like a god by his wife, then his behaviour has to be like a god's ... If he has limitless faults, how can anyone regard him as a god?' (*Malshe* 1975: 2; my translation). *Tarabai* therefore concludes that all the sorrows and evils arising out of the ban on widow remarriage arise out of the moral laxity of the men who surround women.

Tarabai then cites with a great deal of humour contemporary women's novel ways of matching their men's irresponsibility with equal concern for their own ease and comfort. *Tarabai* makes the *dharmaśāstra* and the law-makers themselves squarely responsible for their glorification of totally immoral myths and patterns of behaviour represented in the stories about '*Draupadī, Ahalyā, Satyavatī, Kuntī, Tārā, Sītā*, and *Mandodarī*' *Tarabai's* amazing courage in exposing all these semi-divine figures and fables is reminiscent of *Jotirao Phule's* subversion and mockery of Brahmanical mythology. She justifies her war against the ancient men and their texts by citing the logic developed by the epics justifying fratricide. *Tarabai* argues:

> . . . even your gods are crooked, so is it any wonder that you men are villains too? *Indra* assumed the form of *Gautama* and stained the sant Ahalya's virtue. *Chandravali* was a great *pativrata*, but *Krishna* still wrecked her rows in the guise of *Rahi*, didn't he? Why do you cry so much about *pativrata dharma*, when it's you men that scheme and ruin homes and families? (O'Hanlon 1994:115)

In reviewing the great epics '*Ramayan* and *Mahabharat*', *Tarabai* points out how *Sita, Tara,* and *Mandodari*, after being sexually exploited in convenient patriarchal ways by great men like *Ram* and *Ravana*, were then given the title *pativrata*. She also brings out the contradiction between the origins of ancient sages and the brahmanical Hindu insistence on chastity for women: 'one of them was born of a deer: that is *Shringarishi*; one of a bird . . . one of an ass . . . one of a cow. . . They are all gone now, but women are still stuck with living up to it all' (O'Hanlon 1994: 84). *Tarabai* thus ridicules all the men who used the *sastras* to justify their superiority. She concludes that all those who had written *sastras, purans, pothis,* and so on should feel ashamed of themselves.

Next *Tarabai* exposes the vainglory and the high and empty rhetoric of menfolk in general and the social reform bodies in particular by highlighting the gulf between their precept and their practice. She ridicules the social reformers in these words:

You are absolutely like those rats from the fables of Aesop who give lip service and declare, 'The cat is to be belled'—but who comes forward to do it? ...Your empty meetings have been going on for the last thirty or thirty-five years. What is their use? You may feel great about your-selves, but, looked at honestly, you are as lifeless as a spare tit on a goat (*Malshe* 1975:6; my translation).

Arguing that the divine design demands the interdependence of men and women, husbands and wives, and pointing out women's inordinate capacity for sharing, service, and sacrifice, *Tarabai* states that men's monopoly of power, their control and manipulation of women, their denial of knowledge and education to women, and finally their stupid and ignorant stereotypes about women violate the divine order and promote moral and social decline. *Tarabai* asks pertinently,

Seeing as you're such almighty heroes, why is it so impossible for you to pull poor widows out of this pit of shame? Why can't you break some caste rules, put the kumkum back on their foreheads, and let them enjoy the happiness of marriage again? (O'Hanlon 1994: 85).

Tarabai also cites further examples of male duplicity and double standards in developing codes of conduct in relation to widow remarriage, head shaving, widowhood, marriage between mature husbands and child wives, and so on. *Tarabai* points out how the same set of 'reformers' and 'modernizes' who ape the Europeans in every walk of life, invoke tradition to oppose the colonial government's impositions in social matters. *Tarabai* in fact welcomes the presence of British rule in India as providing Indian women with a strategic opportunity to confront their traditional oppressors.

Ridiculing Indian men who took to clerical jobs under the British *Raj*, *Tarabai* argues that in the contemporary situation men should call themselves not 'pen-pushers' but 'beggars crying for a crumb of bread.' She uses the term '*bhakari bahaddar*' ('masters in producing bread'). She tells men, 'The swords are gone, the pens have lost their sharpness, and all that remains is filling the bellies somehow' (Malshe 1975:9; my translation).

Tarabai's insight into contemporary social, political, and economic affairs finds expression when she demonstrates that Indian men have not been able to take a single step against what we now identify as the processes of de-industrialisation, the decline of agriculture, and the drain of wealth in the colonial context. She recalls the excellent examples set by such great men of the ancient past as *Hariścandra, Śībi,* and *Yauvanāśva,* and tells how they went to the other extreme to honour their promises and values. Making fun of the images of women set up by *Srīdhar* and *Bhartrhari,* and making fun of the reformers and of associations like the Sarvajanik Sabha, *Tarabai* exposes the rampant male ignorance, stupidity, treachery, cunning, corruption, sedition, adultery, moral decay, greed, and pomp of her times.

We can call *Tarabai* the first Indian feminist literary critic. Her exposure of male stereotypes of women appeared almost a century before Simone de Beauvoir's *'The Second Sex'.* In fact, her forthright polemical style stands in sharp contrast to that of de Beauvoir:

> *Tarabai's* language is robust, down to earth . . . As we all know, one of the crucial consequences of colonialism, perhaps on all Indian languages, but certainly in the case of Marathi, has been a kind of a patriarchal, puritanical cleansing and streamlining of the language. As a result, both at the oral and literary level Marathi lost its vibrant, robust and highly expressive character. *Tarabai Shinde's* text . . . refuses to be cowed down by the patriarchal gender-morality . . . *Tarabai* reveals all the subversive linguistic skills of the Indian women brought up in oral tradition and developed through generations. Her imagery is pictorial and full of daily slang (*Bhagwat* 1994:14).

In an autobiographical passage, *Tarabai* describes the tragic results of a marriage alliance secured by a well-meaning father with an educated, indolent, and pretentious man. In the passage immediately following this autobiographical one, she alludes to the double standards followed by *Krishnarao Bhalekar, Mahatma Phule's* close lieutenant, in causing ill treatment to his first wife.

Tarabai also handles the notorious popular text '*Strī Caritra*' and other contemporary works like *Manjughosa, Muktamāla and Manoramā* in the new romantic genres set up by the emerging elites to expose the moral vacuousness and male arrogance and stupidity that characterize these genres. For example, Tarabai echoes a crucial theme in women's oral culture. This theme applauds motherhood and its selfless service to the human race, and reproaches those who hold mothers cheap. She argues, 'It's the one who's always trying to make you happy, that you're heaping all this blame onto—it's her you're trying to push down to the bottom of the earth' (*Malshe* 1975:26).

In forthright language, *Tarabai* also points out that men are too clever for women. She says, 'Men, you are so cunning that you will pass through a sugar cane field without letting those sharp leaves touch you, let alone scratch you' (translation by Maya Pandit). She demands positive governmental intervention, complete with deterrent punishment, to prevent infanticide.

Tarabai argues as follows on behalf of the British *Raj*:

> Well, say the government made it possible for women to remarry. Then each and every one of those women, living happily with their new husbands . . . would become the firm and lifelong supporters of the British government. The government could collect up all those tigers and goats of men, with their swollen lusts, with their minds fuddled with drink and their bellies stuffed with meat, and stick them in a big strong prison (O'Hanlon 1994:27).

Tarabai sums up her argument by throwing light on women's true role as the *archāngīśakti* (the 'better half') and as a *pratiśakti* (a countervailing power) of men. She demands that men not trade upon women merely as objects of passion and urges men to set a true example for women by taking the initiative in following the path of good conduct. She expresses confidence that, if men exercise control, women will surpass them in holding high the banner of purity. The perfect *pātivratya* will then be a reality. Making it clear that she is not making a case for women's license, she requests women to follow the path of good conduct and purity with a sense of determination and integrity. But she also argues on behalf of the prostitutes. She asks, 'Now who are these whores? Aren't they produced on this very earth? Or are they created by some other god? In fact, whores are just some of those women you've seduced and lured away from their homes' (*Malshe* 1975:26; my translation). She ends her classic essay with a prayer to the eternal, ever-compassionate, all-merciful brother of the meek and the poor, the universal-Governor God (*Parameśvara*) to secure this-worldly fulfilment in a state of bounty, happiness, and, most importantly, *saubhāgya*[4].

As I have stated earlier (*Bhagwat* 1994:15), to recover writings like *Tarabai Shinde's* is a political rather than an aesthetic activity. We must read such texts not for the moments in which they collude with or reinforce dominant ideologies of gender, class, nation, or empire, but for the gestures of defiance or subversion implicit in them. At one level *Tarabai* has challenged and subverted Hindu patriarchy's 'purity-chastity' framework; at another level she brings in the issue of the sanctity of the man-woman relationship. It is revealing to see how *Tarabai* appeals to Indian women to become pure like fire in the colonial context.

Comparison

When we juxtapose these two texts, we find that they share some common sensibilities, interests, and positions on concrete issues related to women's lives, and that they reveal some interesting differences in terms of emphasis and nuance.

The two texts provide us with a clue to the cultural upheaval which was taking place in Maharashtra in the last quarter of the nineteenth century. Both the writers belonged to the upper reaches of society. *Ramabai*, as we have seen earlier, belonged, at least until she was 13 years of age, to a high-status *Citpavan* family of good means and a strong tradition of learning. *Tarabai* belonged to a high-class *Maratha* family of aristocratic background (*khandān*) which had seen days of considerable affluence. Both women received a good education in the context of their times and had training in Marathi, Sanskrit, and English (Malshe 1975:2). They had been exposed to new practices and new currents of thought. *Ramabai* had had an unusual exposure to social realities all over the country through her journeys over a long period of time; she moved in high *Brahmo* circles in Bengal and Assam and in *Prarthana Samaj* circles in Mumbai and Pune. *Tarabai* must have been exposed to *Satyashodhak* influence through her father's social and political networks. *Ramabai* was a widow at the time she wrote, and *Tarabai's* marriage was for all practical purposes broken (Malshe 1975:2). Both of them must have seen women's subordination and oppression in their own family circles. Though both of them use powerful expressions, *Tarabai* in particular has control over a clear, lucid, and forthright Marathi. Her text is full of dramatic irony and reveals a command over a rich treasure of phrases, proverbs, and slang handed down by the women's oral tradition.

Ramabai and *Tarabai* seem to take for granted the social and cultural norms of high Hindu families, particularly concerning the domestic sphere and the role and proper bearing of a respectable woman. Behind all the apparent differences between, on the one hand, the Brahmanical and high *Maratha* codes of conduct in these matters and, on the other hand, the Victorian Christian English code, we can identify a common outlook and even the same set of expectations in matters related to marriage and family, to the role and nature of the relationship between husband and wife. But a close look at these texts shows us that their authors have used these traditionalist and Victorian models as a platform for developing an attack on their perversions by the male order. They have turned the tables against dharmasastric orthodoxy and contemporary male solidarity. They use men's prejudices against women, summed up in the form of the various stereotypes, to expose the logical fallacies, inner contradictions, and double standards involved in this game.

In *Tarabai's* text this exposure is direct, unusually blunt, full of bite and ridicule, and highly polemical. By contrast, *Ramabai* has, it seems, followed a deliberate policy of understatement. Besides, her text had the purpose of serving as a guide to practical conduct. But even so her suppressed anger against the *dharmaśāstras* and the tradition manage to erupt once in a while, as, for instance, at the beginning of the seventh chapter of her text. The two authors also agree in their contempt for the contemporary class of western-educated men and for social reform groups. They condemn these people for their fashionable, imitative rhetoric and their blind and ineffectual attachment to orthodoxy.

Tarabai differs from *Ramabai* in that *Tarabai's* universalist framework has its roots in the *bhakti* tradition of Maharashtra. Like *Jotirao Phule* and Justice *Ranade*, *Tarabai* also vents her views on behalf of the whole of humanity. Her narrative is thus the narrative of the community and persistently invokes a rhetoric of love and kinship. By resisting colonialism as a story of universal progress, she is resisting the production of normalized individual and colonized regimes of disciplinary power. While the thrust of her argument has to do with women, she also admits the complementarity between men and women. Her feminist consciousness gives her the strength to produce a cogent critique of colonialism, Brahmanism, and patriarchy in India. *Tarabai* also points to the spaces created by the British *Raj* for women through education. Her text is complex in its weave and is rooted culturally in the tradition and social history of Maharashtra.

The two women's statements also reveal a common strategy. Both of them draw upon examples and models from the ancient and classical texts, but they use these resources for purposes of disruption. Once again *Tarabai's* exposure of the double standards involved in myths related to *Ahilyā, Draupadī, Sītā, Tārā, Mandodarī,* and others is amazingly blunt and expressive of her *Satyashodhak* heritage. *Ramabai's* text adopts a different technique. She was fully at home with the classical Brahmanical tradition. Moreover she had used examples from that tradition in almost all of her talks to men and women in Bengal, Assam, and Maharashtra. But *Ramabai* refused to use the sanction of the ancient texts to support her argument. It is not an accident that the names of great Indian women of the past appear in her book on only two occasions. Her book, despite its Brahmanical and Victorian sets of values, appears as a typical secular text deliberately free from religiosity of the old kind.

Both the texts are based upon full faith in the institutions of marriage and the family. The authors want to secure a household based upon recognition of the reciprocity of needs and a division of labour between husbands and wives, men and women. Both the texts take for granted women's image as the weaker sex. But the texts interpret this image in terms of women's physical constitution and certainly not in terms of any innate lack of strength related to moral, social, or creative achievements. *Ramabai* and *Tarabai* both refuse to see any automatic connection between women's delicate biological constitution and their low social status and alleged moral and cultural decay. Both of the authors take the domestic sphere as the proper domain of women's activities. They seem even to acknowledge a need for an altitude of deference to the husband on the part of the wife. But they expect marital relationships to be based on equality in terms of morality, reason, propriety, customs, the divine design, and even law. This ambivalence is a sign of their transitional times. One can even say that it is still typical of the value system of the Indian elites, and perhaps also of elites in the first world, even in our own times.

In common with their eminent contemporaries, *Ramabai* and *Tarabai* held the right to education, along with practical access to it, to be the key to the solution of women's backwardness. Both of them shared a common belief that denying women access to education was responsible for the state of affairs that permitted the negative and erroneous images of women on the part of men. The texts differ from each other in two basic ways. While they tend to share a common set of values and remedies, *Ramabai's* book is conceived as a manual for guiding women, and so its stress is on positive prescriptions, *Tarabai's* book aims to attack the male nonsense that wanted to overwhelm the just cause of women at the time of *Vijayalaxmi's* trial. In other words, *Ramabai* adopts a constructive posture, in contrast to *Tarabai's* polemical and confrontational posture.

Theoretically speaking, however, they share a common sisterly position. Their upbringing and perhaps also their purposes can account for the other most important difference between them: a difference in linguistic style. *Ramabai* uses a typical modern Marathi prose that was emerging in educated Brahmanical circles at her time. *Tarabai* also uses the same, highly Sanskritized style. But she also shows tremendous control over women's own oral idiom as well as over a simple prose style (*bālbodh*) based on the utmost economy of statement. She employs the latter to create dramatic effect and narrative irony.

Ramabai's book might have gone into successive editions after the first two, but she did not care to print it again after her conversion to Christianity, even when she had good printing facilities at her disposal. Her Hindu counterparts must have lost interest in its revival for opposite reasons. *Tarabai's* work earned for her hostility, it seems, even from the highest Satyashodhak circles. It seems to have been denounced by no less a figure than *Krishnarao Bhalekar*. *Mahatma Phule*, of course, went out of his way to defend both *Tarabai's* integrity and the validity of her argument. Yet the non-Brahman *Satyashodhaks* must have chosen to push *Strī-Puruṣ Tulanā* into obscurity, as the Brahmans had done with *Strī-Dharma Nīti*. No wonder that the third edition of *Strī-Dharma Nīti* was published only in 1967, while *Strī-Puruṣ Tulanā* was salvaged from obscurity by sheer co-incidence in 1975. The eclipse of these two texts from historical memory tells its own story.

Original Source

Images of Women in Maharashtrian Society
Feldhaus, Anne (Ed.)
State University of New York Press,
1998
(pp: - 192-214)

Notes

1. In 1879, from far-off Assam, Ramabai had publicly expressed admiration for Anasuyabai, a woman *puranik* at Nasik (Tilak 1960:74 -75).
2. *Selections from the Records of the Government of India*, Home Department, No. CCXXIII. Home Department Serial No. 3. Papers Relating to Infant Marriage and Enforced Widowhood in India, Calcutta, 15 August 1884.
3. *Pativratya* is the behaviour of the ideal wife, the *pativrata*, who devotes herself to her husband and honours him as a god. This is a concept with many dimensions and many implications.
4. *Saubhāgya* is the auspicious state of a married woman whose husband is alive.

References

Bapat, Ram. 1995. 'Pandita Ramabai: Faith and Reason in the Shadow of the East and West.' In *Representing Hinduism : The Construction of Religion, Tradition and National Identity,* edited by Vasudha Dalmia and Heinrich von Stieteneron, New Delhi: Sage.

Bhagwat, Vidyut. 1994. 'Negotiating Strategies with Hindu Patriarchy' (a review article). *The Book Review* 8, 10 (October): 14 -15.

Chakravarti, Uma. 1989. 'Whatever Happened to the Vedic Dasi? Orientalism, Nationalism and a Script for the Past.' In *Recasting Women; Essays in Colonial History,* edited by Kumkum Sangari and Sudesh Vaid, New Delhi: Kali for Women, pp. 27-87.

Chatterjee, Partha. 1989. 'The Nationalist Resolution of the Women's Question.' In Recasting Women: Essays in Colonial History, edited by Kumkum Sangari and Sudesh Vaid, New Delhi: Kali for Women, pp. 233-35.

Malshe, S. G., editor. 1975. *Kai. Tārābāī Śindekrut Strī-Puruc-Tulanā,* Mumbai: Mumbai Marathi Granthasangrahalaya.

O'Hanlon, Rosalind. 1991. 'Issues of Widowhood: Gender and Resistance in Colonial Western India.' In *Contesting Power: Resistance in Everyday Social Relations in South Asia,* edited by Douglas Haynes and Cyan Prakash, New Delhi: Oxford University Press, pp. 62-108.

———. 1994. A *Comparison Between Women and Men: Tarabai Shinde and the Critique of Gender Relations in Colonial India.* Mumbai: Oxford University Press.

Pandit, Maya. 1991. 'A Comparison of Men and Women' (partial translation). In Tharu and K. Lalita 1991, pp. 223-35.

Pandita Ramabai. 1967 [1882]. *Stri Dharma Niti* (Morals for Women). Third edition, Kedgaon: Kedgaon Pandita Ramabai Mukti Mission.

———. 1997 [1907]. *A Testimony.* Tenth edition, Kedgaon: Kedgaon Pandita Ramabai Mukti Mission.

Tharu, Susie, and K. Lalita (eds.). 1991. *Women Writing in India: 600 B.C. to the Present,* Volume I, New York: Feminist Press.

Tilak, Devadatta Narayan. 1960. *Maharastrachi Tejasvini Pandita Ramabai* (Maharashtra's Glorious Pandita Ramabai), Nasik: Nagarik Prakāśan.

Chapter - 7

Negotiating Strategies with Hindu Patriarchy

Rosalind O'Hanlon's *A Comparison between Women and Men: Tarabai Shinde and the Critique of Gender Relations in Colonial India* is a significant addition to the writing on gender sensitive social history of contemporary India. It is important not only in terms of the history of women and gender relations in India but also in terms of the text it has introduced, since *Tarabai's* writing could be taken as the first major feminist expression in the colonial Indian context. It is noteworthy that Tarabai's Universalist framework has its roots in the Bhakti tradition of Maharashtra. Like *Mahatma Jotirao Phule*, Justice *M. G. Ranade*, *Tarabai* also ventilates her views on behalf of the whole humanity to which she belonged. Her narrative is thus the narrative of the community and persistently invokes the rhetoric of love and kinship. By resisting colonialism poignantly which was generally interpreted as a story of universal progress, she is resisting the production of normalized individual and the colonialized regimes of disciplinary power. While her thrust is on all women and their degradation, she also admits the complementarity between men and women. Her feminist consciousness gives her the strength to produce a cogent critique of colonialism as well as Brahmanism and patriarchy in India. *Tarabai* also points out the spaces created by the British *Raj* for women through education. Her text is so complex in its weave, dialectical in its expression and culturally rooted in the tradition and social history of Maharashtra that translating such a text must have posed a real challenge.

O'Hanlon's book has two parts, translation of the text and an introductory essay which draws out themes from *Tarabai's* text. As O'Hanlon herself has admitted, the book has an 'awkward combination' of translation of the text (original running into 49 pages) and an introductory essay which is much longer than the original text (72 pages for the introductory essay). The introductory analytical essay precedes the original text which makes it rather difficult to enjoy the original flavor of *Tarabai's* text unmediated and undoctored.

To do justice to *Tarabai Shinde's* writing let me first go through the process of comparing the English translation with the original text itself and then review the introduction. O'Hanlon in her introduction has looked at *Tarabai's* text as women's own testimony in matters of politics, power and their perceived relationships with men in nineteenth century colonial India.

Tarabai's text appeared in 1882, at the end of a long line of texts available in Marathi highlighting both the ideas as well as experiences of women as individuals. Her text has a strong sense of identity and reveals outstanding skills in its organizing techniques. Her text, diction and style of argumentation suggest her close familiarity with the *Satyashodhak* discourse initiated by *Mahatma Phule*.

Tarabai's language is robust, down to earth, powerful, highly allusive and bitingly sharp in character. As we all know, one of the crucial consequences of colonialism perhaps on all Indian languages but certainly in the case of Marathi has been a kind of a patriarchal puritanical cleansing and streamlining of the language. As a result, both the oral and literary level Marathi lost its vibrant, robust and highly expressive character. *Tarabai Shinde's* text is written in the robust language which refuses to be cowed down by the patriarchal gender morality which was emerging along with colonialism. *Tarabai* reveals all the subversive linguistic skills of the Indian women brought up in the oral tradition and development through generations. Her imagery is pictorial and full of daily slang and idioms. Translating such a text needs both an unimpeachable competence over the language of the original text and sensitivity towards the social history and cultural context of that particular region. Rosalind O'Hanlon is the author of *'Caste-Conflict and Ideology: Mahatma Jotirao Phule and Low Caste Protest in Nineteenth Century Western India'* and of a range of essays on the social history of colonial India. This background of her scholarship naturally raises expectations of those who are familiar with O'Hanlon's earlier works. By translating *Tarabai Shinde's* text, O'Hanlon has helped to bring it into the mainstream feminist discourse since of a variety of reasons *Tarabai's* text was marginalized in the social and political history of Maharashtra. Until 1975, this text was practically unknown to Maharashtra in general and to the feminist social scientist in particular. When regional language texts are translated into English, it is of supreme importance that the resistance symbolized in the original texts is conveyed as powerfully and faithfully as possible, occasionally even at the cost of the sanctity of the English language. While reading O'Hanlon's translation from this point of view it falls short at times in bringing our *Tarabai Shinde's* robustness and sharp directness. Some specific examples could be cited here.

Tarabai makes it clear that she was talking not on behalf of a particular caste or lineage but on behalf of all her country women being her sisters. In her preface in the opening paragraph she uses the term *Sahas Durgun* (Preface) to describe the sexual encounters of widows resulting in their pregnancies. *Tarabai* wants to convey transgression. O'Hanlon's use of the phrase 'wicked vices' (Introduction, p. 75) does not truly carry this meaning. The term at best could be translated as rash, wild or reckless actions bordering on vices. Similarly, in the preface, *Tarabai's* phrase *angi vasane* does not refer only to 'women's bodies' (Introduction) as translated by O'Hanlon but also to internalization of the reckless values. The body-mind unity of the original phrases is lost in the translation. The second paragraph of the preface is concluded by *Tarabai* with a sharp remark about Indian men. Translated liberally it means, 'they (i.e. Indian men of all castes) would not mind even if widows walk out forsaking (the shelter of) the home (implicit meaning is even if widows take to prostitution) but will not allow them to have a second husband'. The translation however reads. 'If one husband goes off and dies, too bad - they'll never let you have another one' (Introduction, p. 75). The phrase used by *Tarabai* '*uthun jane*' carries a meaning of leaving the honorable life of home and taking to open prostitution. Such women are called '*uthava!*' in Marathi. The translation falls short in creating this sense.

Tarabai is critical of both men and women for imitating the white sahibs and their way of life. When she describes how modern educated women have reduced their size of *kumkum Tarabai* uses the term '*Kapal pandhare fatfatit*' (preface) which could be translated as 'allowing their foreheads to appear as one dreary expanse of white'. This phrase too has a specific colonial context. *Tarabai* is pointing out that the whole nation was suffering from, to use her word, '*avadasa*' (calamity or evil which leads to pauperization) through colonial rupture and even educated women were actively participating in it. In her opinion, though married women in Maharashtra had changed the size of their kumkum in the name of modernity and fashion, underneath was immiserization and deprivation. Again translating it as 'white and bare' does not serve this purpose (p. 76).

Tarabai calls all the new fads taken in by Indian men as '*bhikar chale*' (preface), which means 'deplorable fads'. This phrase refers to deindustrialization, deskilling and creation of clerks. The term '*bhikar*' literally means beggarly, low, vulgar etc. Calling them 'worthless fads' (introduction p. 76) makes it milder and certainly a very poor substitute for *Tarabai's* sharp expression.

In the main text there are some serous gaps which might create problems in the reconstruction of the social history of Maharashtra through the gender perspective.

1) '*Andhar kothadi*' (Original text p.7) Translation: 'dark corner' (p. 88) meaning 'dark confines'.

2) '*Tumchehati kay dagad ahe*?' (Original text p. 8) Translation: 'What stones are in your hand to throw?' (p.88) meaning 'you have nothing in your hand' or 'Do you have anything in your hands?'

3) Ridiculing Indian men who took to clerical jobs under the British *Raj Tarabai* has argued that in contemporary situation men should call themselves not 'pen pushers' but 'beggars crying for a crumb of bread'. Translation: 'Better still, with the way things are, it should be heroes at stuffing yourselves with food that is the name that really suits you!' (p. 89) Here the term '*bhakari bahadder*' (p. 9) comes as a rhetoric. The swords are gone, the pens have lost their sharpness and now what remains is somehow filling the bellies. Tarabai through the phrase '*bhakari bahadder*' is telling everyone that in her time men had taken to begging bowls and were crying for a crumb of bread.

4) Referring to a proverb from Marathi '*Hagawani bayko, nagavani soyara*' (p. 11) *Tarabai* is telling us about the cruelty inherent in the tradition of an old man marrying a child bride. She has pointed out through an imaginary dialogue that these old men are so cunning that they would prefer an 'infant bride shitting in her pants, in order to fob off the father-in-law'.

Translation: 'Money troubles and you need relatives, but it is diarrhoea a wife's best' (p. 91).

This proverb comes in the text when *Tarabai* is ridiculing men ever-ready for one more marriage. She is showing concretely how marriage as an institution is extremely beneficial to men even if they were old. Her use of the term '*soyara*' has a purpose. '*Soyara*' is not any relative but a relative (in fact bride's father) through marriage.

5) While talking about the changes that came about through the British *Raj, Tarabai Shinde* points out that old texts and mythological stories (*Pothya-Purane*) are replaced by 'sphes' (p. 13). Here S-phes does not only refer to learning of English alphabets as translated by O'Hanlon (p. 95) but it is pointing out at the newly emerging 'yes sir' culture, which not only gave a slavish nod to everything that was English, but also displayed a poor and shallow knowledge of English. Even today such a half-baked imitative Anglophilia is scorned at.

6) In the original text while arguing about the complexity of 'man-woman relationship' *Tarabai* says: 'If a woman saps the fine tree of your meritorious self what is it that makes you drive to undertake the burden of a beast?' (p. 17) This question of *Tarabai* is different from what O'Hanlon has translated as 'why . . . put her to like a bullock in every possible daily chore?' (p.100) *Tarabai's* original text and its effort to subvert the cant and humbug of patriarchy is completely vitiated in the translation.

7) While explaining why women willingly participate in their deception and jump into illegitimate relations, *Tarabai* argues that like men, women also have desire and passion. But they are driven into such action as a 'herd-mentality' following one after the other. O'Hanlon's translation 'Because the sex-urge is so strong isn't it?' (p. 105) is missing the point of Tarabai's feminist comment of 'personal is political'. It is not only the sex-urge but women imitate and follow each other in such actions. *Tarabai* suggests that this was the only escape route available to widows for satisfying their desire. *Tarabai's* original statement: 'Because the pull of a herd is very strong' is trying to point out two things. First, that women not as individuals but as a (marginalized) group, commit such acts of overstepping. Second, she is comparing and contrasting men and women. In her typical manner she accepts women's image as illiterate, imitative shepherds, but raises the question that if men call themselves 'gods' and commit the same mistake how can women not follow them. Her use of the word *'sangati'* has a reference to the Sanskrit proverb *'sangati sanga doshen'* which means 'faults are created by the associations you have around you'.

In short, *Tarabai's* Marathi is sharp and succinct because it is earthy and colloquial. The notions of sex, gender, and eros come through in her writing clearly. Her language is close to the processes of life. This could perhaps have found parallels in English as well.

O'Hanlon's well researched introduction brings out how *Tarabai* has put her finger on a set of extremely important processes in colonial culture and gender relations. The introduction has explored various themes in

Tarabai's book, illuminating and explaining at least some of her concerns by setting out the background and circumstances in which they developed. It also evaluates the text in terms of its relevance for the present understanding of the nineteenth century. The introduction is divided into five parts and it covers all the important issues that emerged in nineteenth century colonial India.

O'Hanlon rightly points out that the efforts of rediscovering the writings and lives of such women are worth not only for what they can tell us about women but for '... their value in generating new questions and insights for a wider social history' (p. 60). While pointing out the difference between Jotirao Phule and Tarabai Shinde, O'Hanlon notes that, 'For Phule, brahmanic religion oppressed lower caste people because it had been devised by Brahmans; for *Tarabai* it oppressed women because it had been devised by men' (p. 20). *Tarabai's* genuine authority which gives her the right to speak on behalf of widows and other women living in colonial India also gives her '. . . the wide range of ways in which she herself describes and represents women, contrasting strongly with the impoverished stereotypes of contemporary masculine discourage . . . ' (pp. 53-54). When Marathi was taking a new form as a print language and as a powerful new means of communication and representation, Tarabai saw '. . . this medium not only monopolized by them but employed in a particularly damaging way against women' (p.46). Since widows like *Vijaya Laxmi* found themselves in an impossible position: urged to impossible ideals of the *pativrata* and condemned from either side when they failed, O'Hanlon notes that Tarabai's answering back through this essay was 'pointed and effective' (p. 62). In her earlier essay O'Hanlon has viewed *Tarabai's* project as protest or resistance rather than simply a denial or rejection of contemporary construction of feminine culture (O'Hanlon 1992: 92).

The introduction is full of references from a wide variety of nineteenth century texts, literary as well as historic documents. While pointing out why widow remarriage was increasingly restricted, O'Hanlon notes that the customary law which gave widows the right of inheritance was substituted by statutory brahmanical book law which disinherited them.

The Widow Remarriage Act of 1856 administered by Brahman lawyers and Victorian judges tended to promote brahmanical values. Her observation that restrictions on remarriage, treating it as disrepute were a 'cost-free means of enhancing family dignity' (pp. 34-36) is pertinent. Restrictions on women in the form of purdah or emergence of rigid caste frameworks and identities were a nineteenth century creation. All these were important means of protecting the family's dignity in a strange environment of expanding new towns. She observes that 'Increasingly from the mid-century, political representation, access to education and other forms of privilege came to depend precisely on the assertion of clear and bounded caste identities' (pp. 11-12). The high caste forms of social practice came about for raising the status of the caste. O'Hanlon points out that the Company's government and the Indian elite sought to preserve 'tradition' but women's participation in politics which was prevalent in pre-colonial Maharashtra was certainly not preserved. In keeping family, home, domestic life outside the overview of the State, there was a broad degree of consensus between Indian politicians and the colonial State (pp. 50-51). O'Hanlon has named this new construction of womanhood as '. . . a kind of victorianized *pativrata*, with the implications always of a peculiarly feminine moral vulnerability underlying it' (p. 60). Later on, in her opinion, the nationalists attempted to identify home as a sacrosanct domain for Hinduism's innermost 'spiritual' values. O'Hanlon observes that after *Tilak's* successful campaign to have National Social Conference barred from using the Congress pavilion, social reform issues for women receded from the forefront.

While analyzing how this new womanhood which was a fusion of old brahmanical values and enlightened mother and companion to men, O'Hanlon explains it further. These values were also convenient to the dominant peasant classes who were previously the old warrior peasant communities. For them the colonial peace meant a search for new means both of expressing social distinction and of limiting and controlling social relations between the strata of society that had remained relatively flexible. O'Hanlon convincingly explains why gender assumed peculiar significance for politics and society for India in the nineteenth century. In her opinion, women and development of more restrictive models for their social behaviour became almost an identity need of these groups. She further points out that colonial hegemony was in fact built on such important areas of argument between colonial officials and key groups of elite Indian men.

The introduction in its concluding remarks points out that *Tarabai's* ideas remained limited and constrained by her own Maratha milieu and class. O'Hanlon complains that while deciding all contemporary notions of *pativrata, Tarabai* did not entirely relinquish the idea itself. In her earlier essay O'Hanlon has stated that Tarabai '. . . saw women's suffering in general as the result of men's deliberate viciousness, rather than as a product of complex structures and power that transcended individual intention' (O'Hanlon 1992: 102). In this essay O'Hanlon has further evaluated the new text: '. . . *Tarabai* refused to conform to the ideal of submissive womanhood . . . her refusal brought her a means of self expression and dignity. . . . But these means to dignity and self expression did not represent some neutral space of freedom from Hindu forms of patriarchy. For a part of their cost was precisely the reproduction in an inverted form of some of patriarchy's own forms of sexual essentialism, belittlement and contempt' (O'Hanlon 1922: 103).

When we recover writings like *Tarabai Shinde* in my opinion it is a political rather than aesthetic activity. Rending such texts in a new way is a challenge before the cotemporary social historians trying to develop a gender sensitive perspective. We must read such texts not for the moments in which they collude or reinforce dominant ideologies of gender, class, nation or empire but for the gestures of defiance or subversion implicit in them. *Tarabai's* greatest contribution in this text is when she argues about the existence of prostitutes. 'Tell me this now, what is a whore? . . . In fact, whores are just some of those women you've seduced and lured away from their homes' (p.111). *Tarabai's* some rather 'conventional' and 'old fashioned' ideas about women and their proper rights and duties could be interpreted more creatively keeping in mind her rebellious critique of institutions of marriage and family. O'Hanlon has refused to celebrate *Tarabai's* sheer defiance and apparent antinomy. But in her effort to locate her reading in the context of the contemporary historiography of the marginal and the dispossessed she could have easily gone deeper into interpreting Tarabai's negotiating strategies with Hindu patriarchy. At one level Tarabai has challenged and subverted the Hindu patriarchy's 'purity-chastity' framework, at another level she brings in the issue of sanctity of man-woman relationship. Instead of labeling *Tarabai's* counter models as 'flawed' and 'contradictory' one can read the text against its grain to see why *Tarabai* keeps on appealing to Indian men to become pure like fire in the colonial context.

Original Source

Original Source
The Book Review/Volume XVIII Number. 10
October, 1994
(pp.: - 14-15)

References

O'Hanlon, Rosalind. 1991. 'Issues of Widowhood: Gender and Resistance in Colonial Western India" in *Contesting Power" Resistance and Everyday Social Relations in South Asia*, edited by Haynes Druglas & Gyan Prakash, New Delhi: OUP, pp. 62-108.

Malshe, S.G. (Editor). 1975 (1882). *Stree-Purush Tulana*, Mumbai: Mumbai Marathi Granthasangrahalay.

Section : II

Literature as
Social History

Chapter - 8

Home and the March of Times
in *Wada Chirebandi*

I

For obvious reasons, the concept of home was looked at initially rather one-sidedly by many feminist scholars, with reference to women's existence and lives within it (Simone de Beauvoir 1949; Betty Friedan 1963, etc.), Home and the relegation of women to it was seen as a trap, as a prison set by patriarchal structures and ideology. But gradually, with the emergence of new historiography, an understanding has evolved of 'home' as a site where women have constantly contested, colluded and at times, even made spaces for themselves. Women's consensual, contractual relationship with this so-called private world is now studied seriously by western and Indian feminist scholars, like Christine Delphy (1984), Kumkum Sangari (1992), Susie Tharu (1991), and many others in the context of changing political economy.

Scholars like Partha Chatterjee (1995), while taking a stand against the 'arrogant', 'intolerant', 'rational' subject of modernity, and while resurrecting the virtues of the fragmentary, the local and the subjugated, have pointed out how the home was the principal site for expressing spiritual culture and how women were to take the responsibility for protecting and nurturing this quality. In Chatterjee's opinion, the home was not a complementary but rather the original site on which the hegemonic project of nationalism was launched. According to Chatterjee, the nationalist critique of the colonialist discourse did not succeed in liberating women from male discursive constructions. He has argued that nationalists situated the 'women's question' in an inner domain of sovereignty far removed from the arena of political contest. He further claims that this inner domain of national culture was constituted in the light of the discovery of tradition and the women's question as a problem of 'Indian tradition'. Chatterjee's argument that the material/spiritual dichotomy, to which the terms 'world' and 'home' corresponded, had acquired a very special significance in the nationalist mind. In the inner spiritual domain of home, the East was undominated, sovereign (Chatterjee 1995: 116-34).

This analysis helps us see how the woman-question was constructed in the colonial period and the 'new woman' of the nationalist discourse emerged in contrast with the images of indigenous patriarchy, westernized-modernized women as well as the lower class women. Of course, we all know that the inner world of the home had its material base eroded by the capitalist economy and the outer world also was not devoid of tradition (ibid.: 119-21).

The passage from a feudal to a capitalist civilization is bound to shake the entire social and cultural ethos of any society. In India, this passage, created and mediated by the colonial processes, was not only complicated and truncated in terms of its political economy but resulted in the simultaneous existence of different modes of production. Conflicting pulls of tradition-modernity, community-self, harmony-competition or public-private, no doubt, impose an unbearable burden of living on individuals as well as on institutions. But in India, where the colonial state was kept out of the inner domain of national culture, and where the Indian nation tried to protect and control its language, literature and the institution of family, the situation became still more complex. A new patriarchy was brought into existence which claimed to be different from the traditional order, but also claimed to be different from its 'western' counterpart. This resulted in the emergence of the institution of the home as one of the basic structures of social existence, as a crucial site where all contradictions were felt, fought and worked out.

The changing conditions of life mould the various dimensions of the life lived in a home. The nodal points of all networks which govern the interpersonal relations within and outside the home undergo change in terms of displacements and redefinitions. Gender and property relations, in particular, bear multiple burdens-of an age of social transformation. As compared with all other hierarchical orders, patriarchal hegemony has demonstrated an unusual tenacity in the face of such a situation all over the world.

This paper seeks to examine whether this is also true of contemporary Maharashtra, keeping in mind the colonial past and the fragmentary nature of Indian nationalism. Since modern Marathi theatre has played a notable role in the making of contemporary Maharashtrian consciousness and still continues to enjoy a special status as a preferred mode of expression on the part of the new middle class, which emerged with the advent of the colonial order, I have chosen to read Mahesh Elkunchwar's crucial text woven around the theme of *Wada Chirebandi*, 'Old Stone Mansion', i.e., the never-collapsing home.

We must understand the title *Wada Chirebandi*, in its Marathi context. *Wada* means an old-style mansion built around a courtyard. *Chira* means a stone which is extremely strong. In a popular Marathi children's song, the maternal uncle always has a *Wada Chirebandi*. This is how this theme is familiar to the Marathi mind, as a very reliable natal support. One's mother's brother and his abode is supposed to be very strong, a place to fall back on. *Wada* also offers us the site of analysing the contestations within and between modes of production and modes of reproduction.

This play, written in the form of a family history, tells us the story of the collapse of the *wada* and contains a series of mirror images of the ongoing concerns and anxieties, as well as hopes and aspirations of the new 'modernizing' middle class in Maharashtra.

II

Elkunchwar, as a self-conscious author, has time and again critically evaluated his own work. He began writing plays in 1967. At first, he succeeded in writing six one-act plays and three full-length plays, depicting rebellious characters who express themselves in provocative language, essentially in the modern framework, as if breaking away totally from tradition. At this juncture, from 1975 onwards, Elkunchwar stopped writing for almost seven years. After this long silence, he wrote the play *Wada Chirebandi* in 1982, now breaking away from his own earlier plays.

Elkunchwar, reviewing his journey as a playwright, has said: 'In a sense, this play is of my flesh and blood' (Appendix of *Wada Chirebandi* 1987: 88). He claims rightly that '*Wada* is not a simple family drama, it is more than that, a document of social change, political change. . . .' (Sanyal 1989: ix). *Wada Chirebandi* was followed by *Magna Talyakathi* (By the Pond, Pensive) and Yuganta (End of an Epoch). *Wada Chirebandi* opens with a sensitive and almost nostalgic portrayal of the collapse of the old traditional order. It then proceeds to identify, in a suitable and low-key manner, the unsatisfactory and inauthentic modes of thought, feeling and action which have come into existence with the onward march of time. Refusing to abide by fancies and revival or restoration, the trilogy offers in the end a non-doctrinaire, non-declamatory and yet positive depiction of a transcendental future overcoming the obsolescent order of the past and the modernizing vacuity of the present.

This paper will investigate how far the first play of this trilogy shows awareness of the entire gamut of patriarchal relations which bind women in the social formations of the past, as well as the present, and whether an image of gender relations and a vision of future mark an emancipatory point of departure or a gender-blind confirmation of the age-old patriarchal narrative in an apparently new guise.

The theme of *Wada Chirebandi* runs briefly like this. *Tatyaji*, the head of the *Deshpande* family in the Dharangaon village of Vidarbha region, dies. The death of the head of the family, the dilapidation of the old family mansion, the changing world outside and the suffocation inside are the powerful core of this play.

Tatyaji's family consists of his mother (*Dadi*), his wife (*Aai*), his three sons (*Bhaskar, Sudhir, Chandu*), two daughters-in-law, *Vahini* and *Anjali*, and one daughter (*Prabha*). There are two worlds in this play— the world of people living inside the wada and the world of those outside.

The rituals on the thirteenth day of *Tatyaji's* death are to be observed as soon as *Sudhir* and *Anjali*, the outsiders from Mumbai, arrive. The *Deshpandes* do not have cash for performing the rituals. So the piece of land belonging to the mother is sold off, of course, with her consent, *Ranju, Bhaskar's* daughter, who is lured by the tinsel of Mumbai and filmy 'English', elopes with her English teacher, taking with her the jewel-box containing the *streedhan* (woman's property). She is caught after a brief hunt in Mumbai, but the jewels are not with her. In both these happenings, the honour of the family looms large, towering over everything else. *Prabha*, who is dreaming of higher education and does not want to be married off, has been banking on her share of the family jewels for this. She has to digest this loss. In short, those living inside the *wada* can escape neither the *wada*, nor its suffocation. At the same time, those who have left the wada find no place for themselves. So, *Parag* (Bhaskar's son), who is forever trapped in Dharangaon; *Chandu* (the third brother) whose leg cut on the rusty tractor turns septic; and Dadi stand as living emblems of those caught in the entrapping remains of the *wada*; a living counterpart of the defunct tractor outside. The rusted tractor, the bulldozer carrying up the soil from the land which has been sold to the saw-mill, and the decrepit *wada*, along with the torn palanquin, are silent but significant characters in this play.

This play has raised different types of questions by depicting how the household functions as an important site for the reproduction of class status in contemporary India, and how it functions as the site of production and reproduction and of the primary socialization of children through the structure of the marriage alliance, the nature of marriage payments, the division of labour, the structure of authority, the patterns of consumption, cultural ideas about entitlement and practical problems of distribution of family resources, instead of merely dichotomizing tradition and modernity.

As Kumkum Sangari has pointed out, patriarchies are resilient not only because they are embedded in social stratification, but also because they rest on women's consent, which they constantly and consistently reformulate. Her work tells us that women's consent rests on material arrangements which guarantee women rights, compensations or protection (albeit with the usual asymmetry between rights and obligations). It also rests on ideological ensembles and on forms of coercion, which push women towards normative behaviour. We agree with her that 'families need to be seen not merely as an undifferentiated site of women's socialization and oppression, but also as a site of struggle and of the daily recreation, of inequality in which women participate' (Sangari 1992: 18-19). Let us see whether the text of this play provides us space to investigate the private sphere of the home as a distinct site for the construction and formation of the gendered subject.

III

The *Wada* tells us a story of three generations of a family called *Deshpande*, who belong to the *Deshastha Brahman* caste. *Deshastha Brahmans* have occupied a core place in Maharashtrian politics, society and culture from almost the beginning of Maharashtra's recorded history. Occupying high offices in the state and even other offices at various levels of administration, they were recipients of state honours and, more importantly, land grants of various types. Spread all over Maharashtra as a result of this process, *Deshastha Brahmans* held, in particular, the office of *kulkarni* (village accountant and keeper of land records) at the local level in the village. This gave them not only an unusually high status in the affairs of the community, but also access to the resources of the land and a guaranteed and continuous means of gathering agricultural surplus. *Deshasthas'* socio-economic and cultural background led to the development of the typical culture of landed gentry, common to this class all over the world. It led to a certain *haute couture* of pride, swagger, generosity and *noblesse oblige*. A combined pressure released by the onset of colonization, modernization, and in post-independence years, land reforms and industrialization, gradually but inevitably led to the erosion of their ownership and other rights in landed properties and thus, the basis of their traditional lifestyle. In the process, there came to be an increasing gulf between their pretensions to high culture, based on parasitism, and the actual realities of modern competitive life.

In the text of *Wada*, the invasion of the industrial world comes through the technology of the tractor. The *Deshpande* family from Dharangaon has never worked manually in the fields and has never even touched the old farming instrument, the plough. When the play begins, the tractor lying in the courtyard has sunk into the ground. Its plates have rotted and are falling apart. Obviously, this new technology has come in this household as an object of fascination and not as a necessity. Unused for twenty years, it has become a status symbol—a dead weight.

Vahini, the eldest daughter-in-law, expresses it in these words: 'Didn't rich people have elephants parading in their courtyards in the earlier days, *Bhavji*? Now, in these modern times, the *Deshpandes* have a tractor on show in front of their house. Whether they need it or not, what matters is that you show your wealth. In the front yard, you have the tractor and at the back, you have a palanquin' (Sanyal 1989: II). The eldest brother, *Bhaskar*, tells the story of the tractor, which was purchased twenty years back, in these words: 'Our lands are fanned by tenants. They thought, now that the landlord has bought a tractor he is going to till the soil himself. So all were against it. And once that happened, nothing could be done' (ibid.). The *Deshpande* family's refusal and inability to make use of the tractor and their total dependence on the tenants show that while the old material order is practically dead, traditional values still persist.

Old privileges come to an end, but the family continues to live as in the past on an unearned income, although with the vital difference that the sources of revenue are getting scarcer and scarcer. One by one now, all the household articles are treated as commodities and sold. The carpets, rugs, mirrors, copper pots and huge utensils to serve food, are all gone, sold—but not in an open bourgeois manner; rather through stealth.

The same is the case with the rituals. The norms of collectivity continue. Feeding the whole village on the thirteenth and fourteenth day of *Tatyaji's* passing away becomes a compulsion for the family. Even the mother's rightful share of property is sold for the occasion.

Women in the family previously had helping hands to assist them in carrying out the daily work. Now, they have to carry the burden of daily household chores: *Vahini*—'Haven't they all gone, one by one? Once, there were four servants for each person here. They have a point. Do we pay them as much as they get outside?' (ibid.: 12). Women of this household have lost the privilege of having domestic servants and are forced to carry the burden of domestic work. They have lost touch with women from different caste/class backgrounds, not because of their consciousness of themselves as 'New Women', but because of the collapse of the old economic order.

This process of transition leads to an isolation of the *wada*. Previously, the village and the *wada* were organically linked with each other. Now, the village is distanced from the *wada*. The old connectedness and reciprocity is over.

This isolation, poverty and brokenness provide *Wada* with its background of feudal or pre-modern patriarchy in transition.

IV

It would be revealing to see how the gendered subject is constructed under what remains essentially a pre-modern patriarchal social order. In other words, we will examine the texture of the patriarchal hegemony operative within this framework. Kumkum Sangari's statement provides a good starting point. 'Unless certain distributions of power are made within patriarchal arrangements, it is difficult to imagine how any degree of consent from women can be obtained' (Sangari 1992:10). We see two sets of values interacting in the realm of socialization—feudal and patriarchal. Both are in the transitional phase.

As is well known, collectivity was obviously a supreme norm of the feudal framework. The individual and individuality were yet to gain social recognition. All the major decisions in this play are taken by collectivities. But, in family situations, women seem to be able to form only an uneasy collectivity, if any. Their subordination comes through their dependence rather than their submission. Women in this play belonging to one household are torn in multiple ways from each other, in terms of their age, material interests and their roles in the household. *Dadi*, who has lost all sense of time, keeps calling her dead son and her god by the same name '*Vyankatesh*'. Though *Aai* and the unmarried daughter have some closeness and communication, their survival itself places them against each other. Two daughters-in-law are torn apart from each other due to their different locations, one residing in the *wada*, the other outside it. The youngest female member of the family, *Ranju*, has no possibility of sharing her dreams nurtured by the world of cinema with any woman residing in the *wada*.

For festivals and funerals, the family is bound to come together. *Bhaskar* expresses his anger this way: 'Shouldn't he have brought the boy? Your dear brother-in-law did not feel a thing, comes after five days have gone by. Like an indifferent visitor' (Sanyal 1989: 6).

Bhaskar goes even further, challenging the authenticity of the problems of modern life, of travel arrangements: 'I am angry. Your father-in-law is dead and you are worried about reservations? What can one say?' (Sanyal 1989: 6).

The family network is tightly knit through a clear-cut hierarchy between the brothers and between male and female members. One can see how the eldest brother in the *Deshpande* family has both control over material resources and answerability to the outside world on behalf of the whole household. *Chandu*, the youngest brother, suffers in every respect and lives the life of a beast of burden.

All women here are subordinate to all the male members of the family. *Prabha*, the daughter of the house, vents her feelings: 'When a father dies, the daughter has no future. Now I shall have to survive on whatever little you throw at me in charity' (ibid.: 8).

When the mother gives away her share, the daughter is utterly depressed. Their dialogue then is telling —

> Prabha: Sleep, Aai.
> Aai: Look at me.
> Prabha: Aai, what is to become of us?
> Aai: He up there will look after us, my dear. (ibid.: 42)

At this point, the daughter clearly sees through the selfishness of her mother. By consenting to sell her share from the *wada*, the widow-mother regains her power. By choosing to be a sacrificing mother, she incites the male-dominance in the household at the cost of the daughter's interests. Notions of false status and a tendency to extravagance dominate such frameworks. *Bhaskar* himself admits: 'We cultivated our lands. But how? By sitting here on the swing. Idly swinging away, issuing orders. And we lost our estates just by whiling away time chewing *paan* . . .' (ibid.: 22).

On the thirteenth and fourteenth days of the death of the father, the whole village; four or five thousand people, is to be fed. *Bhaskar* says: '*Arrey baba*, that's the tradition here. On the thirteenth day of the death, the whole village is to be fed. Or else we won't be able to show our faces' (ibid.: 32).

In this framework, the patriarchal values which subordinate women are manifested in a direct and undisguised way. As Bina Agarwal states in her recent book about the land rights of women:

> The term 'gender relations' refers to the relations of power between women and men which are revealed in a range of practices, ideas and representations, including the division of labour, roles and resources between women and men and ascribing to them the different abilities, attitudes, desires, personality traits, behavioural patterns and so on. Gender relations are both constituted by and

help constitute these practices and ideologies in interaction with other structures of social hierarchy, such as class, caste . . . (Agarwal 1994: 51).

Most of the women in this play are *Deshpande* not by birth, but by marriage. Their incessant efforts and struggle to keep the family honour intact at any cost can be seen as their negotiations with patriarchy, caste and class. The daughters of this household have no legitimate place in it and are very easily abused, either physically or by being robbed of their material base. The power relation between men and women in this play is as evident as that between women.

The patriarchal value system differentiates between married women on the one hand, and widows and unmarried women on the other. *Prabha*, the unmarried daughter of the family, observes:

> ... It is not even five days since *Tatyaji* is gone. Five days. In these five days, *Vahini* has changed. There was no delay in the house keys reaching her waistband and no delay before *Aai* was shoved into the darkness of the backroom . . . (Sanyal 1989: 9).

Dedication to the husband and to his family and giving birth to a son confer status within this framework. *Aai* bursts out in tears after *Tatyaji's* death, saying, 'Our Shelter is gone forever.' Widowed Aai becomes a helpless woman and *Vahini*, as the eldest daughter-in-law, gains some power in this process. Women here have apparently willingly accepted the division of leisure for men, and drudgery and a service-giving role for women. They take pride in their husbands laziness and dependence on them. *Anjali*, the second daughter-in-law, remarks in an indulgent tone, while serving her husband: '*Deshpande* . . . ! Catch him doing one thing for himself' (ibid.: 16).

These women proudly declare that their men will not look at another woman or that their men may sell land, but will never touch their jewellery because it is *streedhan*.

One must note that there is some recognition of female property rights in the concept of *streedhan* (literally meaning a woman's property), although there were varied and changing interpretations of what *streedhan* could include, how much control a woman could be allowed over it, and how it would devolve on the woman's death. Broadly, it appears that in the very early *shastric texts*, *streedhan* could consist only of movables (such as ornaments, clothes and household utensils), given to a woman by parents, brothers or relatives before or at the time of her marriage, and by her husband after marriage. Over this property, she was allowed absolute control, and it devolved on her female heirs in the first instance. Here, we must note that the elder daughter-in-law in the household perceives of her *streedhan* as a source of connection between women from earlier generations. *Prabha*, the unmarried daughter, looks at it as a possibility to escape the trap of patriarchy in the form of marriage and overall dependence. Bhaskar, the eldest son, wants to have control over the jewel-box. But his wife defeats his selfishness with her inner realization that the *streedhan* has to devolve on the female heirs. The selfish husband is shocked to see his wife's commitment towards the family network and because of her selflessness, he retreats from his greed.

The women in *Wada* also live through their children, particularly their sons. *Aai* tells *Prabha* that as soon she was widowed, her innings were over. Now the reins were in the hands of her eldest son and daughter-in-law. 'After all, it is they who are going to be in charge. I will have to spend my days with them' (Sanyal 1989: 43).

This powerlessness of women is seen very clearly when *Prabha*, the daughter of the family, has refused to marry and wishes to take further education. The dialogue between mother and daughter tells us that the mother has internalized her subordinate position as a strategy of survival. She says:

> *Prabha*, sorrow is not something one puts on display. It belongs to oneself. When it is unbearable—there are many dark rooms in this mansion where one can go and shed tears, quietly—all *Deshpande* women have done that (ibid.: 43).

Prabha, the daughter of the household, is victimized in this process. How do we understand her act of locking herself further in the *wada*? Her refusal to participate in the reunion of the family comes through more as resistance than defeat. Her mother explains the event of loss of jewellery in a philosopher's mode. The *Deshpandes* had earned it not through their labour but through appropriating others' labour. Though the jewellery was *streedhan*, it would have created more conflicts in the family. *Prabha* refuses to buy this argument and remains shut in her room.

Since the mother was totally dependent on her eldest son and daughter-in-law, she gives away her belongings, including her legitimate share of property. *Prabha* refuses to exist as a dependant.

In terms of the right to property, women have, at the most, a right over their jewellery, but their share in immovable property like land is tenuous. Widowed *Aai* mortgages away her share of land. Her philosophy is that if you do not get something you want, it is best to reject it. *Prabha's* mother and brothers feel sorry for her trapped situation, but they feel that it is natural to give priority to a brother's education. *Bhaskar* tells her: 'All decisions about you were taken by *Tatyaji*, why blame us? The fact is *Sudhir*, too, was studying then and it would not have been possible to pay for two people' (Sanyal 1989: 30).

In short, the decision-making power is in the hands of men in this framework. When *Aai* decides to sell off her portion of the estate, she does have that power in her hands for the time being. But while negotiating with the patriarchal structure of the household, she gives consent to selling her own immovable property—a piece of land. In this contestation, *Aai*, as a disadvantaged person, has perceived the conflict between her self-interest and the socially defined order. She uses her share of the property to create a better deal for the family, in terms of her honour. At the end, the eldest daughter-in-law compliments Aai for her immeasurable strength and capacity to bear pain. Thus, *Aai* by giving up her material property, earns honour and dignity by becoming a saviour of the family.

V

The above sections now help us understand the intricate and yet differing constellations of relations and values which go into the making of the life of the principal set of women in this play.

Dadi: Dadi, the senior most member of the family, has seemingly entered the world marked by timelessness. She is not even aware of the death of her own son. In the end, we find her approaching the arena marked by the tractor. She is pulled back from oblivion with the sad realization that this was the end. The *Deshpande wada*, with all its glory and eternal prosperity, was headed for irrecoverable demise. The rusted tractor, mired into the earth reflected this slate.

The tractor and *Dadi*, who had never had anything to do with each other, suddenly become partners and symbols of this decay.

Aai: Aai's widowhood changes her position in the family. Her relationship with her children and grandchildren is complex. Her wisdom gives her the capacity to survive with honour through her marginalization. Particularly, when she promises Prabha to fight for *Prabha's* share in the family jewellery, she becomes a 'new woman.' At the same time, she tells *Prabha* that *streedhan* or ornaments were not just money, they were the links between women from different generations. At the end, when *Ranju* has gone off with the jewellery, *Aai* declares: 'Let the gold go. It's a nuisance anyway. As long as the girl is found. Let not the *Deshpande* honour be further torn to shreds' (Sanyal 1989: 51). Her understanding of the total reality and her calm acceptance of the so-called calamities demonstrate the ripeness of her worldview.

Vahini: Vahini is the eldest daughter-in-law of the household. She is a typical, ordinary woman, who grabs power when it comes to her. Her imitative use of English phrases, her vicarious ways of using her power, her blind love towards her children, all this leads her inevitably to a circle of maintenance and nurturing. In her old age, *Vahini* is still bound by home and hearth, that too, her daughter's.

Ranju: The world of fantasizing, which appears to us in the too familiar form of a Hindi cinema, constitutes *Ranju's* inner and outer life. Her dress, her language, her so called 'love', elopement, her casual attitude towards marriage, children and housekeeping and her endless indulgence in the movie world exhibit her total submergence in the world of fantasy, devoid of even a minimum understanding of domestic and external realities.

Prabha: Prabha is the intelligent daughter of the household. She is ready to fight for her rights and has dreams of and aspirations toward freedom. She has realized that the old order has lost its vitality and thus wants to participate in the life offered by the new order. But in the given situation, such opportunities are denied to her and she is driven to a reality where even the will to live becomes a burden.

Anjali: Anjali is the second daughter-in-law of the household. She comes from Mumbai and initially has a practical outlook towards the *wada* and kinship. Slowly, she changes and becomes a part and parcel of the inner life of the *wada*. She has her own problems. Her repulsion towards the sexual demands of her husband is shared with *Vahini*. Nuclearization of the family in an urban setting has resulted in women's loss of control over their own bodies. She extends her love towards the other children of the family. *Anjali* thus creates, on her own, an authentic space for herself in the family.

VI

The play depicts the life of three generations within the boundaries set up by *Dharangaonkar Deshpande's wada*. In a setting of transition, where different modes of hierarchy are being reformulated, the multiple identities of men and women also go through a fluid and complex process of formulation and reformulation. The text puts forth the dichotomies of conflicting emotions; hope and despair, sullenness and understanding, and the will to live and to die. A primary reading of the text tends to get caught up in the stereotypical dichotomies with reference to the women characters. One who refuses to be a part' of the new order loses her sense of time and space (*Dadi*); one who tries to take advantage of both the worlds ends in the cyclical maintenance, nurturance role (*Vahini*); one who gains power through the old and new order has to give up her material base (*Aai*); one who tries to break away ends up in madness and suicide (*Prabha*); one who is pulled into the glamour of the new order turns to an animal-like existence (*Ranju*). We can go on adding to this list, but the point I want to make here is that the deeper reading of the text takes us beyond this, and tells us that in such transitional situations, women are neither passive victims, nor heroic agents. They do not have the space or the possibility, or the will, to break away from the boundaries or to make new spaces. But as the text reveals quietly, what we see is a transgression of boundaries.

Such prominent plays written in the period of post-independence India around the theme of home will definitely give us a better understanding of the way the category called 'home' is being constructed in present-day Maharashtra. This will help us in understanding the complex nature of man-woman relationships in transitional societies like that of India.

Original Source

Home, Family & Kinship in Maharashtra
Glushkova, Irina & Vora, Rajendra (Eds.)
Oxford University Press,
1999
(pp: - 113-1)

References

Agarwal, Bina. 1994. *Field of One's Own Gender and Land Rights in South Asia*, London: Cambridge University Press.

Beauvoir, Simone. 1949. *The Second Sex*, Harmondsworth: Penguin Books, 1981, reprint.

Chatterjee, Partha. 1995. *The Nation and Its Fragments: Colonial and Post-Colonial Histories*, New Delhi: Oxford University Press.

Delphy, Christine. 1984. *Close to Home—A Materialist Analysis of Women's Oppression* (translated and edited by Diana Leonard), USA: University of Mass-achusetts Press.

Elkunchwar, Mahesh. 1994. *Wada Chirebandi*, Mumbai: Mauj Prakashan.

———. 'Magna Talyakathi' and 'Yuganta' (unpublished).

Friedan, Betty. 1979, reprint (1963). *The Feminine Mystique*, Harmondsworth: Penguin Books.

Sangari, Kumkum. 1992. *Consent, Agency and Rhetorics of Consent: Occasional Papers on History and Society, Second Series*, New Delhi: Nehru Memorial Museum and Library.

Sanyal, Kamal. *Old Stone Mansion* (transl.). 1989. Calcutta: Seagull Books.

Tharu, S., and K. Lalita. 1991. *Women Writing in India: 600 BC to the Early 20th Century*, vol. I, New Delhi: Oxford University Press.

Chapter - 9

Mumbai in
Dalit Literature

The word *dalit* means 'ground down', 'depressed', 'oppressed', 'broken'. It is intended to avoid the negative connotation of 'untouchable' and also of the Gandhian expression '*Harijan*' (children of God). *Dilip Chitre*, writing on dalit literature, pointed out that the term was first used in the 1960s for the writing that has come chiefly from ex-untouchables, many of whom in Maharashtra are now Buddhists, or other oppressed groups (Chitre 1982: 95). *Gangadhar Pantawane*, a professor of Marathi and editor of '*Asmitadarsh*', a major platform for dalit writers founded in 1967, expands on the implications of the term. He writes:

> . . . there is a specificity to the Dalit consciousness. Dalit writers are part of Indian counter-culture and its core is made of protest against exploitation and oppression. Dalit consciousness denies all institutions of exploitation and is innately connected with the universal consciousness up against exploitation. Dalit writers do not believe in fate, holy books, rebirth and discord and enmity in human beings. They stand for change and ultimately revolution.

Dalit literature marks an authentic breakthrough in an otherwise dreary literary scene in Maharashtra. Its immense merit lies in representing a rebellion in life as well as in letters against the white-collared Hindus who had up till then monopolized cultural expression. Dalit literature signifies the emergence of a new group of writers who, through a language of their own, describe a new set of experiences. They have forced their way into an area of life previously dominated by high castes. Dalits came to Mumbai as members of the traditionally oppressed sections of the society. In addition, they were made to bear the burden of the colonial order. Uprooted from the villages, the dalit consciousness which took shape within the framework of the upstart city of Mumbai was bound to be critical in nature. A comprehensive chronological review of Dalit expression in the city over the years would be a formidable task, beyond the scope of this article. I shall endeavour to note some markers the journey accomplished by dalit literature in the Marathi language. In the case of Mumbai, as with other Indian cities, the line between city and countryside is not sharply demarcated. The continuous interplay of rural and urban elements informs dalit writings. In this connection, two outstanding dalit literary figures, *Narayan Surve* and *Daya Pawar*, address the crucial questions: what is at the core of the irresistible temptation that draws people to Mumbai and what is it that brings about their intense love and hate relationship with the city? In an interview given to *Shri G. M. Kulkarni*, an eminent professor and a critic of Marathi literature, *Narayan Surve* says

> I find it artificial to differentiate between urban and rural dalits. In fact, the difference, if any, is in their language and the environment. To tell the truth, the debate of the city versus the village seems phony to me. This is because the half-way industrialization of our country has not achieved a genuine urbanization at all. A worker living in the city longs to return to his village. His roots are in the village. He is in the city merely for a living . . . Mumbai gives him his daily bread, but for relationships he looks to his village. Our country has neither absorbed capitalism in full, nor has it completely shed feudalism. I therefore consider the village-city debate redundant (Kulkarni 1986-89).

Daya Pawar in his now famous autobiographical novel, *'Balute'* (a customary harvest share due to village artisans and menials who serve the cultivating peasants), pointedly brings out the complexities and contradictions that the dalit youth faces in Mumbai:

. . . this kind of a mad attraction for Mumbai was deeply entrenched in my blood. After all these years, I now wonder what has this city really given me. They say that *Krishna* tore *Jarasandh*a in two pieces and threw them in opposite directions. In the same way in this city we are torn in two opposite directions. As I seek a place to merely rest my heart at the end of the hard day, all I have come back to is a wretched hell that this city can offer . . . The life I see from a distance, the life of indulgence that I can see from afar is different. She appears as a temptress (*Mahanagari*), an illusion . . . like a ruby in a ring. It dazzles me, beckons me. But I can never escape the realization that this dazzling ruby has always eluded me (*Pawar* 1982: 132).

To these writers, Mumbai represents a post-feudal world that struggles to escape from the feudalism still gripping the rest of the country. Yet, as an almost pure product of market economy, it treats money as the measure of all things. For the Dalit in the city, the new situation takes a tragic form. His flight from the culture of feudalism and face-to-face repression in the village offers him both the reality as well as the illusion of becoming a member of a free universe. But he soon realizes that once again he remains an unnoticed, expendable stone at the base of the edifice of modernity, the ugly city dominated by the rich and the powerful.

The interaction between this brand new city and the oppressed sections finds its first expression in the ballad by *Shahir Parsharam* (circa 1754-1844). True, *Parashram* was not a dalit in our present sense of the term, but a *shimpi* (tailor). Yet in the social order of his times, his status as a *shudra* in the brahmanical regime of the *Peshwas* was not much better than that of the dalits. More important, his audience which consisted of the toiling sections of the society gave his work the character of a popular voice, defiant of the dominant culture. His poetry is both an expression of the pre-industrial ethos of nostalgia for the bygone world, and at the same time of a hesitant fascination with the novel and exotic. His short fifteen-line ballad, amazingly, contains almost all the themes which reappear in the works of later poets. It depicts both the outward appearances of Mumbai and the inner contradictions of the city's life.

Balled of Mumbai

Look, on the island came up a settlement
surrounded by the water of the sea.
Like another Lanka of Ravan,
No one loves anyone here.
In this demonic state mountains of sins are a reality.
The sinners of the four *yugas* descend and live here.
Herein are some converted to Parsis and Christians,
Millions of creatures and animals are slaughtered and devoured.
In addition men and women gulp down daily their ration of toddy, and
other spirits.
The prince and the pauper end up in the graveyard.
The high and low are beaten into the same shape.
Mumbai is a good bet if you are a drifter ready to bear the burden.
To make it in this city one must bear the hectic frenzy of life.
The skilled turn mud into gold.
In the world of palatial, ornate mansions, tall and big,
With their coloured glass chandeliers and mirrors,
Uniqueness of human being is here turned into animal existence.

- Translated by Vidyut and Sharmila

He succeeds in capturing the maritime character of the city with its long
sea-frontage and at the same time, its ephemeral character as a group of
wayward floating islands. In a reference to the demon enemy of the
hero of the *Ramayana*, he calls Mumbai '*Ravan's* Lanka'. The vast
numbers of sinners are emphasized by the invocation of Hindu tradition
which divides all time into four *yugas.* The cosmopolitan character of
Mumbai is signified by the mention of Parsis and Christians. Meat eating
and alcohol symbolized the vices, the pollution and corruption oozing from
the mansions of the neo-rich. The poet is dazzled by the city; disturbed
by the absence of a clear-cut feudal hierarchy and the egalitarianism

produced by the market, the ruthless leveler of all pretensions. Mumbai beats the individual into a mould. The luxurious mansions of Mumbai (*rangamahals*) serve merely as backdrop. Everyone, high and low, is caught in a whirl of hectic frenzy (*belpatee*) or sucked into a culture of drift and wandering (*paypeeti*)

Let us now skip about a hundred years and take a look at another text, *Patthe Bapurao's 'Mumbaichi Lavani'* (The *Lavani* of Mumbai). *Lavani* means, literally, that which is immensely beautiful. As an art form, *lavani* is an essential part of the *tamasha* (folk theatre) of Maharashtra and dates back to the era of the *Peshwas*. In the modern form of *tamasha*, this part is presented after *gan* (the invocation of Lord Ganesha) and *gavalan* (description of the erotic relationship between Lord *Krishna* and 16,000 maidens - the gopis). *Lavani* celebrates the beauty of women; it often takes the form of questions and answers. It serves as the polar opposite to the *powada* (ballad) which focuses on the valour of men.

Even though he himself was a brahmin, *Patthe Bapurao's* audience (dalit and non-dalit), his identification with popular culture and his standing among the rural Marathi-speaking masses makes it appropriate to take account of his lavani. It will help us to understand the popular conception of Mumbai's material and cultural personality and the moods of the city in the first two decades of this century.

Mumbaichi Lavani is a fairly long work (52 stanzas), full of details of Mumbai's physical environs. Like *Parsharam*, *Patthe Bapurao* refers to Mumbai as another Lanka of *Ravan*. It appears to him as a flirtatious, voluptuously youthful dilettante (*gulhoushi*). Yet this coquette becomes a Kashi (a site of pilgrimage) to all the high and mighty who come to court her. Every coin minted here tightens the noose around someone's neck. All the *mawalis* (ruffians) of the world pass through its waterfronts. Some hit the jackpot while others end up with a begging bowl.

Mumbai's high society women-poised, proud, self-conscious, confident and overbearing - appear in Patthe Bapurao's lavani. Wealthy high-class

Gujarati wives as well as enterprising and self-reliant fisher-women constitute one set of the city's women. The others, the pleasure-women, Bapurao, anticipating many dalit writers in later years, catalogues in terms of their diverse geographical and caste origins: Punjabi, Mindi, Sultani, Muslim, Jewish, Chinese, Sindhi, Gujarati, Bengali, Telangini, Wani, Parbhini, Japanese, English and Germani, Malni, Salni, Teli, Tambolini. Bapurao adds that the red light areas - Golpitha, Foras Road and Duncan Road, are to be found side by side with the mansions in the Malabar hills and Colabas of Mumbai. To *Bapurao*, Mumbai can be expressed in a series of pairs: the Taj Mahal hotel and the chawls; the share market and the streetwalkers; the electric railcars and streetcars as opposed to the horse carts and the helpless pedestrians. He sees a veneer of affluence masking the world of poverty.

When we move on to the post-Second-World-War scene, we come upon a fresh, creative and radical expression of dalit consciousness as formed by the city, together with a bold bid by the dalit writers to impress upon Mumbai the stamp of their poverty-stricken yet robust rhythm of life.

In *Anna Bhau Sathe* we hear a voice which is as urgent and full of anguish and protest as the voice of the American Black poets from Harlem. A product of Mumbai city, an accomplished creative writer who has handled various genres in Marathi literature, a Marxist in terms of his commitment and practice throughout most of his life, *Anna Bhau* had become a household word in the dalit and working class slums of the big city as well as in the hamlets of dalits and toilers all over the Marathi-speaking region. A lowly *matanga* by caste, he was able to make his presence felt in the company of both the giant *mahar/nava Bauddha* (neo Buddhist) writers and the upper-caste Marxist intellectuals surrounding him. His song *'Mazi Maina'* (My Myna) even now strikes a chord of identity and concern which haunts the dalit consciousness. Saddened by the pain of separation from his beloved by the compulsions of hunger and want, the protagonist relates how he was compelled to migrate to Mumbai. He feels guilty of betrayal when he offers empty promises to his *Maina* that he will make it rich in Mumbai. Heavyhearted with the premonition that Mumbai was par excellence 'a land of dead machines, deadening techniques, and of the walking dead' he soon realizes that it was also 'a factory endlessly producing thieves, parasites cheats, knaves and capitalists'.

Yet exposure to this new world, enriched by its very rootlessness, makes alive and sharpens his creative consciousness. He notes that his horizons expand, crossing the boundaries of Mumbai, reaching every nook and corner of Maharashtra and finally culminating in an outright revolutionary stance towards the whole world. He declares that he would turn to Mumbai now not to secure a paltry job but to liquidate the mighty house of pride, prejudice, discrimination, repression, coercion and theft. *Anna Bhau* once again invokes the metaphor of Mumbai being *'Ravana's Lanka'*, now presided over by *Morarji Desai* and *S. K. Patil*. His attachment and devotion to Maina now takes a new form. Instead of promising gold and ornaments, he offers to her the fruits of victory gained over the exploiters by the combination of a white-hot anger at the plight of the exploited and the solidarity achieved through sharing the woes produced by the city.

Anna Bhau continuous to handle this theme through two additional *lavanis*: 'A Tale of Mumbai' and *'Lavani* about Mumbai'. The tale notes the overcrowding, the piling up of people. It contrasts the masses of the unemployed, beggars, paupers, wanderers, the maimed and the diseased with the ranks of the wealthy, the sophisticates and the gentry. In common with his predecessors and successors, *Anna Bhau* depicts the juxtaposed universes of Malabar Hill and Parel; Vincent Road and the *'Sandas'* (toilet) Road (punning on the name Sandhurst Road); the funeral grounds of Chandanwadi and Sonapur for the rich and the gutters and garbage heaps of the city which serve as the final resting places for the nameless dead among the destitute; the Share Bazar as against Golpitha and Foras Road. Yet 'Mumbai's *Lavani'* ends on a note of optimism, not the petty bourgeois sentimental optimism of the white collared world but a faith born out of the revolutionary dalit and working-class consciousness in the coming birth of a new world to arise over the ruins of the demolished megalopolis.

Narayan Surve, the tallest of the Dalit creative writers in Maharashtra and perhaps in the whole country follows *Anna Bhau*. In his poems we note a perfect balance of protest, anger and denunciation accompanied by poise, determination and clarity.

The new relationship of dalits to the city is expressed in *Surve's* poem 'Mumbai' (Mumbai). The dalits and the workers alone, he declares, are truly entitled to call themselves the architects of the metropolis. The dalits and the toilers go on enhancing the beauty of the city day after day all through their lives, yet he and his people find themselves on the rotting heaps of garbage produced by the other half of the same city. In guileless query, his kids ask why the true makers of the city are surrounded with high cruel walls like those of a jail or a concentration camp, while the parasitic few are allowed to exhibit their power and arrogance through their sky-high mansions and gaudy festivals. The poet in utter sadness points out the only two roads which are open to roaming, jobless and starving masses - the road to the soulless factories and assembly lines and the road to the funeral grounds. Nonetheless the poet insists the poor in their utter desolation manage to maintain hope in the future by joining hands with others in a similar situation (Surve, 1985).

Along with other evils, the common folk of Mumbai have suffered from Hindu-Muslim riots. *Surve's* wonderful poem titled to:'*Usman Ali*' is a timely reminder of this hidden character of the city. [This poem is reproduced in translation in the following chapter]. *Usman Ali*, a Deccani from Hyderabad and a former sailor, is a vibrant affectionate person, full of the fire of life, exemplifying the values of sharing, compassion, solidarity and care for children. His message is that - if we share a common place for work, why not share a common residence and a common meal? *Usman Ali's* regularly demonstrated faith in his own religion goes hand in hand with a capacity for friendship with one and all. But a day comes when the poet finds *Usman Ali* drained of life, a stick of a man and pale of face. *Usman Ali* reports that he has just returned from Hyderabad where he had to bury no less than eleven members of his family - victims of communal frenzy. How can the poet find words to offer solace to this noble person? The poet sadly recalls *Usman Ali's* earlier words about the end of the 1946 naval uprising. 'We were not really vanquished but it almost amounted to losing.' The poem in reality is as much, in fact more, about Mumbai as about Hyderabad. Mumbai figures as an ugly city which carries the stores of Hindu-Muslim riots as if they are the ornaments of its sophisticated self.

Another of *Surve's* poems, 'My Remark in the Diary of My Country' (*Mazya Deshchya Nondbookat Maza Abhipray*), presents striking images of the city. He depicts it as an arid stretch of land witnessing the play of the light and the shadow according to its ever-changing moods. In the surrounding world day-old puppies in search of the milk of life only once a while manage to snap the iron bonds tying them to the steel-hearted monster of the city. The city's endless miles of roads are assimilated to over-worked arteries that somehow sustain the megalopolis giving off a sound like the throbbing of a dilapidated boiler (*Surve* 1985: 62-5).

In his *Lavani* about a mill, *Surve* remarks that the traditional focus of this form is on the beauty and majesty of woman. Nowadays he says ironically we perforce have to write lavanis about the mills which offer the same promise of fulfillment. The poet is aghast at the fact that the actual producers of wealth appear as thieves appear as overlords (*Surve* 1985: 102-3).

It would be appropriate to say goodbye to *Narayan Surve* by invoking his celebrated poem on Karl Marx. The metropolis has no longer the power to keep its toiling progeny voiceless, meek and mute. One day, the poet happens to come across Karl Marx. The poet was reflecting on the root cause of his mental depression and the true source of festering poverty. He dreams of a day when a toiler, as a creative person in his own right, declares his new-found identity as the maker of history and the hero of all future biographies. Marx appears out of nowhere and tells the poet that after all both of them at heart are creative individuals in love with Goethe and his evergreen tree of life. This transformation of a meek toiler, devoid of courage and lacking the time to acquire the rudiments of culture, into a creative, cultivated person represents the long journey of the dalits from the colonial days to the present, apparently clouded by despair but full of hope for the joyful morrow to come.

Like *Surve, Baburao Bagul* is a Marxist and also a follower of *Phule* and *Ambedkar*. *Bagul* is an outstanding short story writer. His short story, 'When I had Concealed My Caste!' (*Jevha Me Jat Chorli Hoti*) illustrates the myth and the reality of metropolitan Mumbai. A city generating modern consciousness with attachment to secular norms and practices a fearless individual, who puts his faith in these values. But when he leaves the city (in this case, Udhna), the naked reality destroys his pretensions and reduces him to his caste position. *Bagul* calls upon his hero to carry his dalit identity as a red badge of honor. The story, *'Maran Swasta Hot Ahe'* (Death is Getting Cheaper) opens with a conversation between the writer and his poet friend about how to obtain a true understanding of Mumbai. Finding no solution in terms of dry literary discourse, they decide to explore in person all the neighborhoods of the city. At the end of the day their steps take them to a nameless railway station. At this point the story ends dramatically.

> . . . There was a big crowd at the water tap. People were fighting for water. A railway policeman was there with two goondas, looking for a girl for himself while he was controlling the crowd. And the grandchild of the old uncle with an old iron pot in his hand was wandering in and out of the crowd like a cat.
>
> My friend said, 'I'll throw away what I wrote. I'll keep just one line:
>
> 'This is Mumbai. Here men eat men. And Death is Getting Cheaper.'
>
> - Translated by Vidyut Bhagwat and Eleanor Zelliot

Daya Pawar, almost a member of the same team, has offered a vivid depiction of a dalit's life in Mumbai in his famous autobiographical novel, *'Balute'*, published in 1978. He relates how his mother was bound to a daily grind of work like a draught animal. Her world was that of the rag pickers, scrap collectors and searchers for morsels of thrown-away food.

The protagonist expresses his shame as he realizes that his illiterate old mother has to function as a beast of burden while her literate son, an unemployed youth, is withering like a young plant drained of its vitality by termites. In despair he asks, 'What after all is social status? My notions of status are after all the product of my education. No one around me is bothered about it. They are leading a carefree life, innocent of the pain arising out of the consciousness of deprivation. And here was I, I alone, languishing, as my strength ebbed away day by day' (*Pawar* 1982: 133-45).

The dalit belongs to Mumbai and Mumbai belongs to the dalit. He is the anti-hero who strides on the metropolitan stage turned upside down. *Daya Pawar's* novel dares to portray the multidimensional and multilayered universe of dalit consciousness and dalit life practice. It portrays the woes and agonies of the rising dalit middle class occupying a transient and unstable (*trishanku*) position in its relations to the city and to the dalit masses. Daya Pawar charges that the dalit movement is subjected to slow poisoning by opportunist leaders who use the name of Ambedkar as a stepping stone for their selfish political pursuits. *Balute* is essentially a metaphor of a rock capable of supporting the high edifice of the free future. The rock is reduced by design and neglect to a piece of chalk, thrown at random into the nameless foundations that underlie the garbage heap known either as Mumbai or as the modernizing social order of today (Pawar 1982: 189).

The current roster of dalit writers is led by *Namdeo Dhasal. Vijay Tendulkar*, the well known playwright, in his Introduction to *Golpitha* - Dhasal's first collection of poems - writes:

In the calculations of the white-collar workers, 'no man's land' of Mumbai begins at the border of the Dalit world and it is here that the world of *Namdeo Dhasal's* poetry (Mumbai's Golpitha) begins. This is the world of days and nights; of empty or half-full bellies, of the pain of death; of tomorrow's worries; of men's bodies in which shame and sensitivity have been burned out; . . . of Mafia bosses and pimps; of Muslim tombs and Christian crosses; of smuggling;

of naked knives; of opium. No one can escape Dhasal's Golpitha, where prostitutes waiting for clients sing full-throated love songs; from here no one can run away to save his life. Anyone managing to do so is necessarily thrown back - that is Golpitha. In *Dhasal's* Golpitha, all seasons are pitiless and have no heart. [*Tendukar*, in *Dhasal*, 1975: 8-9]

Namdeo Dhasal's poetry reminds us of the creativity, vitality, anger and defiance represented by the Black American poetry of the Vietnam days. Dilip Chitre notes:

Dhasal communicates an angry energy even when he is depicting pain or anguish . . . The anger of Golpitha rises to the level to the level of architecture because it both systematizes disparate images from an authentic world hitherto invisible in literature, and uses the energy of anger to encompass a whole range of negative feeling and positive visions [Chitre 1982: 94].

Two of *Dhasal's* poems in *Golpitha*, 'Their Eternal Pity' (*Tyanchi Sanatana Daya*) and 'Mumbai, Mumbai, My Dear Slut' (*Mumbai, Mumbai, Mazhya Priya Rande*) are representative of his whole work. They depict with great insight and fury the city which produces situations in which dalits are trapped. Here are the first and a part of the second:

Their Eternal Pity

There Eternal Pity no taller than the pimp on Faulkland Road
No pavilion put up in the sky for us.
Lords of wealth, they are, locking up lights in those vaults of theirs.
In this life carried by a whore, not even sidewalks are ours,
Made so beggarly it is nausea to be human,
Cannot fill our shriveled gut even with dirt.
Each new just day supports them as if bribed

Not a sigh slips through the fingers of day's plenty as we are cut down.
- Translated by Eleanor Zelliot and Jayant Karve
with the assistance of A. K. Ramanujan

Mumbai, Mumbai My Dear Slut
(An extract)

. . . Laxmi, Saraswati
the discriminating harlots.
We invited them but they never came.
We asked them to spread under us but they refused.

Dear Mumbai, you be true and loyal to us,
Keep our beds alive,
Play on the flute of eternity,
Tantalize our semen to yield fruit.

You the wander-lust,
the Atishudra,
Murali of Khandoba,
Nautch girl,
My harlot of a soul mate.
I will not leave you like a worthless upstart.

I will make you mine
shorn of your draperies
Throw wide open sesame
of your precious self

Mumbai, Mumbai
O my dear slut
I may say a good-bye

But not before
I will take you
in multiple ways
Not before
I will pin you down
here and how
thus and thus

            - Translated by Vidyut and Sharmila

Among other contemporary dalit poets we may mention *J. V. Pawar, Arun Kamble, Keshav Mesharam* and *Arjun Dangle*. Their poems, like Dhasal's, elaborate on the love-hate relationship between the dalits and this megalopolis. They reveal the emancipatory spaces as well as the forces of regimentation that characterize this upstart, neo-rich conglomeration, called not Mumbai but Mumbai. To take one example, *Arjun Dangle*, a powerful poet and a leader in dalit politics, asserts that

Hunger says yet to our dreams
Don't snuff out the orphan huts upon the shore
we'll see later
the gold-threshold struggle
between the snail of pain
and the sea

            - (Dangle 1992: 43)

In the literature of the Dalits, as we have seen, Mumbai acts as a magnet promising great possibilities and rewards to those who arrive from the hinterland suffering from burdens of the present and the past. We have noted how Mumbai continues to tempt her marginalized children despite that the meek of the megalopolis can achieve a reconstitution, however tentative, of their own so as to inherit the city, if not today then tomorrow, in this protracted war between the rulers and the ruled.

I would like to express my gratitude to *Narayan Surve* for helping me in locating some very rare poems that I needed for this paper.

Original Source

Mumbai - Mosaic of Modern Culture
Patel, Sujata & Thorner, Alice (Eds.)
Oxford University Press,
1995
(pp: - 113-125)

References

Bagul, Baburao. 1976. 'Jevha Mi Jat Chorli Hoti!' in *Jevha Mi Jat Chorli Hoti*, Mumbai, Abhinav Prakashan, pp. 105-201.

_____. 1992. 'Dalit is Getting Cheaper', trans. Vidyut Bhagwat, Eleanor Zelliot in Nissin Ezekiel and Meenakshi Mukherjee, *Another India*, New Delhi, Penguin Book.

Chitre, Dilip. 1982. 'The Architecture of Anger: On Namdeo Dhasal's Golpitha', in *Journal of South Asian Literature*, Asian Studies Center, Michigan State University, Vol. XVII, Winter Spring, pp. 93-5.

Dangle, Arjun (ed.). 1992. *Poisoned Bread, Modern Marathi Dalit Literature*, Mumbai: Orient Longman.

Dhasal, Namdeo. 1975. *Golpitha*, Pune: Nilkantha Prakashan.

_____.1983. 'Mumbai, Mumbai, Mazya Priya Rande' in *Khel*, Mumbai: Press Publishers.

Kulkarni, G. M. 1986. *Dalit Sahitya Pravaha ani Pratikriya*, Pune: Pratima Prakashan.

Kulkarni, Patthe Bapurao. 1969 (1954). 'Mumbaichi Lavani' in *Jintikar*, Bapurao Mahadeo, Editor, Rangabaji Lavanya.

Parsharam, Shahir. 1828. 'Mukbaicha Powada', in *Nave Navnit*.

Pawar, Daya. 1982 (1978). *Balute*, Mumbai, Granthali.

Sathe, Anna Bhau. 1985. '*Mazi Maina . . .*' & '*Mumbaichi Lavani*' in V. V. Bhat, Editor, Mumbai: Manovikas Publications.

Surve, Narayan. 1966. *Maze Vidyapeeth*, Mumbai: Popular Prakashan.

_____. 1985. 'Mazya Deshachya Nondbookat Maza Abhipray' in *Sanad*, Mumbai: Granthali, pp. 62-5.

_____. 1990. 'Usman Ali' in *Mauj* Diwali issue, p. 25.

Zelliot, Eleanor and Jayant Karve. 1982. translation of Namdeo Dhasal's poetry, 'Their Eternal Pity' in *Journal of South Asian Literature*, Asian Studies Center, Michigan State, University, Vol. XVII, Winter, Spring, p. 98.

Section : III

Histories of Women's Studies : Institutional and Intellectual

Chapter - 10

Engendering and Developing Curriculum : A Tightrope Walk

This paper focuses on Women's Studies curriculum in higher education while drawing upon the experiences of the Women's Studies Centre, University of Pune. At the Centre, teaching 'gender' has always been on the agenda; so I thought of presenting a specific institutional history as it is located in larger discussions about engendering disciplines and disciplining gender. Issues of curriculum cannot be divorced from intellectual and organisational debates and to that extent this paper is about syllabus design as it is related to academic and organisational practices in a university.

The first part of the paper focuses on the lack of linear history of Women's Studies Centres and their programmes and will seek to explain the institutional constraints in developing curriculum within such a context. The second part discusses the instructional programme in Women's Studies as structured at the Centre in Pune and the planned expansion of its teaching programmes. Under this, I would like to reflect on issues related to:
1. Post Graduate Interdisciplinary Certificate Course
2. Proposed Diploma Course in Women's Studies
3. Gender in Social Sciences (Refresher Courses)
4. Engendering disciplines (Sociology)

Women's Studies in Higher Education: Engagements and Disruptions

A lot of thinking has gone into how to really present a specific institutional history because the UGC sponsored Women's Studies Centre at the University of Pune, like all other Centres, does not have a clear linear heritage. I must clarify that it is a case not just full of experiences of disruption, but also one of several periods of empowerment and engagement. However, the history of Women's Studies curriculum and programmes cannot be seen outside the larger structures such as changing policies for Higher Education, the debates in Women's Studies and the micro-politics of everyday life in the University. One of the major intellectual debates in Women's Studies, which has influenced curriculum development, has been on the autonomy vs. integration model.

Autonomy / Integration

There have been complex arguments for and against autonomy, as well as, integration models for Women's Studies Centres. It is generally assumed that autonomy would give more freedom for innovative methods which promote experiments in teaching and learning. The arguments in favour of an integrated Women's Studies state that this will give to the new subject the solid supportive base of an established discipline, thus helping to open up fresh possibilities for research. But both these models also have their own danger zones. Autonomy may, in practical terms, result into Women's Studies becoming a narrow compartment or a kind of a ghetto. Integration might result in Women's Studies being swallowed into or becoming an appendage to the parent discipline. Women's Studies started by filling in the gaps and exposing the silences in traditional syllabus. Since disciplines were not necessarily formulated from a feminist perspective, the expectation was that with the introduction of Women's Studies, the mainstream disciplines would give up authoritarian power and gain the benefit of new intellectual enquiry. But in practice, when we began our work through the Women's Studies Centre in 1987 located in the department of Sociology, we neither had autonomy nor integration for almost ten years.

When UGC finally granted autonomy to the Centre in 1997, in fact made it compulsory, we experienced this status in two ways To begin with, a functional autonomy was worked out as a via media. It was assumed that Women's Studies as a vibrant intellectual stream had a lot to offer to the tired discipline of Sociology and the 'non-disciplinary' status of Women's Studies would be made less troublesome by the steady structure of Sociology. During this period we learnt the 'nuts and bolts' of university administration and the intricacies of academic bodies (Board of Studies, Academic Council etc.). Simultaneously, we daringly produced our resource kits and monograps:hs which were different from mainstream textbooks.

In the second stage, functional autonomy was thrust on Women's Studies, not out of deliberations or serious academic consideration but due to micro-politics of university structures. In this context, we struggled for two things -

1. Actual concrete space (classrooms)
2. Figurative space (recognition as a discipline)

This autonomy also took the form of partitioning not only of major physical resources of teaching programmes such as books, but also of our professional identities. We were denied the claim to being a part of Sociology and came to be called 'only Women's Studies persons.' The student community, which had earlier been offered both courses (Women's Studies and Sociology), had to encounter the problem of divided loyalties. Since our funds had been shared and books purchased on a combined basis, when libraries were divided, we had to convince the mainstream social science that Women's Studies also needed books on social theory. In brief, having started from an integrated model and later having autonomy thrust upon us, we realised that developing a Women's Studies curriculum meant more than designing courses and workshops. It involved dealing with the micro-politics of 'doing' Women's Studies within a complicated, entrenched structure of a university.

Problems Faced

1. Recruitment in Women's Studies meant temporary appointments with the perpetual sword of termination hanging over the head. It meant a location on the margins. The assumed interdisciplinarity of Women's Studies was understood as either no discipline or a double-day i.e. one shift in teaching courses in the parent discipline, the other to prove yourself as an interdisciplinary Women's Studies scholar. This also meant negotiating strategies, for instance, organising a series of workshops on popular films, presentations on Marx and Marxism, etc. to gain cross-disciplinary visibility.

2. Secondly, there was unpleasant academic ridicule faced by first generation research students (M.Phil, Ph.D) who worked on gender issues. Their work was often mocked at as chanting of mantras of 'patriarchy', 'gender' and as lacking rigour. A presentation on domestic labour was commented upon by a 'senior professor' as 'I help my wife by carrying a vegetable bag. What do you mean by the sexual division of labour?' The theoretical seriousness of Women's Studies was lost in such banal asides. Though such examples may seem trivial in a single instance, they acquire significance when located in a wider analysis of power relations. A lot of our 'achievements' have been at the cost of invisible labour like being 'guest' lecturers (not authentic teachers) and consultants for a 'politically correct' curriculum. In the last three years, there have been at least seven Junior Research Fellows (JRFs) in Women's Studies but the faculty at the Centre has been denied the status of research supervisors despite the obvious demand from talented students. Consequently, some faculty members serve as invisible guides, or at the most as co-guides, because of the uncertain disciplinary status of Women's Studies.

Women's Studies in Practice

Besides this, there have been several other occasions for discussion and sharp dialogue. Positive thoughts opened up with others who were also on the margins—students, teachers from mofussil colleges and the peripheral faculty in the mainstream disciplines. As those who lobbied for the Cell against sexual harassment and asked for a crĕche on campus, we found ourselves caught in the nitty-gritty of creating these services. The UGC mandate requires networking with colleges. We realised that they, along with governmental and non-governmental organizations could be channelled into legitimate activities on campus. Our work with college students, women's groups and other progressive groups thus could be given a strong public face. Such joint enterprise proved occasionally useful. Interventions could be made on the issues of beauty-contests, religious fundamentalism (e.g. when controversies on films such as Fire and Water were rampant) and globalisation. A long-standing relationship of co-operation with Autonomous Women's Groups emerged and the Centre became a locus for mediations and potential coalitions especially when differences between AWG and dalit feminist groups seemed positioned for a divide (e.g. an issue like celebrating 25th December as Indian Women's Day). There could be mutual exchanges with feminist magazines and newsletters. A kind of interactive culture developed whereby every year, besides the academic seminars, there was at least one workshop on contemporary issues and campaigns in which women's groups were engaged. Open forums talked of hysterectomy, rapes faced by Zabua nuns or the debate over legalisation of prostitution. In turn, this manner of public engagement has inspired several persons— housewives, journalists, NGO workers—to enrol for the courses in Women's Studies.

The UGC mandate has proved useful in many other ways too. The programme for combining teaching, research, extension and documentation has been effective. Each kind of work builds into the other. A teaching programme in Women's Studies necessarily entails extension and research. Documentation and publication of teaching and learning materials is imperative for the growth of the discipline. In significant ways the organisational culture of the University has been, at least in some moments, transformed by our activities. For example, there were 'morchas' demanding a safe campus, issue-based street plays on the University Foundation Day, and slogan shouting by women's organisations against a sexual harassment case.

Having told this story of opportunity carved from within institutional constraints, I would like to underline here that this crisis for the very survival of Women's Studies is not separable from the prevailing crisis in higher education. The issue of autonomy for departments is proving extremely tricky for us. Though several social science departments are lobbying for 'academic freedom' and a credit course system for individual subjects, we as a Women's Studies Centre are apprehensive about the outcome. We are already conducting a self-financing P.G. Certificate Course in Women's Studies and hope that autonomy and a credit course system will mean better interdisciplinarity. More students from Social Sciences and Humanities would offer credit courses in Women's Studies if given a chance.

In the midst of present anxieties, we look back at the last decade and see our own vision of doing Women's Studies in a university structure changing. Our enduring vision has carried us across our research, teaching, extension and publication. For example, what began as an ICSSR funded project on 'Gender and Caste-based Occupations in a Changing Political Economy' in the year 1991, got translated into our engagement with dalit and minority women's groups. Several seminars and workshops on the theme followed, and several publications such as 'Moving in the direction of non-Brahmanical historiography' materialised. This has extended into the classrooms of the Refresher Course for the social science teachers as well as the Certificate Course.

The challenge is to avoid both an 'advocacy approach' and, at another level, esoteric theorisation. The emphasis is on practising Women's Studies in a way that keeps the original promise of integrating political, personal and intellectual engagements. With all the institutional obstacles, are we ready for MA and Ph.D. programmes? There are always arguments against this. Refined and high quality textbooks that a discipline needs are said to be lacking. At other times, it is said that there are as yet no job opportunities in academics for Masters in Women's Studies, since the subject is not taught at the undergraduate level. We bypass the objections through some positive methods. Our strategy has been one of publishing teaching-learning material and of regularly translating these into regional languages. The entire discourse on issues of labour, violence, sex work, communalism has been made available in the regional languages. In a sense, we prepare ourselves for 'disciplining gender' but more effort is required to mobilise and lobby for introducing Women's Studies as a subject at the undergraduate level This will help to launch MA and Ph.D programmes.

Curriculum

With this, I move on to the second part of the paper, i.e. a more detailed look at the curriculum in Women's Studies at four levels.

1. Post Graduate Interdisciplinary Certificate Course
2. Proposed Diploma Course in Women's Studies
3. Gender in Social Sciences (Refresher Course)
4. Engendering Discipline

POST GRADUATE INTERDISCIPLINARY CERTIFICATE COURSE

What was our rationale for this Course?

We argued that Women's Studies is a relatively new and unique academic discipline. It seeks to redefine knowledge by overcoming the barriers created by the 'taken-for-granted' dichotomies between theory and action, knowledge and experience, and objectivity and subjectivity. The discipline is unique in that it emerged from activism and experience, and therefore underlines the connections between knowledge, experience and social transformation. Knowledge must initiate action at individual and collective levels.

Women's Studies is not to be understood as merely a critique of male perspectives. Being a discipline that seeks to assess and challenge the interlinked axis of oppression in society viz. class, race, caste and gender, it re-discovers the experiences and knowledge of the marginalised sections in history and in contemporary societies. At the core is an attempt to understand the material and ideological structures of women's oppression. For this objective to be realized, Women's Studies adopts an interdisciplinary thrust examining social, cultural, historical, political and economic structures.

Having thus determined the rationale, we underlined the local specificity of the courses. Pune city boasts of a long lineage of political consciousness and political activism on the woman's question. Mahatma Phule and Savitribai Phule started the first school for girls in 1848 in this city. Ever since, whether it was the debate on education for women or widow remarriage, Pune has occupied a central place. *Pandita Ramabai's 'Sharda Sadan', D. K. Karve's* educational institutions all have their roots here. Thus, the very name and location of the Centre at the University of Pune, we argued, are such that there is much to draw upon and many ideals to live up to.

About the Course

Since 1995, the Centre has been conducting a P. G. Interdisciplinary Certificate Course in Women's Studies. This course was the first of its kind in the country and today brings together modules in feminist theory, issues in Gender and Development and issues in Gender, Religion and Culture. A unique element of this course is the training it imparts in the Social History of Maharashtra from gender, caste and class perspectives. Every participant in the course works on an annual project, thus integrating the book and field view. Teaching methods are participative and collaborative, thus collating intellectual, emotional and political engagement. Our visiting faculty includes renowned scholars and activists. Moreover, courses are taught in English as well as Marathi and resource kits/reading material are provided to the participants. Since, the Centre is a part of the national network of women's organisations, activist groups, NGOs and institutes committed to human rights advocacy, the course participants gain opportunities for internships, on-the-field training and assignment based work with organisations and the community.

Across the 4 papers, the issues taken up could be seen as modules on Feminist Theory, Gender and Development, Social History of Maharashtra, Culture, Religion and Politics.

TERM I

Module I

What is Women's Studies? Its emergence, growth and significance; Its relationship with the women's movement.

Module II

Women's Movement: Global and local contexts (Movement in Europe, U.S.A., Russia, Asia, Africa, Latin America and the Middle East)

Module III

Women's Movement in India (The women's question in 19th and early 20th century India, Women in the nationalist movement, Women's question in the non-brahmanical movement. Women's movement in its second phase: post-1975 campaigns/issues.)

Module IV

Introduction to concepts in Feminist Theory
- Feminism
- Woman/Gender
- Sexual division of labour
- Patriarchy

Module V

Feminist Thought and Theory: An Introduction
- Vintage Feminism
- Feminist Classics (Beauvoir, Kollantai)
- Liberal Feminism, Radical Feminism, Marxist Feminism, Socialist Feminism

- Challenges to Feminist Theory: Black and Third World centred Feminism

Module VI

Feminism, Development and Culture (The emergence of women as a constituency in Development, the Theoretical underpinnings of WID, Perspectives on Gender and Development)

Module VII

Connecting, Extending, Reversing: Development from a gender perspective. (A detailed review of the perspectives of Shiva and Mies, B. Agarwal, Gabriele Dietrich and Naila Kabeer)

Module VIII

Gender, Development and the Indian Nation State (The five year plans, Towards Equality, Shramashakti Report, NPP, NCW and Beijing and after)

Module IX

Issues at Stake in India: An Introduction to Gender Concerns in:
- Work
- Politics
- Family
- Health and sexuality
- Law

TERM II

Module X

In Search of our Pasts: The Significance of History (Why study social history, different perspectives, debates on feminist historiography)

Module XI

Doing Social History - from a gender and caste perspective (Readings from Tarabai Shinde, Phule, Gandhi R. Periyar, Dr. Ambedkar)

Module XII

Rewriting Histories: Four case studies over four historical periods
- Who was the Vedic Dasi?
- The 'Sant Poetesses of Medieval India'
- The 'prostitute' in colonial India
- Women in the Telangana movement and the Ambedkar movement

Module XIII

Controversies and debates on gender in Modern Indian History:
- Widow remarriage
- Sati
- Education for women

Module XIV

Gender, Culture and Ideology (Basic concepts, approaches to the study of culture)

Module XV

Studying Cultural Practices: A gender, caste and class perspective (women writing in India, gender and Indian television, gender and cinema, global cultures/local cultures, and oral traditions and gender)

Module XVI

Myths/Mythology, religious practices: Gender concerns (The Mother Goddess, Reading 'Sita', Women in Islamic tradition the Buddhist Bhikunis and Therigathas)

Module XVII

Untangling contemporary cases/issues:

- The Shah Bano controversy
- The Roop Kanwar case
- The *Fire* controversy and the debate over *Gaddar*
- Making sense of gender and religious fundamentalism

Module XVIII

Writing the Research paper (Basic guidelines - A workshop)

PROPOSED DIPLOMA COURSE IN
WOMEN'S STUDIES

Eligibility for this Course: Those who have completed the P.G. Inter-disciplinary Certificate Course in Women's Studies can seek admission to the Diploma. The first term of the Diploma can be taken by students of semester I and III of the Master's programmes in social sciences and humanities as a credit course.

Course Description: This course is spread across two terms, the first consisting of 60 teaching hours and the second consisting of 40 teaching hours plus 20 hours of the optional course. Every participant has to complete a supervised research project on which he/she will work throughout the year.

Rationale of the Course

This course is designed for participants who have been introduced to the basic concepts, debates and controversies in Women's Studies. It seeks to engage participants in the following:

- Mapping feminist interventions in knowledge.
- Issues and gender concerns in the context of globalisation.
- Issues in feminist epistemology, methodology and methods.
- Doing a research project - from drawing up a proposal to writing the project.

TERM I

Module I

Feminist Epistemology & Methodology and Introduction to Qualitative Research

- Vintage Feminism
- A brief history of Methodology
- Science, Nature and Gender
- Feminist Epistemology, Methodology & Method
- Debates in Feminist Ethnography
- Introduction to Qualitative Research
- Major debates in Qualitative Research
- Drawing up a Research Proposal

Module II

Major themes in Gender Studies in India.

- Feminist assessments of the Political Economy
- Gender and Family and the Household
- Gender in Indian Agriculture and Industry
- State, Sexuality and Social Reform
- Constitution and Law as subversive sites
- Women, Community, Rights
- Women's Writings and Voices
- Gender and Environment
- Feminification of Theory
- Victimhood vs. agency
- Conceptualising gender, caste and class in India
- Engendering Disciplines - Disciplining Gender

TERM II

Module III

Globalisation: Gender Concerns

- Globalisation in a historical context

- Globalisation and changing patterns of employment in the Third world
- Late capitalism and gender transformations
- Issues in globalisation and the culture-industry
- Globalisation of poverty - feminisation of poverty
- Rise of the NGOs and challenge for people-centred development
- Issues and controversies in Human Rights

Module IV

This is an optional module (20 teaching hours). The choice of the modules should be in keeping with the area of the research project of the participants who can select any two of the following:

A. *Social History of Maharashtra:*
A caste, class and gender perspective

Rise of the middle class and recasting of gender, the *Satyashodhak* and non-Brahman movement, debates and controversies on widow remarriage and Restitution of Conjugal Rights, trends in Political Thought and the Women's Question in 19th & Early 20th Century

B. *Literature and Feminisms*

Debates in feminist literary criticisms, understanding what feminist critics do, 'Reading' - working class, dalit and feminist literature

C. *Gender, Community and Nation*

The 'sacred' and the 'secular': Gender concerns, issues of citizenship, embodied violence and resistance. Women in the Right wing movements

D. *Gender and Cinema*

Theoretical perspectives in reading cinema; Issues of history, pleasure and consumption; Nation in the cinema; The 'female ideal' in popular cinema

E. Gender and Sexuality

Theoretical perspectives; Debates in reproductive technology; AIDS and the gender question; Sexuality: Issues of race, caste and class; Sex-work debates

F. Gender and Mental Health

Theoretical perspectives; Gender and mental health in India and in a globalising context; Decoding stereotypes in the Media. Legal concerns

G. Advanced Feminist Theory

With and against Marx, Post structuralism / Postmodernism and Feminism, Post colonialism and Feminism. Theorising difference

H. Gender and Caste: Issues in Theorisation

Gender, Caste, Class: Case studies. Reading from *Phule, Ambedkar,*

Periyar on the gender and caste question; Under-standing the debate on 'difference' and Dalit feminism; Issues of violence and representation)

GENDER IN SOCIAL SCIENCES
(REFRESHER COURSES)

Having participated in the effort at developing curriculum on gender, I turn to another of our attempts at 'engendering the mainstream curriculum.' We have been taking this up through the UGC Refresher , Course on 'Gender in Social Sciences.'

In the last two decades, theoretical and empirical work in the area of Women's Studies has seriously challenged the accepted theories and methods of the Social Sciences. These developments in Women's Studies have been across the disciplines of Literature, Sociology, Economics, Political Science, History, Anthropology and Philosophy. In this context, the Refresher Courses at the Women's Studies Centre seek to mainstream these challenges.

I will briefly outline the highlights of the Refresher Course on 'Gender in Social Sciences' which is attended by 40-50 college and university teachers from all over India.

1. Introduction to Feminist Theory and its impact or the disciplines
2. Introduction to Feminist Methodology: Issues of Empirical Research and Epistemology
3. Complexities of Gender, Caste, Class in the Indian Context (especially in the context of cultural practices, labour and sexuality)
4. Social Movements on Issues of Caste, Class and Gender
5. Gender and Issues of Religious practice, debate on secularism and communalism

The method of teaching is innovative and participatory

- Specialists in the area and renowned scholars deliver lectures
- Use of Audio/Visual material
- Regarding material in English and Marathi provided as resource kit
- Teachers work on curriculum transformation from a gender perspective in their own discipline for their assignments.

Finally, another of our attempts has been to engender the curriculum of mainstream departments in the University. Obviously, because of our earlier location in Sociology, we have been integral to the curriculum development of this Department and have insisted upon engendering the basic/foundational courses and not just having courses on Sociology of Gender. Contextualising the larger requirement for engendering disciplines taught at universities in India, I end this section with questions that should be addressed by Women's Studies practitioners:

1. What kind of a model do we adopt for a master's programme? Who will administer/teach this programme? Who will enrol in these courses? Towards what end? How do we make degrees in Women's Studies usable without vulgarising the content?

2. How do we ensure meaningful interventions in other disciplines even while we nurture our independent MA Courses? We must not allow mainstream courses in Social Sciences and Humanities to go ungendered.
3. How do we develop meaningful correspondence and capsule courses to reach out to the larger audience?

Interdisciplinarity has become the rhetoric in our university structure, however almost no effort goes into operationalising it. Interdisciplinary work has in no way become an intellectual critique, lesser still a critique of organisational and institutional arrangements of the existing compartmentalisation of social sciences. It lacks political clout to alter the present structures. How do we develop Women's Studies Centres that understand interdisciplinarity not just as the use of more than one discipline but as an integration of disciplines to create a new epistemology?

Original Source

Women's Studies in India: Contours of Change
Lal, Malashri & Kumar, Sukrita Paul (Eds.)
Indian Institute of Advanced Study, Shimla
2002
(pp: - 281-295)

Chapter - 11

'Dalit Women:Issues and Perspectives Some Critical Reflections'

The theme of Dalit Women is of a crucial importance in the contemporary Indian situation, particularly in the context of new social movements silenced today by the narrowing of their democratic space. By using the term *'dalit women' we are creating an imagined category. This imagining is necessary because we hope that Dalit women in the near future will give new critical dimensions to Indian feminist movement as well as to Dalit movement.* As Gabriele Dietrich in her extremely balanced article 'Dalit Movements and Women's Movements' points out while discussing the interrelationship between *caste and patriarchy* that caste should be looked at as a marriage circle and endogamy which is related to patriarchal controls over women. Scholars like Gabriele Dietrich and Gail Omvedt point out that Morton Klass and Babasaheb Ambedkar both give the most comprehensive and coherent explanations of the caste system. Dietrich further states that 'in his early writings of 1916, Ambedkar comes very close to Morton Klass' version of *seeing caste as a "marriage circle"* which regulates access to resources as well as exchange of services based on territoriality and kinship' (Dietrich 1992: 90). Her conclusion is that '. . . neither Morton Klass nor Dr. Ambedkar goes into an analysis of how the closing into endogamous marriage circles is related to patriarchal controls over women' (Dietrich 1992: 92). She further states '. . . intermarriage and even fantasies about intermarriage and inter-dining are major factors in triggering off caste riots in Tamilnadu today. There is a need to work on a feminist position on this issue by Dalit women themselves since otherwise the debate deviates into the rape fantasies of men' (Dietrich 1992: 91). I would only make an addition here by saying why talk about intermarriages, even marriages within kinship by choice are opposed vehemently by the dalit-caste panchayats to chop off the heads of young couple e.g. the recent case in U.P. (August, 1993). As we are all aware, the term dalit is meant to skip from the negative connotations of the word 'untouchable' and from the Gandhian framework of the word *'Harijan'*. Though the term dalit is chiefly used for those who are ex-untouchables, now Buddhists or lower castes, Dalits really are a part of Indian counter-culture. The core of dalit consciousness is made of protest against exploitation and oppression. In short, the term Dalit stands for change and revolution. *By using the term Dalit women we are trying to say that if women from dalit castes and of dalit consciousness create a space for themselves for fearless expression i.e. if they become subjects or agents or self, they will provide a new leadership to Indian society, in general and to feminist and dalit movements in particular.* In spite of Dalit Panthers and Republican Parties, in spite of Dalit literature marking an authentic breakthrough in the white collared Hindu culture, and in spite of strong women's movement since 1975, *we feel that voices and protests of Dalit women are almost invisible.* This invisibility is so deep that leaders from left politics and leaders who are trying to build up new *'Hindutva'* do not take due *cognizance of 'dalit women' at all.* In fact when we use phrases like, marginalization of women in the development process, or feminization of poverty or women's contribution in the unorganized sector we are referring to dalit women without even being conscious about their specificity. Dalit women were actively participating in the Ambedkar led movement in the pre-independence period. Today we see no protest against so-called 30% reservations for women in the local self government which further denies the possibility of dalit women getting any representation. Women who are part of the toiling masses are leading their life as beasts of burden and often as victims of dominant caste onslaught. It is but natural that they are mute. But dalit women living in urban centers, taking care of their homes and children at times teaching in schools and colleges or most of the times playing the role of housewives have not yet come out. We do know how they *perceive themselves and the world around them*. Particularly, wives of political leaders, professors, doctors, executives are strangely silent. On the contrary, to take an example from Maharashtra, we can surely say that women from Brahmin and related castes are visible in various professions as well as are taking leadership in various social movements by showing their readiness to pay a heavy price inside and outside the household. We also witness some mobility on the part of dominant caste women and Jain women. *But what is happening to dalit educated women is peculiar and it is destroying their potentials*. Though there are some autobiographical writings, and some literary texts, dalit women's writings has not become a force as yet. *Mallika Dhasal's* autobiography *'Mala Uddhvasta Vhayachay'* was in sense a significant contribution; however critics read it as an outburst and questioned its authenticity in the light of continuance of her marital life in the same *Dhasal* family. Today dalit women are working in various government offices, they are active members of *Zilla Parishads* but they are still bearing the burden of a double-day, sexual division of labour and overall patriarchal ideology and not saying anything about it. Why is it so? It is not sufficient to answer it only in terms of political economy or brahminical ideology.

Amongst other social movements, women's movement is unique in many ways. Feminist consciousness not only makes one aware of the forms of power relations that men and women have with each other but is also adds to our understanding what it means by the common saying that *'all women constitute a caste' i.e. 'baichi jat'*. This truth or reality is camouflaged by glorifying womenhood on Hindu patriarchal terms and dividing women into different castes. Male dominance or patriarchy is so deep rooted in us that both men and women in India will readily say that patriarchy is a western phenomenon and a western problem. Women in the developed world are living in a degraded status because of 'their' permissive value systems, market orientedness and consumerism. It is generally argued by many social thinkers that in India women are protected by community, caste, kinship and family networks. This neglects the fact that women are the gateways of the caste-system and the crucial pivot on whose purity-sanctity axis the caste hierarchy is constructed. Every caste not only controls 'their' women's sexuality and labour power but in the process of reform or upgrading the community or the caste a new agenda of morality and efficiency is designed at every stage of history for women in such a way that at one level women from each caste are coerced into as if consenting for this change in fact 'trapping' and at another level they are further divided and estranged from the collective consciousness of '*baichi jat*'.

Moreover, the growing communalist and casteist forces today have mobilized 'Hindu Women' who are given a promise of '*Ram Rajya* as a fantasy of a happy family. This is of course in direct counter position to the women's movement which had pointed out the cracks and violence against women in 'happy families'. '*Stree Shakti*' was counter posed to marginalize 'stree mukti' and *'Sita'* and *'Durga' were picked up as symbols to oppose the 'liberationist ideology'* of the 'western' feminists. This poses a threat for both the women of the majority community who are being shown the carrot of restricted mobility within a Hindu patriarchal order and for the women of minority community it means the postponement of issues like uniform civil code because of the ever impending threat of rape and violence from the majority community and increasing restrictions from the fundamentalists of their own community who seek to reinstate the communal identity through women.

The participation of women in the anti-mandal agitations and caste-based violence (*Gothala*/Pimpri-Deshmukh) has implications for both the women's movement and the Dalit Movement. The women's movement has in its enthrallment of 'sisterhood' failed to note the 'caste' factor while *the Dalit Movement has remained patriarchal and sees that dalit women's oppression merely as caste oppression.* At this juncture we need to go deeper into the new construction of a concept of 'Hindu Religion', which is fundamentalist and patriarchal in many ways. *Sandeep Pendse* in his incisive article '*Sadhvi Ritambhara Va Jamatvad*' (Sadhvi Ritambhara and Communalism) given us clues how women's leadership within the framework of neo-Hinduism is perverted and vicarious and how women like *Ritambhara* are further pitted against any space of emancipation or transcendence for 'all' women. (*Pendse* 1993: 11-20) *Sadhvi* by being n :'Sadhvi' i.e. one who has controlled her sexuality is not only uncommon but is 'allowed' to incite the manhood of men who are young, confused, and frustrated. In *Dr. Pendse's* opinion when the new capitalism in India is facing a race of hurdles, when people are entrenched in bargains, sales, indulgence, leaders like *Sadhvi Ritambhara* encourage a kind and convenient religiosity which does not disturb any one at the root. The ruling party has also not criticized Ritambhara who in a sense serves to hinder any mobilization among the disenchanted youth by this opiating religiosity. *Ritambhara* creates a fear of castration in the minds of young men constructing them as Hindus, sweeping aside/ up all the caste, class consciousness in them. In her framework, she promises men of virility and also puts a fear in their minds of turning them into eunuch if they do not listen to her and act. The othering process of Muslim community, positing them as backward, animal like or non-cooperative, cruel has made use of gender in subtle and open ways. Hinduization of dalit youth in Mumbai riots is an extremely alarming situation. In this context again we will have to make a conscious effort to build up our understanding of interrelationship between caste and gender.

Technically speaking brahminical Hindu religion is natural religion which was not found by a single person. It is not based on a single text and it possesses no single church. Therefore it speaks in multiple ways, in multiple voices. At the philosophical or rather than metaphysical level, it sees the ontological reality in terms of *Prakruti-Purush* dialectics. At this level it ascribes creative, dynamic role to women. This has inspired scholars like *Vandana Shiva* to build up a new paradigm in the form of eco-feminism. It is true that both the elite and the populist currents of Hindu opinion and sensibilities regarding woman carry a deep impress of mother-goddess cults and forms of worship. As a religion of a great agricultural civilization it stands in awe, respect and yet fear and an anxiety about the role of a woman as a source of fertility and creativity. But barring the various modes of ritual and worship like *Vamachari, Tantrik* and *Shakta*, all the so-called higher traditions of Hinduism ascribe to Hindu woman a complimentary or supplementary role. At the level of social reality Hindu religion has so far functioned within the context of a caste society. The woman of the so-called higher castes pays for the dominant role gained by her male counterpart over the rest of the society. A rigid control over higher caste women in the context of their body and granting a lot of room for lower caste women not as freedom but as a space for brahminical male licentiousness are results of brahmanical patriarchy. Women from lower castes were considered so lowly and degraded in life that their body was a free terrain for colonization.

This process has given rise to various complicated situations for the practices of women's movements in the Indian context. Women from *Devdasi* or *Kolhati* castes might find marriage and the legitimacy that is granted through it as a liberating space from their trapped situation. Brahmin woman while analyzing family and marriage as patriarchal structures will have to understand this need as a historical stage. Similarly those women born in Dalit castes will also have to produce their *own critical interpretation* of the issues prioritized by the other feminists in India like *securing control over body, sexuality, fertility, and labour and the need to practice the slogan of 'personal is political'*. We must keep in mind that both the *dalit and non-dalit women are on the margin of Indian society*. The upper caste women have put up resistance and made some space, but we all know that this is not sufficient. Moreover, in order to create a challenge to patriarchal structures we in India need to know all the details of patriarchy's open and subtle modes. Feminist scholars not belonging to dalit castes might not be able to carry this task. Conscious women from dalit castes will produce this critique more ably. This research has to come from within and with critical consciousness.

Dalit Panthers particularly in their initial phase were extremely aggressive in their expression. Their dissatisfaction about their placement in the caste hierarchy came out in open through literature and politics. But dalit literature constructed dalit woman in the similar patriarchal framework of *'glorification of motherhood'* and overall subjugation of women. Similarly dalit politics also looks at the issues of *empowerment of women as a non-issue. Women in dalit politics figure only in number and are also caught in a trap of 'our women' framework*. This *results into further marginalization of dalit women.*

All those who are on the margins of social milieu will have to come together for creating an alternate world-view through critical perspectives. *Dalit women's agential collectivity is a fundamental necessity to build up a feminist movement in the Indian context.* Otherwise 'all women' coming together will end in privileging and *empowering high-caste Hindu women and degrading women from dalit,* Muslim and other minority communities. The process will subjugate all women in many ways but this will affect the working class, dalit caste women the most. This is the time when we need very strong and firm and broad-based women's movement *which will subvert the populist essentialising meaning of 'Baichi jat' and create unity amongst all women in India, giving new meaning to the reality of baichi jat!*

Original Source

Dalit Women: Issues and Perspectives
Jogdand, P. G. (Ed.)
Gyan Publishing House, New Delhi,
1995
(pp.: - 1-7)

References

Dietrich Gabriele. 1992. 'Dalit Movement and Women's Movement' in Reflection *on the Women's Movement in India,* New Delhi: Horizons India Books.

Pendse, Sandeep. 1993. 'Sadhvi Ritambhara Va Jamatvad' in *Stree-Uvach* 7th issue, Mumbai.

About the Author

Vidyut Bhagwat has taught Literature, Linguistics and Women's Studies at the undergraduate and postgraduate levels for more than two and half decades. She is the founder director of Krantijyoti Savitribai Phule Women's Studies Centre, University of Pune, from where she superannuated in 2008. Much of her research emerges from an explicitly stated commitment to bringing the complex category of region to the centre of historical, literary and gender studies. Teaching in a State University, she has been involved in designing and conducting innovative teaching Programmes in gender studies and courses on Indian Society, Globalisation and Social Justice for international exchange programmes. Her engagement with the anti-caste, peasant and women's movements in Maharashtra have influenced her research and teaching. Several of her projects on translation - seek to open new 'dialogues' across different linguistic and institutional locations.

She has written and published extensively both in English and Marathi on broad ranging themes including social movements, social history of Medieval and modern Maharashtra, feminist literary studies, feminist thought and theory. She is the recipient of the prestigious 'Samajvidnyan Kosh Puraskar' for the year 2004-2005 and 'Maharashtra Saraswat Puraskar' for the year 2006

www.ingramcontent.com/pod-product-compliance
Lightning Source LLC
Chambersburg PA
CBHW052029020726
47501CB00004B/1324